HOT PROTECTOR

Hostile Operations Team® - Strike Team 1

LYNN RAYE HARRIS

The Hostile Operations Team® and Lynn Raye Harris® are
trademarks of H.O.T. Publishing, LLC.

Printed in the United States of America

First Printing, 2022

For rights inquires, visit www.LynnRayeHarris.com

HOT PROTECTOR
Copyright © 2016 by Lynn Raye Harris
Cover Design Copyright © 2021 Croco Designs

ISBN: 978-1-941002-1-17

Chapter One

"OH, THANK GOD YOU'RE HERE. I NEED YOUR HELP."

Chase "Fiddler" Daniels stared at the woman standing on his doorstep, his brow furrowing. He didn't need to look at his phone to tell him it was around three in the morning or that he'd fallen asleep about an hour ago. His eyes were gritty and his brain wasn't quite up to speed.

He shook his head, but she didn't go away.

And holy hell, she was gorgeous—if she was here to fuck, then he was down with that. Wouldn't be the first time some chick had shown up with a lady boner for him. He'd been in Buddy's Bar earlier with some of Strike Team 2's guys, shooting pool and bullshitting. He'd flirted with the waitresses, as usual. But he didn't remember this one, which was strange because he should have.

He put his hand on top of the open door—because he knew it made the muscles in his chest and abs flex—

and gave her a look. "What kind of help do you need, sweetheart?"

She had violet eyes. Pretty violet eyes framed with dark lashes. They were wider now than they had been a few seconds ago. Her red-gold hair hung in waves over her shoulders and down her back. She was on the curvy side, not at all skinny or waiflike. She had hips a man could hold on to while he thrust deep into her body. Chase liked a girl with curves.

She threw a glance over her shoulder, almost as if she was afraid, before turning her gaze on him again. "You don't recognize me, do you?"

He was too tired for bullshit games. "Nope."

She dropped her lashes over those incredible eyes and sucked in a breath. "Please let me in. I'll explain everything."

He was starting to get annoyed. "Honey, it's after three in the morning, and you woke me up. I have no idea who you are. If you want to fuck, just say so. You can get naked, and I'll take you to paradise at least once before I fall asleep again. Promise."

Her jaw had dropped during this speech. He felt a little guilty, but hell, what did she expect?

"You think I'm here for sex?"

He leaned forward, the movement popping his biceps as he held the door. "It's nothing to be ashamed of, sweetheart."

She stiffened her spine as if she was somewhat outraged. "I'm Sophie, you jerk. Sophie Nash."

And just like that the ice water of reality splashed down on his head and cooled every illicit thought he'd

2

been having about the sexy woman on his doorstep. He dropped his hand from the door and stood straight and tall, as stiff as she was now.

"Sophie Nash." He couldn't help the bitter twist on her last name. "Well, how about that? Not a kid anymore, I see."

"No, not a kid anymore." Her gaze slipped over him, from his bare chest to the faded jeans he'd tugged on when the doorbell kept ringing and right on down to his feet. "You aren't sixteen anymore either."

He was tempted to close the door in her face, but he didn't. Instead, he stepped back and silently agreed to let her inside. She swept in like a queen before turning to face him again. He shut the door and leaned back against it, studying her through hooded eyes.

"You were fourteen the last time I saw you." And he'd barely paid any attention to her at the time, though he'd actively disliked her because she'd had the things he didn't. She'd been unremarkable, a chunky girl who'd followed him around and talked entirely too much while he completely ignored her. It was quite a shock that she'd changed so drastically, though it was to be expected in ten years.

She clasped her hands in front of her body. Her knuckles whitened. "I know you and your father have had a strained relationship over the years. But it's not my fault—and it's not my fault he married my mother."

Chase swore. Two minutes ago, he'd been thinking about taking her to bed. Technically she was his stepsister, though he'd never looked at her like family. Impossible since he'd never thought of his biological dad as his family either.

"I haven't talked to Tyler in about five years. I like it that way."

"I think he misses hearing from you."

Chase closed his eyes and swallowed the rage building inside. "Don't," he growled. "Don't even go there. He's never fucking cared about me or my mom. I don't even have his last name. So don't you tell me he fucking misses me. He damn well doesn't."

Sophie's tongue darted out to lick her lips. He hated that it sent a sizzle of electricity down his spine. *Off-limits, dude.*

"I'm sorry. I... I didn't mean..." She shook her head. "Your mom gave Tyler your address. I have nowhere else to turn, Chase. I need you."

Chapter Two

SOPHIE GULPED DOWN HER FEAR AS SHE STARED AT Chase leaning back against the closed door. She told herself she wasn't trapped, that she could walk out at any moment, but she sure felt trapped. Trapped between a rock and a hard place.

He looked so calm and casual. She knew he was anything but. He was taller than he'd been at sixteen, probably about six-three, and broad enough it was breathtaking. His chest... Oh my heavens, his naked chest. All that tanned muscle. The dog tags lying between hard pecs. The valley of his abdomen and the peaks—the delicious peaks of his hipbones jutting out above the loose, faded jeans that were torn across one knee.

He looked like an underwear model come to life. A scary, intense underwear model with a moody disregard for the world and a specific dislike for her in particular.

He hated her. She understood why. His father hadn't married his mother when she'd gotten pregnant with him. And when he'd been about twelve, his dad had married her mother—and adopted her a year later. She was a Nash, and he wasn't.

Chase had come to California once a year to spend a month with them, and he'd always had this moody resentment of her. She'd tried to make him like her, but it had never worked. When she was fourteen, he'd been sixteen and so utterly gorgeous he'd made her mouth dry.

That was the last summer he came out to California. After that, he'd never been back. And her parents didn't talk about it.

"What could you possibly need my help with?" he drawled in that slight Tennessee twang he had. "You're the stepdaughter of a rich and famous blues musician, honey. Let him buy you the help you need."

"Tyler can't help me. No one can."

He lifted an eyebrow. "Thought he was *Dad* to you."

"You know he prefers to be called by his name." Tyler Nash was nothing if not vain. Being called *dad* made him feel too old, he'd said.

"If he can't help you, I don't know what makes you think I can. He's got money and connections. I'm a soldier."

She licked her lips. She didn't miss the way his gaze narrowed or the sudden tension in his muscles. Worse, a little prickle of awareness flared to life in her belly.

"That's it exactly," she forced out, her voice barely more than a whisper. "This is a matter of life and death."

Her life and her death.

He pushed away from the door and ranged toward her, all rippling muscle and hard-edged male animal. Wow. He'd been attractive before, but nothing like this.

She told herself it was wrong to feel even a frisson of excitement over a man who was supposed to be her stepbrother—but in reality they weren't family and never had been. Chase was a boy who'd come to visit for a month during three summers of her life. He'd spoken to her with ill-disguised hostility most of the time. He'd sat in the guest room and strummed a guitar or swam in the pool or played video games and always ignored her as much as possible.

"If you've come to tell me that Tyler needs a kidney or something, you're out of luck. The fucker can rot for all I care."

"I'm not here about Tyler."

Chase's chin lifted. "Good thing. Now what do you want?"

Sophie pulled in a breath. Now that she was here, it almost seemed silly. It was just so abstract, so unbelievable. Like a Hollywood movie. And Chase was Jason Bourne from the Bourne movies, a man with lethal skills and the ability to save her life. The whole way here from New York, all she'd kept thinking was that if she could reach Chase's apartment, she'd be fine.

When she'd gotten to Union Station, she'd hailed a taxi and given them this address. As the taxi took her into the suburbs of Maryland, she'd started to wonder if she'd made a mistake. When they'd turned onto a remote road with no houses, she'd been convinced of it. She'd had her hand on the door handle, ready to escape.

And then the taxi driver stopped and motioned toward a darkened house sitting off the road. Once she'd paid and been left standing in the dark, it had taken her a moment to realize there was another building, a garage with an apartment over the top. That was Chase's place. Now that she was inside and could see his living room, she was surprised to find it tastefully furnished despite its small size. Surprised because there wasn't a board with concrete blocks to hold up his television or anything.

There was, however, a guitar on a stand and an amp sitting near. There were also pictures of album covers on his walls. None of Tyler's, but plenty of other famous guitar players.

His mouth tightened as her gaze slipped over his walls and back to him. "Out with it, Sophie. It's late and I want to go back to sleep. If you aren't here to beg for a kidney or some bone marrow, what do you want?"

"I wish it were that simple," she said softly. "But it's not. It's nothing to do with Tyler. It's me."

His eyes narrowed. "We aren't actually related, you know. I can't give you blood or marrow or an organ."

She felt her teeth grinding. "Actually, that's not necessarily true. You wouldn't know without tests." His nostrils flared and she realized she was getting distracted. "But donations aren't why I need help. It's…" She swallowed. "Have you ever heard of Grigori Androv?"

It was kind of a stupid question in a way, considering that Grigori owned Zoprava, a Russian technology firm that sold a popular antivirus software. He'd been in the news a lot lately, not all of it good, but that was to be expected when a man was as powerful and controversial as he was.

She'd grown up with people who lived in the media spotlight, so she knew to take it with a grain of salt. And yet sometimes what they said was true. She'd learned that too.

"What does Androv have to do with you?" Chase demanded, his sexy green eyes flashing fire.

Sophie swallowed. "I met him at a charity event. We seemed to connect, and he asked for my number. I gave it to him."

Chase swore. Not the reaction she'd expected.

"He was nice to me. He sent flowers every day. He was… romantic."

It felt so stupid to say that now, but it had been the truth. He'd been romantic, hitting all the right notes as he sent flowers and cards and whisked her to fancy dinners and Broadway shows. He'd romanced her the way a girl wanted to be romanced. Slow, deliberate, attentive. And since she hadn't had a lot of romance in her life, she'd fallen for it hook, line, and sinker.

Chase was looking at her with a hard expression. "Any guy who sends you flowers every fucking day is a stalker, not a romantic." He shook his head. "I don't care how many orphans he donates money to, Androv is bad news. You need to stay away from him."

Sophie shivered. She'd come a long way tonight and she still wasn't safe. She wrapped her arms around herself and rubbed. Tears threatened to spill over. "I didn't know that at the time. I thought he was just a rich guy with enemies." She swallowed. "But I know better now."

Chase looked a little furious. Or maybe a lot furious. "What happened? Did he assault you?"

She shook her head even while her throat burned. Assault her? He'd never even kissed her.

"No, he didn't assault me. But I... I heard him arguing with someone on the phone, threatening him if he didn't do what Grigori wanted." Chase frowned and she hurried on. "I know that doesn't necessarily mean anything. I thought it was just business, quite honestly, even if it wasn't very nice. Sort of like when you're pissed at someone and you say you could kill them, but of course you don't literally mean that. B-but that same man was found in the East River four days ago."

She had Chase's full attention now. She could tell it by the way his nostrils flared and his eyes flashed. "A coincidence," he said—and she didn't blame him because she'd said the same thing when she'd seen the news report. Grigori's argument with the man had chilled her, but even then she couldn't say that Grigori had anything to do with his death.

Until tonight.

"It looks that way, but it's not."

"How can you be sure?"

This was the part she hated. The part that made her sick. It still wasn't a smoking gun, so to speak—but she knew the truth. She'd seen it in Grigori's eyes. He was unbalanced, vicious.

"I went to his apartment tonight to tell him I needed space, that I wanted to take a break for a while. He was having a small party, so I felt safe. He took me into his home office to talk—and then he got very angry. He asked me if I'd seen the news—and then he said the same thing would happen to me if I tried to stop seeing him."

Chase's face was a study in controlled rage.

Sophie swallowed as she tumbled on. "I thought he might hit me, but he didn't get the chance. He grabbed me—but his butler interrupted and Grigori let me go. He left me in his office and told me not to move until he came back."

"But you did move."

"I was scared, so I ran while I could." She hadn't left his apartment empty-handed, however.

Chase shoved a hand through his dark hair. It stood on end, but in a sexy way. "I'm sorry, Sophie—but exactly what do you expect me to do about this? You had a fight with Androv. He's a bully and an egomaniac, but I doubt he's going to kill you because you argued. It's risky to go around killing everyone you don't like, and he knows that. He's a fucking bully, and you don't need to see him again. Go to the police and file a restraining order."

She clenched her hands into fists. "You don't know him."

"Neither do you if you thought he was just a nice man with enemies."

She deserved his sarcasm. "I'm afraid, Chase. I need your help."

"Why my help? Why not the police?"

She swallowed. She'd thought about going to the

police, but what could they do? It was her word against Grigori's—and they weren't going to arrest him because he'd threatened her. Not to mention she had technically stolen his property when she'd fled his apartment.

"You're a soldier. An elite soldier. You do counterterrorism work—"

His brows lowered and he looked pissed.

She hurried on. "That's what Tyler said. He told me you could protect me."

And God, she hoped it was true. Because if Chase turned her down, what would she do?

He swore, long and hard. She wasn't encouraged by the look on his face.

"I'm not a fucking bodyguard, Sophie. Tyler is wrong. You need the police for this, not me. I can't help you."

Chapter Three

CHASE COULDN'T REMEMBER THE LAST TIME HE'D BEEN so pissed. He didn't give Tyler Nash much thought these days, and he certainly never thought of Sophie. He knew she'd gotten advantages in life because of Tyler's influence, and that used to piss him off. Now he couldn't care less.

But knowing that Tyler had called his mom and gotten his address? Knowing that his mom had told Tyler—because who else would have?—that he worked in top secret stuff and could help? Was the man ever done taking advantage of Carrie Daniels?

Sophie was looking at him with wide eyes, her cheeks flushed though her skin was pale. He could see her pulse beating in her throat, that soft fluttering like a hummingbird's wings. He felt a rush of sympathy for her and immediately stomped it back down.

What kind of dumb twit got involved with Grigori Androv? Even if Sophie didn't have the advantage of working for HOT, which maintained a dossier on

Androv and knew precisely how he'd built his fortune—it wasn't in software but rather in the ugly world of organized crime and petty arms dealing—the Russian had been in the news recently for an alleged assault of a hotel maid.

The details were ugly and brutal—and the maid was being systematically taken apart in the court of public opinion by Androv's spin doctors.

"If you don't help me, I'll be dead by the end of the week," she said. "Maybe sooner."

Yeah, he was pissed at the idea of Androv threatening her, but if the man hadn't eliminated the hotel maid by now, he wasn't going to kill Sophie. "He's not going to hurt you. He's smarter than that. He has too many other interests to protect, and you're nothing to him in the scheme of things. You wounded his pride. Nothing more."

She didn't look relieved. If anything, she looked even more desperate. "I took s-something from his office. A flash drive. He'll have realized it by now—and he'll want it back. He'll stop at nothing to get it."

Interest sparked deep inside even though he told himself it was probably bullshit. "Do you know what's on it?"

"No. But I never saw him without it. It's important to him."

"It could be anything. Or nothing. Lots of people use flash drives. It doesn't mean anything. It could be pictures of his vacation—or dirty pictures he gets off on."

"But what if it does mean something? What if there's information he doesn't want made public?"

She looked hopeful. And, damn, he had to admit he was hooked. She'd thrown him the fucking bait and she was reeling him in bit by bit. She tumbled on before he could speak.

"He told me he doesn't trust the cloud with what's on it—and I know that's crazy because he makes a living selling antivirus software, so presumably he should have the best firewall protection there is. But it's true. He told me he doesn't trust the cloud and that it was better if his enemies didn't get this information."

Chase could only gape at her. "Why would he tell you this? And how did you get ahold of it if it's so important to him?"

"He was using his laptop in his limo when we were going somewhere once, and he inserted a flash drive. I asked why he didn't just use the cloud. He told me he didn't trust it. As for how I got it… it was on his desk with his papers. When the butler interrupted, he left me in his office. I grabbed it and ran."

Chase's senses were tingling now. He held out a hand. "Better hand it over and let me have a look."

Her eyes dropped away. "I… I don't have it. I mailed it before I left town. I thought it was safer that way."

"You mailed it? To me?" He turned his head to the pile of mail he'd brought in earlier. If she'd just mailed it, it wouldn't be here yet. But fuck, this was not at all what he needed right now.

She reached for him, her fingers grazing over his arm for the briefest of seconds. He felt as if someone had touched him with a hot iron. His head whipped around, his eyes boring into hers. She licked her lips again, a quick maneuver that had him thinking about pink tongues and pleasurable uses for them.

"I didn't mail it to you," she was saying as he dragged his mind into the present. "I sent it to Tyler's apartment… in Paris."

Chase felt his brows arrow down. Of course the fucker had an apartment in Paris. Chase's mother had always said she wanted to go to Paris someday. And Tyler had a fucking apartment there. Figured.

"You sent it to Paris. And I suppose you want me to go get it, right?" He really couldn't believe the nerve of this girl, but then why not? She'd been raised in privilege and splendor. She'd never had to work a day in her life while he'd always worked for everything he had. He resented the fuck out of her for that.

"Yes… but I want to go with you. It won't be there for three more days, so there's time. But we should be there when it arrives."

He blinked at her for a second before the truth of what was going on here hit him. Holy shit, she was crazy. Too many fucking conspiracy theory movies probably. And he wasn't about to play along. She was a drama queen, fishing for sympathy and trying to drag him into her own twisted world of intrigue and danger. Hell, for all he knew, she was making up the existence of the flash drive—though the why of it eluded him.

But she did seem genuinely scared, which didn't help.

He raked a hand over his head. Fuck, he hadn't had enough sleep for this shit.

"Look, sweetheart, even if I wanted to help you, I can't just take off for Paris. I'm a soldier and there are procedures to be followed. I go to Paris with you, I'm AWOL from my job. And I can promise you I'm not doing that."

Technically, since they'd just returned from a mission in Qu'rim where they'd rescued a group of archaeologists, his team was off duty for another week. The guys were all taking holidays, going to beaches and mountains and relaxing until time to return for duty.

But the difference was that everyone was staying within an eight-hour radius of HQ. That was the requirement unless officially on leave. The eight hours was travel time, not distance—and Paris was over eight hours when you added airport delays and car time.

"I'll pay you, if that's the issue."

Chase stiffened. He was just about to tell her to get the fuck out when the neighbor's dog started barking like crazy. Sophie whirled and stared at the door. The hair on Chase's neck prickled, but he dismissed it. Crazy night. Lack of sleep.

"Relax, it's probably a possum or a raccoon. One time, that idiot dog got worked up over a skunk—didn't work out well for his owner, I can promise you that."

She threw him a look over her shoulder. For the first time, he was looking at the rear of her—and it was a mighty fine rear to look at. Baby had back, that's for sure. Sophie might be the privileged stepdaughter of a wealthy man, but she didn't look like someone who had a personal trainer and a chef who fixed salads for her.

No, the girl looked like she liked her fries and milk-shakes a bit more than that—and yet she was still fucking gorgeous with her red-gold hair and killer curves. No wonder Androv had been interested.

"I really need to get out of here," she said, her voice tinged with panic. "When Grigori figures out I've left New York, he'll come looking for me."

He had to admire the depth of the conspiracy theory scenario she had going. Yep, Sophie had watched too many *Mission Impossible* movies.

Chase sank onto the couch and propped his feet on the coffee table. "I don't think I've seen you in about ten years or so. Why would Androv assume you'd come to me?"

Sophie looked suddenly disgusted with him, like he was the one a few bricks short of a load. It was not a good feeling.

"How do you think I got your address? By carrier pigeon? I called Tyler for help and he told me to come to you."

Chase felt the first prickle of warning slip down his spine. Maybe she was blowing the whole thing out of proportion… but what if she was right?

"Do you think Androv tapped your phone?"

"I put nothing past him."

The bad feeling in his gut was growing stronger. "Why didn't you use a fucking pay phone then?"

She looked distressed. "I didn't have a lot of time. I left Grigori's place and went straight to the shipping office and then the train station. I didn't even go home first!"

If she wasn't just doing this for attention, if this wasn't a joke—

The dog's frantic barking ceased abruptly.

Fuck, that probably wasn't good.

"You don't have the phone with you, right? Please tell me you ditched it."

She frowned. "Well, yes, I have it. I turned it off though. I thought you could wipe it for me."

Chase erupted from the couch and stalked to where she stood. Her eyes widened and alarm skated over her features.

"Hand it the fuck over. Now."

She dug into her purse and pulled out an innocent-looking Android phone. Chase snatched it and went down the hall to the bathroom, Sophie on his heels the whole way. She might be doing this for attention, making mountains out of molehills, but he wasn't taking fucking chances.

You didn't stay alive in his world by ignoring your gut when it started giving you funny vibes.

"What are you doing? Wait a minute, why—?"

Chase dropped the phone in the toilet and closed the lid. Sophie stood there with her mouth hanging open. Indignation crossed her face as he stalked past her toward the bedroom.

"Why did you do that? It could be debugged—every contact I have is in there! Everything I am—my photos, my texts—"

He spun on her, wanting like hell to grab her shoulders and shake her. Then he wanted to smash his mouth to hers and take her in a hard kiss.

Whoa, where the fuck had that come from?

"Androv is the big time, sweetheart. Turning it off—shit, you probably *can't* turn it off. If what you say is true, then it's very likely been recording everything and transmitting it back to your *boyfriend*."

She gasped, her hand slapping over her mouth in horror. Not entirely stupid then. She knew what it meant if Androv had heard what she'd just said about the flash drive and Paris.

He shoved past her and went to grab his bugout bag with his weapons and papers. It might be a false alarm, but he was taking her to HOT HQ and figuring this shit out there.

Something pinged against metal. And then it happened again. Chase threw himself at Sophie and grabbed her, dragging her down to the floor as he did so. There was a whoosh—and then his apartment erupted in flame.

Chapter Four

SOPHIE WAS TOO SHOCKED TO SCREAM. THE WEIGHT OF Chase's body pressed her into the floor for only a moment before he scrambled up and jerked her to her feet. The front of his apartment, where they'd been standing only moments before, was ablaze. Fire licked at the walls and glass shattered.

"Come on," he said roughly, tugging her toward the back of the apartment and away from the flames.

Sophie's heart hammered, but she did as he asked. This was not her area of expertise, that's for sure. Chase grabbed the bag he'd dropped when he'd tackled her and then raced into another room. He jerked on a pair of boots, then fell to the floor and shoved an area rug aside to reveal—a trapdoor?

Sophie blinked. Who the heck had a trapdoor in their apartment?

Chase produced a weapon from somewhere, and then he yanked the door open and waited a few seconds. When nothing happened, he snagged a pillow from the bed and dropped it through the opening. Still nothing. He looked up at her.

"I'll go down first, but you better be right behind me. If you're scared of heights or the dark, now's not the time to let that stop you. Your life depends on it, got that?"

Sophie nodded. Chase dropped his bag down the hole and then started down the ladder. Sophie scrambled over and found the rungs of the ladder with her toes. Her heart rocketed and her breath came in pants. Slowly, she let herself down, her legs and arms shaking. The heat from the flames was growing unbearable, pulling her breath from her body, wrapping around her throat.

A hand gripped her hip, and she nearly jumped out of her skin. But it was Chase, of course. He grasped her hips with both hands and steadied her as she came down the ladder. Before her feet touched the ground, he picked her up as if she weighed nothing and set her on the floor.

It was hotter down here. The room glowed orange with the flames licking against the exterior. A dark, low-slung car sat in the garage like a predator waiting to pounce.

"Get in," he said as he went around to the driver's side and opened the door. He tossed his bag into the back and dropped down into the seat.

"My purse," Sophie gasped. "I left it in your apartment."

She'd dropped it when he tackled her and she hadn't picked it up again.

"Too late. Get in the car."

"But my credit cards, my money—"

Chase looked utterly furious. "Get the fuck in the car, Sophie. You can't use a credit card if you're dead."

He was right. She ran over and yanked open the door before throwing herself into the seat and grabbing the seat belt. The car was a Corvette. An older model, not the newest one, but nice with a dark interior and a black body. The car growled to life as he turned the key, and she had to drag her gaze from his face before she could think clearly enough to realize what he was about to do.

The garage door was closed and he was planning to put the car through it. With them inside. Oh God.

"Hang on," he said tightly.

He jerked the car into gear, pressed a button on a handheld remote—and the door blasted open on its own. Sophie shrieked, but the scream died in her throat as she was thrown back against the seat. The car growled and shot out into the open, tires spinning and rubber burning.

"Get down," he told her about the time she heard a pop.

Sophie slipped down in the seat as far as she could. The sky was orange and red as the building burned. Chase's face was orange and red too, his jaw set firmly, his eyes flashing with anger as he drove the car like he'd just robbed a bank.

There were more pops and then some shouting, but the noise grew faint pretty quickly as they flew down the road she'd traveled up in a taxi just a short while ago.

Sophie lifted herself up and turned around to look back. The sky glowed, but she didn't see any movement behind them.

"He found me that quickly," she said in shock.

Chase glanced at her. "Yeah, that quickly."

"If I'd been delayed at any point—his people could have grabbed me." Her stomach bottomed out. "I have to get to Paris."

He snorted. "One step at a time, sweetheart. Let's get somewhere safe and figure out what happens next."

"I guess you believe me now, huh?"

Because it had been pretty clear at one point that he'd thought she was making it all up.

He glanced at her, his expression grim. "Hard not to after that."

A car appeared on the road ahead. Chase tensed his fingers on the steering wheel as the lights grew bigger far more quickly than they should have. Someone was heading toward them at a high rate of speed.

"Fuck," Chase said before downshifting the Corvette and whipping onto a side road. The tires spun and the car bounced across grass and gravel before finding purchase on asphalt again.

Sophie clutched the door, hard. She was positive that her fingers would need to be pried free eventually. The car flew faster than was comfortable for peace of mind. The road was dark, illuminated only by the headlights. If they came to a curve too quickly, or if a deer leapt out in front of them—

She didn't want to think about it. She told herself to close her eyes, but she couldn't manage that either. All she could do was hold on and pray they made it without crashing.

Chase glanced into the rearview. "These guys don't give up."

"Can you outrun them?"

"Probably not. I'm going to guess they've set up checkpoints along the road—" He seemed to listen for something, then nodded. "Yep, they've got a helicopter. This isn't going to end well, Sophie."

She could barely breathe. "It has to. You have to do something."

He shot her a glance. "Why me? I'm not the one who got myself into this mess." His hands tightened on the wheel. "In fact, if I just stopped and handed you over, I imagine I could be on my way."

"You wouldn't!"

His expression hardened. "No, I wouldn't. But what kind of person shows up unannounced in the middle of the night with a bunch of criminals on her heels and almost gets a guy killed?"

"Chase... I'm sorry. I don't know what else to say, but I really am."

"I don't even fucking like you, you know that?" He glanced up in the rearview, downshifted the Vette suddenly, and spun into a turn.

Her stomach bottomed out as she gripped the door and the console and held on for dear life. Chase straightened the Vette and shot forward again.

"You don't like me? But why not? You don't really know me. You never even tried."

His words hurt because she was nothing but nice to

everyone she knew. Always had been. In the world she'd grown up in, where being thin and gorgeous was the highest currency possible, she'd had to find something to protect herself with. She'd become a people pleaser, because who could hate someone who was nice to you all the time? Someone who only wanted you to be happy?

He shot her a look. "Really, you have to ask that? You can't figure it out for yourself?"

It was hard to think when they were flying down the road and she could die at any minute, either from Grigori's men killing her or from this car crashing and erupting in a ball of flame.

"You barely talked to me when you visited us—and when you did, it was mean. I thought you didn't know I existed most of the time."

He snorted. "Oh, I knew. Sophie Nash." He emphasized the last name. "I'm his only biological child, did you know that? The only one, and he always acted like he'd rather I didn't exist. Gives his name to you, raises you as his—and you wonder why I never liked you?"

Her chest ached. "It's not my fault, Chase. I was a kid."

"So was I," he ground out.

She wanted to reach out and touch him, squeeze his arm or something, but she knew he wouldn't welcome it. She sucked in a breath, hoping to find some words, but he spoke before she could.

"We're going to have to ditch the car." His voice was calm, matter-of-fact.

She was almost relieved for the change in subject, no matter how serious. "Ditch? But how will we get away?"

"We're under heavy tree cover at the moment. The helicopter can see the glow from the headlights, but they can't pinpoint to the exact degree where we are until we emerge again. Which we aren't doing—though you'd better pray they don't have thermal-imaging capabilities."

Sophie gulped. "What would that do?"

"It means they can find us by our heat signature. We can't hide that. But take heart, I doubt Androv's men have access to a military helicopter on such short notice. It's probably a local job, so I wouldn't worry too much."

Wouldn't worry too much? Was he crazy?

He turned off the road and drove into the grass, and she began to think he definitely was crazy when she saw the bushes up ahead. He switched off the headlights and kept going. Branches scraped and slapped the car as they passed into a cluster of foliage.

Sophie cringed. If he hated her already, he'd want to murder her with the way his car was getting beaten and scratched. He didn't say anything as he came to a stop and killed the engine.

It was eerily quiet, like that strange calm right before a storm.

"What now?" she asked in a whisper that hurt her throat because it was so tight.

He turned to her. "You ever take a survival course, Sophie?"

Chapter Five

HE KNEW THE ANSWER TO THAT QUESTION ALREADY, BUT even if he hadn't, the way her breath shortened would have told him she'd never taken a survival course. No way had this little princess ever roughed it a night in her life.

She shook her head in the darkness, and he could feel the fear emanating from her. A twinge of guilt speared him. He hadn't helped her just now by telling her he'd always disliked her. Of course he had, but he'd been a kid. So had she. They weren't kids now, and logically he knew she wasn't to blame for the actions of his father.

Didn't mean he didn't resent her though. Or resent the mess she'd just landed him in.

"No," she finally squeaked out. "Why?"

"We're going into the woods, Sophie. There will be no hot showers or soft beds. No room service."

"All right."

He blinked. "All right? You're good with that?"

"I don't think I have a choice, do I? Tell me what I need to do and I'll do it."

He reached into the back of the car and grabbed his pack. "All you need to do for now is follow me—and keep your mouth shut."

He got out of the car, wincing at how hard he had to shove the door. He'd buried them good in the bushes, which meant his Vette was probably scratched to hell. Couldn't be helped though. Getting out alive was more important than a car, no matter that he'd worked hard to buy the damn thing or that he'd done some of the restoration work himself.

He'd learned growing up that things were just things. His mother had taught him that with quiet dignity and hard work.

Sophie stumbled out of the car on the other side. She had nothing but the clothes on her back, which was good for his purposes. He thought of that scene in *Romancing the Stone*, a movie his mother loved, where Jack Colton took Joan Wilder's suitcases and threw them over the side of a cliff. At least he didn't have to do that to Sophie. She hadn't had any suitcases.

"We're going to have to do this in the dark," he said. "No lights to guide the way."

She laughed, which surprised him, even if it was nervous laughter. "Bet you say that to all the girls."

Her answer shocked him. "Honey, no way. I like to look at everything while I'm sampling the buffet."

It was her turn to be surprised, judging by the silence. In the distance, he could hear the helicopter sweeping overhead. They had to get out of here before

Androv's men figured out where they were. They were most likely thugs, not Special Operators like he was, so he definitely had the advantage. But he had to use it while he had it.

"Follow my voice, Sophie, and come to my side."

He heard the rustle of bushes in the dark and then a curse. But a moment later she made it around the car. His vision had adjusted and he could see her. He wished like hell he had his night vision goggles, but that was part of his gear back at HOT. No taking those home for fun.

"Can you see?" he asked her.

"Do I look like a cat?" she grumbled.

"Not especially."

She sighed. "Sorry. No, I can't see well. I can tell that the big shape in front of me is you, and that's about it."

He set the bag on the roof of the car and rummaged through for a T-shirt. Then he pulled it over his head and zipped the bag again. It was chilly, but as soon as they started moving, he'd heat up.

"Keep your eyes on my shape and follow me. If you feel like you can't keep up, for God's sake let me know. I'll be finding a trail and I can't look back and make sure you're there every ten seconds."

"Chase," she said as he turned away.

"Yeah?"

"Thanks for helping me."

———

SOPHIE HAD no idea how long they had walked, but she was utterly miserable. It was dark and dank in the woods, and her mind began to conjure up all kinds of critters hiding in the gloom: snakes, bears, foxes, wild-cats. Bigfoot. She stayed on Chase's heels, as close as she could get, and prayed nothing would get her.

She kept listening for the sounds of pursuit—cars, motorcycles, horses maybe—but she heard nothing. The helicopter had stopped flying overhead about an hour ago. But that didn't mean Grigori had given up or that she was safe. She knew that.

For the first time in hours, she could think about everything that had happened tonight and just how close she'd come to dying. New York City was big, and she'd thought it would take Grigori quite some time to realize she'd left the city instead of hiding out at a friend's. But his men had been so close on her tail that it was impossible to believe they hadn't been tracking her through her phone. Chase was right and she'd been a fool to keep it.

When they'd found her, they'd set Chase's apartment on fire. With her and Chase in it. Sophie shivered.

Eventually, Chase stopped and she walked right into him, colliding with his hard body and bouncing backward. Somehow he turned and caught one of her flailing arms before she fell. Her heart skittered as he tugged her up and she hit him again, only this time she hit softer—and she felt the impression of all that hard muscle against her body.

He was a temple of muscle. A monument to working out, with taut peaks and hard planes in all the right places, a rippling fantasy man come to life. She practically moaned, except that would be weird.

Weird because they were running from men intent on killing her and weird because he was technically her stepbrother. Though in the few visits he'd ever made to California, all she'd done was think how intriguing he was. Her thoughts had not been sisterly in the least.

"Steady," he said, and she nearly laughed. Steady? Oh no, she was anything but steady.

"Why have we stopped?"

He tilted his head up, and she realized that she could see him much better now. The shadowy outlines of his face had coalesced into a beautiful portrait.

"It'll be light soon. We need to stop."

"But shouldn't we keep going? Keep distance between us and them?"

He shook his head. "Are you ready to do that, Sophie? How much farther can you go? Another hour? Two? Ten?"

It hit her then that he was stopping for her. If he'd been on his own, he'd have kept going.

"I… No, not much farther. My feet hurt and my back aches."

Not that she hadn't felt worse after a day at work, but that was different somehow. She could go home and soak her feet or get a massage from her massage-therapist roommate.

There would be no massages tonight. She looked at the pinkening sky. *Today.*

"All right, we're going up this tree here," he said,

placing his palm against the side of the tree he was standing near.

Sophie tilted her head back to look up into the thick tangle of branches. "Uh, I don't think I'm much of a climber, Chase. Unless you have a ladder."

"Actually, I do. There's a deer stand in this tree. And there's a ladder up there. Just have to go up and get it."

She peered into the tree but didn't see anything. "How do you know that?"

He was scowling, but even his scowl made her heart skip. "I'm from Tennessee, darlin'. We like to hunt—and I know the guy who owns this land. He put a stand in this tree, and I've used it a few times."

He dropped his bag on the ground and eyed the tree. Then he started to climb. She watched him—and realized with a start there was a small wooden structure up there. It was camouflaged so well that it wasn't easy to see at first.

"Better step back," he called down. "Don't want to get hit by the ladder."

She did as he said and then a rope ladder unfurled and slapped the side of the tree. Chase came back down and dropped to the ground.

"You first," he told her.

She looked at the rope ladder doubtfully. But it had held him when he shimmied back down on it, so she gripped the rope and put her foot on the first rung. It was a shaky climb, but she made it up. She pulled herself into the stand and looked around. It wasn't quite what she'd expected—in fact, it was more like a tree house than a deer stand. It was dark inside, but there

33

were windows with screens and what appeared to be a twin-sized Army cot. In one corner, there was a stack of bottled water and some boxes that she hoped contained food.

She stepped into the little room, wary for the sensation of swaying with the tree, but nothing happened. The room was solid. And surprising as hell.

She turned as Chase came through the opening. He threw his bag and it slid across the floor, hitting the bed. Then he turned and pulled the ladder up, rolling it and leaving it near the entrance. He tugged a door down and latched it, then faced her.

That's when she realized he could stand up in this darned thing.

"Who in the hell builds a tree house and calls it a deer stand?" she asked.

Chase laughed. "Guy who owns the land is kind of a doomsday prepper, but on a smaller scale. I don't think he really expects doomsday—but he likes being ready for anything. He stockpiles supplies, weapons, and ammo in various locations on his property. Kinda nutty, but a nice enough guy."

Sophie turned around to look at the space. With Chase inside, it was suddenly a whole lot smaller than it had been. And the only surface to sit on besides the floor was the cot.

"Now what?" she asked, chafing her arms as if she were cold. She wasn't, but her skin prickled from the circumstances. Or maybe it was just Chase's nearness.

He shrugged and retrieved his pack. "We eat and rest. Tonight we'll head out again."

"Where are we going?"

He speared her with a look. "Somewhere safe."

She hated the way he was so cryptic with her, but she knew it was no good to press him. She rubbed her arms again. His gaze followed the motion, and then he turned away and went over to the boxes in the corner. He ripped one open and started rummaging through it.

"I need to let my mom and Tyler know I'm okay," she said and then immediately regretted it when he stiffened. She knew that any mention of Tyler made him angry.

But when he came back over to her with a pack of peanut butter crackers and a bottle of water, he looked cool, at ease. He thrust the food and drink at her and she took it.

"No can do, sweetheart. No contact with anyone outside. It's too dangerous."

She wanted to protest, but there was no point in arguing. She didn't have a phone anymore, and she doubted there was a pay phone on a tree trunk somewhere. Besides, she'd asked for his help and she had to trust that he knew what he was doing.

She sank onto the edge of the bed and ripped open the crackers. She was usually so careful with food, but she was starving right now. Chase retrieved crackers and water for himself, then reached into a dark corner and produced a folding chair. He proceeded to sit down and tear into his food.

"How will we get to Paris?" she asked when the silence stretched uncomfortably.

"The usual way, I'd imagine."

"My passport is in my apartment and my ID was in my purse." She spared a pained thought for the Louis Vuitton bag that was nothing but ash by now. "I lost the tracking number for the package as well."

She'd had the receipt with the number on it. She hadn't sent it signature required, but she'd been comforted by the fact she could track its progress if she needed to.

"Doesn't matter. You know when it's getting there. That's enough."

She finished a cracker and blew out a frustrated breath. "You're becoming very terse, Chase. Am I bothering you or something?"

"Are you bothering me? Hell yeah, you're bothering me. I was asleep when you woke me. If you'd been a waitress wanting to fuck, that would have been far better than what we've got going on now."

She really wanted to throw something at him. Surly asshole.

Surly asshole who saved your life…

Thus far.

And she wasn't even touching that comment about fucking. Though God help her, she had a moment of picturing him naked. Picturing them together naked.

She shook her head to rid herself of that much-too-hot image. "I *am* a waitress, asswipe."

He snorted. "Sure you are."

"No, really. I am. I want to be an actress, so I decided to wait tables for a while, study people. You'd be surprised what you learn when you wait on people."

He was sitting back in the chair now, long legs

sprawled out in front of him, bottle of water held casually in one hand. And she knew he was dismissing her. Scoffing at her. "You decided to wait tables for the *fun* of it. How noble and self-sacrificing of you. Most people who wait tables do it because they need the money."

She sniffed, but a wave of heat washed over her at his words. All right, maybe it did sound silly. "It's still work, and I still did it. *Am* doing it. It's not a lark."

"Yeah, but you don't need the money."

"What makes you think that? For all you know, I've been paying my own way in New York."

"Maybe. But I doubt it. Tyler lowered himself enough to call my mother and ask for my address—if he'd do that, he wouldn't make you fend for yourself in the big city."

She was glad it wasn't bright in this room because he'd see how red her face was. Naturally, he was spot-on in his assessment—but not for the reason he thought. It had always been her mother's policy to throw money at Sophie as if that was all she needed to be happy. Sophie wasn't sure her mother was capable of guilt, but if she was, money was how she made up for her lack of involvement in Sophie's life when she'd been growing up.

And Sophie spent it too. Why not?

"Fine, I don't need the money to live. But if you think I'm living in a Park Avenue penthouse, then you'd be wrong. I live in a nice brownstone in the theater district, I have a roommate, and I work hard at my craft and my job. I have an audition next week, by the way."

She was proud of that because she'd gotten it all on

her own. Through hard work and not giving up. It was only a small off-Broadway production, but it was a start. And not one that anyone else had helped her to get.

"I'll try to have you back in time, princess." His tone dripped with sarcasm.

Far from wounding her this time, it made her angry. "You know, no matter what you think, I'm a good person. I don't deserve your attitude. If you don't like me, fine. But you don't have to be an asshole about it."

He didn't say anything for a long moment. "All right, you're a good person. A good person with poor judgment. Sorry if it offends you, princess, but I *can* be pissed at you for that. Your lack of judgment has so far cost me a place to live and a car I loved, so forgive me if I'm not feeling all cuddly toward you at the moment."

Guilt pricked her. "I'll pay you back, Chase."

"With your waitressing money, of course."

"Of course," she said, returning his sarcasm.

He downed half his water and then looked straight at her, his dark eyes boring into hers. "If you think I'm going to turn down Tyler's money because I hate him, you'd be wrong. The least the fucker can do is replace my shit if I get you out of this in one piece."

Her heart thumped. "You will. That's why I came. You're the only one who can."

He stood and went to peek out a window. The sky was getting lighter, but they were hidden in the tree and the branches and camouflage helped obscure them—or so she hoped.

"Go to sleep while you can, Sophie. It's going to be a long day, and a long night ahead."

She stared at his back. It was broad, and the T-shirt he'd put on clung to taut muscles. His biceps bunched and flexed as he lifted an arm and pressed his palm to the wall beside the window as he peered out.

"What about you? When will you sleep?"

He turned and speared her with a look. "Don't worry about me. Worry about yourself."

He unzipped his pack and took out a pair of binoculars. Then he went over to the door and unlatched it.

Sophie stiffened. "What are you doing?"

"I'm going to check out the surroundings, make sure no one's out there."

Her stomach flipped. She didn't want him to go, didn't want to be alone out here in the woods. What if he didn't come back? What if she had to find her own way out again? If she had her phone, she'd use GPS— but she had nothing.

"Do you have to?" She sounded breathless and a little scared, but she couldn't help it.

His gaze softened for a second before hardening again. "Yes. Go to sleep and don't worry about it. I need you to be ready to go when it's time."

He dropped out of sight and Sophie was alone.

Chapter Six

THERE WAS NO SIGN OF PURSUIT IN THE IMMEDIATE AREA. Chase did a perimeter sweep, but all was clear. Which was good because he still wasn't quite sure what the fuck he was going to do with Princess Sophie.

His team was scattered after the last mission. He'd planned to take her to HOT HQ and sort it out there, but that was before someone had set his apartment on fire. Before he knew without a doubt that Androv really did want her dead.

If he took her to HOT now, Mendez would have to turn her over to the FBI. Domestic crime wasn't part of HOT's mandate, and they couldn't get involved in this kind of thing. Yeah, Androv owned Zoprava and supplied antivirus solutions to companies worldwide. He also owned quite a bit of property in New York, and he did a lot of business there.

But none of that involved the military or national security, which meant no HOT. He was on their watch list as someone of interest, primarily because he had a lot of money and he'd dabbled in selling Russian military technology at one time. It hadn't been as profitable as his other enterprises, so he hadn't done a lot with it, which meant he wasn't a HOT target at the moment.

Yet if there was something incriminating on that flash drive, something big... Chase gripped his weapon tighter and dragged in a breath. Yeah, that would be amazing.

If Androv was willing to use lethal force to get it back, which he appeared to be, then it was entirely possible there was something on there he didn't want falling into the wrong hands. Which made Chase really want to know what was on the flash drive.

There was only one way to find out. He had to go to Paris and get it. No matter what he'd said about Androv's ability to record Sophie's conversations when her phone was off, it was possible it hadn't happened that way. That all Androv had installed was a tracking device.

If so, there was still a chance to get the information before Androv or his people recovered it.

They just had to get the fuck out of this forest and get some help—though not HOT because Mendez wasn't going to authorize government assets for a mission against a private citizen, which Androv still was. He wasn't a military target, and he wasn't going to be unless something significant turned up—which meant Chase needed to seek alternative help for what was essentially a personal mission.

Chase continued his careful circuit of the area, checking for signs of human trespass. When he was satisfied there was nothing out of order, he returned to the stand, bare-climbing the tree and popping in the door. When he spotted Sophie, he paused and watched her for a long minute.

She was curled on the bed with her back to the door. Her long, strawberry blonde hair lay against the pillow, revealing the vulnerable column of her neck. Her skin was creamy, pale, and soft-looking, like silk. She had a small beauty mark on that luscious neck, a blemish that marred the otherwise-pristine swath of skin.

He'd noticed it earlier. It was a small spot, barely discernible in the dim light—and yet he wondered what it would be like to press his lips just there, right over the mark and near the soft pulse beat of her throat.

Chase had to shake himself like a wet dog to dislodge the image—and the corresponding heat that kindled in his groin. Jesus, what the hell was wrong with him? Even if she weren't his stepsister—or his father's cherished adopted daughter, more like—he wasn't attracted to pampered princesses. He liked girls who could shoot. Girls who drank beer and told dirty jokes. Girls who liked to fish and didn't squeal about having to touch worms.

You don't know she squeals over worms.

Yeah, right. As if she'd ever been fishing or baited a hook in her life.

She walked through the woods without complaint.

Yeah? What choice did she have?

Chase forced himself to turn away, to stop studying the rise of her shoulder, the dip of her waist, the sweet curve of her hip. The luscious roundness of her ass.

Fuck. He whipped open his bugout bag and took out the burner phone he kept there. He had to solve this situation and soon. The less time he spent with Miss Sophie Nash, the better. Chase flipped open the phone and sent a text to the only person he could think of who might be able to help him out of this mess without getting HOT involved.

Nothing to do now but wait.

————

SOPHIE BLINKED AWAKE, confusion settling into her brain for a moment. The cot was stiff, she was cold, and the air smelled woodsy and kind of musty at the same time. Her body ached as she shifted, her muscles protesting with sharp soreness in her legs and back.

When it hit her where she was, she sat up, wincing with pain as she searched the room. It was every bit as dark as it had been when they'd arrived earlier, so she figured she must have slept until almost nightfall. She would have thought that impossible considering the danger she was in, but apparently she was wrong. Her gaze settled on Chase lying on the floor. He was asleep —but then he cracked an eye open and stared at her, proving her wrong.

Her heart pattered, but if Chase was on the floor looking at her with annoyance—and he was—and they were still in the tree, which they were, then they were safe. Still alive, still hopeful.

Her stomach rumbled, and she put a hand over it because it was so loud. Chase pushed himself up to a sitting position and shoved a hand through his hair. His jaw cracked as he yawned, and she felt a pang of guilt that he'd had to sleep on the floor while she took the cot.

Still, she was glad he hadn't made her take the floor. If her body hurt this much after sleeping on a cot, she hated to think what it would feel like if she'd spent the day on a plank floor.

Chase reached for something beside him and then threw it at her with a "Here, catch."

Sophie caught the plastic package as if it were a fish, fumbling it back and forth until it plopped onto the bed beside her. "What is it?"

"It's an MRE—Meal, Ready to Eat," he said. "It's what we eat in the field. It'll fill you up, trust me."

The plastic was thick. She tried to tear it, but nothing happened. Chase pushed to his knees and came over to her. He bent his head, taking it from her. He was so close she could feel the heat emanating from him. He smelled like the outdoors, fresh and clean—and a little sweaty too. She bit her lip as he flipped open a knife. He cut the package open and looked up at her.

Her breath stopped in her chest as their eyes met. His were green, rimmed in brown with golden flecks dotting the iris. She had a sudden insane urge to reach out and touch his cheek, to skim her fingers over the hard plane of his jaw that had a day's growth of stubble.

He shoved the package he'd opened into her hand and turned away before she could do anything so stupid. Sophie took a deep breath, trying to calm her fluttering heart and make it beat normally again. Then she upended the MRE, and several envelopes spilled out.

She picked them up, reading each one, focusing on them as if they were the most important thing on earth. It was the only way to get her mind off Chase and that weird moment just now.

"Spaghetti? Really?"

"Just follow the directions and heat it up. It's not the best thing you've ever eaten, but it'll do the job."

She blinked at the packets littering the bed and wondered for a second if he'd hit his head on something. "Heat it? With what?"

"The ration heater. It's in there."

Sophie poked around until she found a plastic envelope that said Heater on it. *Really?* She turned it over, studying it. It was nothing more than a plastic bag with instructions on it. She glanced up at Chase, but he was busily sorting through his own stack of envelopes. She opened the heater bag, placed the spaghetti pack inside, and filled it to the line with water from the bottle she'd left beside the cot. Then she closed the bag and held it until it started to feel warm.

"How does this work?"

It really was getting hot. She set it on the floor, propping it against one of the cot's legs since the directions said to prop it up.

"It's a chemical reaction," Chase said with a shrug. "Magnesium, iron, and table salt. Add water and voila, you get heat."

For some insane reason, that excited her more than she'd have thought possible. She kept watching the bag as if it would do a magic trick or something. "That's pretty cool. I didn't do so well in science—I was more of an arts and humanities kind of person."

She babbled when she was nervous—and she was definitely nervous.

"Arts and humanities won't keep you from starving when it's just you and the environment."

"No… but at least I can quote Shakespeare and provide some entertainment to the rest of the campers."

Chase actually stopped what he was doing and looked at her long and hard. Sophie couldn't help but giggle at the look on his face—horror, and maybe fear she was an idiot at the same time. He didn't crack a smile when she giggled, but that didn't stop her. In fact, she giggled harder—and that made him frown even more.

Finally, she shook her head and tore open the candy bar from her MRE with trembling fingers. *Stop it.*

"It's a joke, Chase. I'm not planning on quoting any Shakespeare."

"Thank God for that," he grumbled.

She cocked her head as she sniffed the candy bar. Ordinarily she didn't eat candy, but these were extraordinary circumstances. She took a bite—oh, yum—and chewed. When was the last time she'd eaten chocolate?

Too long ago, that's for sure.

"You don't appreciate the Bard?"

"The what?"

She rolled her eyes. "Shakespeare. The Bard of Avon. To be or not to be and all that."

"Had to read *Julius Caesar* in high school. Boring as fuck."

Sophie's heart actually squeezed. What kind of barbarian didn't appreciate Shakespeare? Her finest role in high school had been Lady Macbeth. *Out, damned spot...*

"You should try *Hamlet*. Or *Macbeth*. *Romeo and Juliet*. *King Lear*."

Chase took a bite of bread. "Nope. Life's too short to read stuff you don't like."

Not reading Shakespeare was a travesty, in her opinion.

"So what *do* you like?"

His gaze sharpened for a second. Then he gave his head a little shake and snorted. "Stuff with pictures. Dirty pictures, preferably."

Sophie's mouth dropped open. And then she closed it in a hurry. He was trying to shock her. Derail her. And she'd started trembling again. Damn him.

"How about when it doesn't have pictures? What do you read then?"

"The newspaper, where I learn things like the fact Grigori Androv is accused of assaulting a hotel maid in Manhattan. Nothing as important as Shakespeare, obviously."

The heat of embarrassment rolled through her. "You know, you don't have to beat me over the head with my stupidity. There's nothing you can say that I haven't already said to myself."

His gaze remained sharp and hot on her face. And then he made an expression of dismissal, as if he'd decided it wasn't worth pursuing. "I get how you got involved with Androv—but why did you keep going out with him? You had to know he'd been accused of assaulting that woman."

She stared at the envelopes arrayed around her and swallowed. "He was charming. Attentive. Gentlemanly. And it was entirely possible that woman was looking for a settlement because he's wealthy. That's what he told me—and I've seen similar things growing up, so it wasn't impossible to believe."

"You still believe him?"

Her eyes blurred a little but she swiped the moisture away. She was ashamed of herself for what she'd thought about the poor maid. For what she'd believed. "No, I don't."

Their gazes met, tangled. It was a long moment before she managed to rip hers away. She reached for the MRE for something to do.

"Careful," he said. "It'll be hot."

It was indeed. She tore the packet open as directed and let some steam escape before she dipped the plastic spoon into it. It didn't smell too bad, so she touched her tongue to the sauce.

It wasn't gourmet, but it was pretty good when you were hungry. She spooned the bite into her mouth and swallowed. When she looked up, Chase was still watching her. His brows lowered, making his handsome face into a thundercloud.

"What?"

He dropped his gaze and ripped into his own MRE. "Nothing. Eat the food."

"I *was* eating it. You're the one who looked irritated about it."

"I'm not irritated."

"Sure you aren't. You're just Mr. Happy Sunshine all the time. I love that about you."

He shot her a look, the spoon halfway to his mouth. Sophie laughed at the confusion on his face, though it was nervous laughter. There was something going on here, and she didn't know what.

"Anybody ever tell you that you talk too much?"

"It's been mentioned a time or two."

"And you didn't learn a damn thing, I bet."

"What's there to learn? That I need to be quiet just because people like you don't like it? No thanks."

He frowned even harder. His voice, when he spoke, was tight with anger. "How about that you need to be quiet so your Russian pals don't follow the sound of your voice straight to this stand?"

Chapter Seven

Her eyes went wide, and Chase felt like a dick. Well, fuck, she did need to be quiet, but not because they were in danger right now. He'd checked the perimeter thoroughly, and he'd set up a couple of alarms that would trigger an alert to the monitoring system in the tree stand. Thank God for paranoid guys like Don who outfitted their land with state-of-the-art equipment just in case anarchy or the zombie apocalypse set in.

If Androv's men got within a two-mile radius, Chase would know about it. Which meant she could talk all she wanted, even if it did drive him insane.

"I'm sorry," she said softly.

Ah, Christ. "It's fine," he said, guilt pricking him. "Just keep it down a bit."

She nodded and went back to eating. But her eyes remained downcast and the fiery attitude she'd had a moment ago banked. It shouldn't bother him, but it did.

It wasn't that he'd wanted her to be quiet so much as

he'd been stunned at his reaction when she'd stuck her tongue out to lick the spoon. The sight of her pink tongue, the way it stretched toward the sauce, the dainty swipe she'd taken—and then the way she'd attacked the food once she determined it was good—that combination had been lethal to him, assaulting him on a primal level that made his dick start to tingle in reaction. *Not good.*

He wasn't supposed to get a hard-on over Sophie. He just wasn't.

Chase finished his MRE and cleared the trash. When Sophie finished with hers, he collected her trash as well. He suddenly wanted to say something, wanted to take them back to those moments when she'd been asking him what he liked to read. He wanted to go back and not be a jerk this time, but that was impossible.

"I like thrillers," he said, and she looked confused. "Novels. James Patterson, Stephen Hunter, Lee Child, Clancy—stuff like that."

"Oh. That's cool."

He shrugged. "Yeah, I guess so."

She cleared her throat and their eyes met for a long moment before she dropped her gaze. "You play guitar too."

His gut twisted with familiar anger. "Yeah. I fiddle with it here and there." He snorted softly. "Guess it's in the DNA, though a lot of good that does me."

"But you enjoy playing or you wouldn't do it."

His eyes burned, probably from lack of sleep. "I hate it and I love it."

Hell, he didn't know why he'd admitted that to her.

Even worse was the look of sympathy she gave him. Give him enough time alone with Sophie and he'd be curled in a ball, telling her about all his childhood hurts while she stroked his hair and crooned lullabies. That image was enough to make him want to puke.

His phone pinged and he reached for it, happy for the distraction.

I'LL BE THERE.

CHASE TEXTED a quick response and then started to gather up supplies and stuff them in his bag. Just in case it took longer than anticipated or if he had to change the plan.

He could feel Sophie's gaze on him, but he didn't make eye contact. He'd hurt her feelings and then he'd tried to make it up to her by not being a dick. Instead, he'd revealed too much of his soul—and she pitied him for it.

"We're heading out in another hour. Better get prepared."

"I don't have anything to prepare," she said softly. "Unless you want me to carry something."

"Nope, no need. We'll be out of the forest tonight and into a safe house."

He could see her sit up taller out of the corner of his eye. "We will? Where are we going?"

He finally let himself look at her again. And he felt a little thump in his chest as he did so. She'd twisted her red-blond hair into a knot on her head, but the knot was coming loose and hair escaped to fall around her face.

He'd tried not to pay too much attention to her clothing before, but he let his gaze skim the dark jeans and boots she wore, the white tank top displaying luscious breasts beneath a black jacket. And all the gorgeous hair that was slipping free of its knot.

She had full, generous lips, and the hint of cheekbones beneath plump skin. Her violet eyes were fringed in dark lashes. Her eyeliner had smudged, but it gave her a just-got-out-of-bed look rather than a gothic appearance. Some women looked like zombies the next morning when their mascara had run, but not Sophie. A whole day of sleeping in her makeup and she looked sexy, not scary.

"I've got a friend," he said. "He's going to help us."

Her breath hitched. "Are you sure you can trust him?"

He wasn't offended by that question. "He's a teammate. Or used to be. He started his own security firm recently. They protect high-profile clients—movie stars, rock stars, billionaires. I trust him with my life because he's saved my ass more than once with his skills."

She nodded. "Then I guess I'll trust him too."

———

THE WOODS WERE dark and wet. Apparently it had rained today while she'd been asleep in the tree house. She hadn't heard a thing. Now she squelched along behind Chase, her suede Christian Louboutin boots no doubt ruined beyond all repair. Her feet were wet, and she shivered inside her light jacket, wishing she'd been wearing something a little heavier when she left New York.

But it was late April and the temperatures had been mild. When she'd gone to Grigori's yesterday, she hadn't anticipated hiking or camping only a few hours later. Sophie shivered again. Maybe she should have just stayed home and avoided all his calls instead of going to see him. Maybe that would have worked better.

She shook her head to dislodge that line of thinking. It wasn't true. Grigori would have come to her apartment, and he would have made a scene until she let him in. Which she would have.

No, far better that she'd gone to him. At least there had been other people around, though a lot of good that did her now.

She thought she heard a noise behind her, and she whipped her head around, trying to see if there was anything back there. Sophie peered into the darkness surrounding them. There was nothing but woods, woods, and more woods. Chase showed no concern, his pace not slowing at all. Sophie hurried to catch up before he left her behind.

Something cracked again in the distance, and Sophie turned once more to look. There was still nothing, so she faced front again—and collided with something solid. It knocked her back a step, and she windmilled her arms as she lost her balance and started to go down.

Chase grabbed her and jerked her upright. She

collided with him once more, only this time she didn't bounce off him. This time he held her steady. Dammit, she'd crashed into him last night too. And here she was doing it again. Such a klutz… though it was hard to feel bad about it when he was so solid and warm. Her fingers curled in the rain jacket he wore, her knuckles brushing hard muscle.

"You're shivering." His voice was angry, but that was certainly no surprise. He stayed angry with her.

"I'm cold and my feet are wet."

She sounded petulant, which she knew he would hate. Hell, she hated it. But it was too late to call the words back and try again.

He didn't let her go. Instead, he chafed her arms with his big hands. Warmth buzzed in her veins, but it wasn't from the mere act of rubbing her arms. No, its origin was somewhat deeper. Somewhat illicit, truth be known.

Sophie told herself she should step away, rub her own arms. But oh, that so wasn't happening. Her blood thickened to molasses and her insides tingled suspiciously.

"You'll have a hot shower at the end of this. I just need you to hang in there a couple of more hours."

She sucked in a breath. "I will."

"Good girl," he said, squeezing her shoulders before letting her go again.

"Are we being followed?" she asked, worried once more now that he wasn't touching her.

"Possibly."

Her chest squeezed—and then a noise that sounded

like a dog baying cut through the night. Chase's head snapped up, and Sophie's heart hammered. Tears pricked her eyes. Why in God's name had she ever said yes to Grigori? And why had she taken that flash drive from his apartment? Why?

"They're going to find us, aren't they?"

Chase's attention jerked to her. His jaw tightened. "No."

Despair arrowed into her. She didn't believe him. She was going to die in a cold, dark swamp, and no one would ever find her body. Grigori was too powerful, too determined. He'd eliminated a business rival and no one blinked. A hotel maid accused him of assault—and got painted as a lying tramp. If he wanted to get rid of one more person, who was going to stop him in the end?

"Don't lie to make me feel better, Chase. I want the truth."

Chapter Eight

HE GRASPED HER SHOULDERS ROUGHLY AND LOWERED HIS head until he could look her in the eye. Sophie's stomach flipped at the ferocity of his gaze. The utter determination.

"They aren't going to find us. It rained all day, and we've been walking through water for a mile. That's not an accident. A good tracking dog can still find the scent, but it takes a little more time. And time is our friend right now."

"You led me through water on purpose?"

Her poor boots—and oh how she really didn't give a crap about them right this second!

"That's right." He gave her a brief grin. "This isn't my first time around the block."

"I think I love you right now," she breathed. "More than chocolate, I might add."

He straightened—and then he laughed softly, shaking his head. "You're a mess, Sophie. But I might end up liking you in spite of myself."

57

For some reason, his words infused her with warmth. She returned his smile. "I think you will. I'm determined you will."

Briefly, she felt twelve years old again, an awkward girl who wanted the tall, good-looking boy to smile at her at least once before he left for another year.

He lifted his head to peer into the distance. And then he took her hand and tugged her forward. "Gotta move fast now. No time to waste."

Sophie's boots slipped and slid in the muck, but she managed to find her balance and tripped along with Chase through the night. She was very conscious of his hand on hers, though she told herself it was nothing. He was hauling her along beside him, making sure she didn't stop or slow. There was nothing more to it than that—but the pressure of his hand, the feel of his skin, still made an impact on her senses.

She ignored her aching knee, the stitch in her side, and the muscle spasms in her left arch. Chase wasn't going to slow down for any of that—and she didn't want him to. She couldn't hear the dog anymore, but that didn't mean it wasn't back there. It might not be a tracking dog at all—maybe it was a hunter's dog or a stray—but she didn't want to stop and find out.

They pounded through the night, feet slapping into puddles, Chase's hand still firm on hers. She wasn't cold anymore. She was hot, sweating, and she wanted nothing more than to stop and rest for a while.

She was ready to collapse, certain she couldn't make it another inch, but he kept pulling her forward, relentlessly driving her toward something. And then he stopped, and she was so accustomed to running that she kept going and jerked up short, tripping when he snatched her backward and into his arms.

She went immediately still, her back pressed to his front. She was breathing so hard, her blood pounding in her veins and her ears, that she couldn't hear a damn thing except her own breath razoring in and out of her lungs.

Chase had an arm around her, across her breasts, his hand gripping her waist, holding her tightly to him. Her body was exhausted, and yet a new feeling began to drip into her system. His chest swelled against her back as he dragged in air, though he wasn't panting anywhere near as hard as she was. His entire body was hard as stone. He was a pillar against which she could rest, and she let her body melt just a little.

His breath gusted in her ear, and a shiver rippled down her spine. Goose bumps rose on her neck, her arms, and her nipples tightened.

"We have to wait here," he told her, his voice barely a whisper. "Not long."

She nodded, her skin prickling and tingling. It was as if he'd nibbled the shell of her ear when in fact he'd done no such thing. But try telling her body that as parts of her that had no business being awake right now decided to respond.

Her nipples were tight little points now. And then there were the itchy, achy, gotta-have-it sensations zipping around in her nether regions. She turned her head to ask him what they were waiting for, but his face was still near her ear and her mouth hit his jaw—

and maybe part of his lips. She gasped, and he stiffened.

When she would have jerked away, he held her tightly and wouldn't let her go. He shifted so his face wasn't there anymore, so her mouth wasn't touching him, but he didn't let her escape the prison of his embrace.

She was already hot from the run, but her face flamed even hotter. God, what must he think? She was certain she was the only one who felt this odd sexual heat. If he had felt it, she knew he'd let her go like a hot potato. No, pretty much the only thing he felt for her was anger and disdain.

Her ears throbbed with heat, but the pounding of her blood was beginning to subside enough that she could make out other sounds. One of those sounds became tires on pavement. She turned, searching for the road—and then she saw it, a dark, wet ribbon stretching into the night.

An SUV came around a corner, headlights shining bright. And then they went out and the parking lights shone for a second. On again, off, on.

"That's our ride," Chase said, easing away from her and starting down the embankment that lay before them.

"How can you be sure?"

He turned to look at her. "Would you rather stay here and wait for the dogs to catch up?"

Sophie gulped. And then she took the plunge over the side of the embankment, her wet boots squelching as she hurried to catch Chase since he'd started toward the road again.

The SUV inched forward until whoever was inside spotted them. The window slid down and a man leaned out.

"Hey, Fiddler. Heard you needed a ride."

Fiddler?

"Yeah, got a bit of a problem here," Chase said as he came up to the SUV and grasped the rear door handle behind the driver.

"And this is the problem, I take it?" the man said as Sophie approached.

"Yep." Chase dragged the door open, threw his bag in, and motioned for Sophie to get inside. She didn't like being called a problem, but she did as instructed without calling him on it. Besides, from his perspective, it was certainly true.

The door slammed and Chase went around to the passenger side. When they were situated, the man at the wheel flipped on the headlights and smashed the gas. Sophie was thrown back against the seat as the SUV accelerated.

"Who is she?" the driver asked.

Chase rolled his neck from side to side before answering. "Hawk, meet Sophie Nash. Sophie, meet Jack 'Hawk' Hunter, the best sniper to ever take aim at a target."

The man's gaze met hers in the rearview.

Sophie smiled. "Nice to meet you, Mr. Hunter."

He laughed. "Just Hawk. Or Jack. Polite," he said to

Chase. "Gina would love that. Any chance you and Sophie are, uh, a couple…"

Chase snorted. "No way in fucking hell, dude."

Sophie's heart pinched, but then Chase turned and speared her with a look. "Technically, Sophie's my stepsister."

"We weren't raised together," Sophie interjected. She didn't know why she felt the need to say it, but she did. Maybe because of the way her body had reacted to him earlier.

"Nope, we definitely weren't." Chase's eyes glittered as he stared at her, and then he turned to face front again.

Hawk shrugged. "Sorry. It was just a thought. You know how Gina is these days. The mere hint of romance and she's planning a wedding."

Chase laughed. "Jesus, dude, she just held a wedding at your place a couple of weeks ago."

"Yeah, but now she's waiting for the next teammate to fall and gleefully plotting where to put the swans."

"Swans? Shouldn't she be writing songs or something?"

Sophie had no idea what they were talking about, but she was damn glad to be in a closed vehicle for a change. She melted against the seat, her body tired and achy and ready for the promised shower and some sleep. She had no idea what time it was, but she felt as if she hadn't actually slept most of the day.

She stifled a yawn as Hawk and Chase continued to talk about this Gina person and her desire to host weddings. Sophie gathered at some point that Gina was Hawk's wife and that they had two children.

"You got somebody for this case?" Chase asked after a while, and Sophie's ears perked up.

Hawk shook his head. "Sorry, dude, I don't."

Chase's jaw flexed. "Her daddy"—he put a twist on the word daddy—"can pay a lot to protect her. Surely you have an operator willing to take this on."

Sophie sat up straighter. She didn't want someone else. She wanted Chase. But before she could protest, Hawk spoke again.

"Man, I wish I did. But Hunter Security Services is too new, and all my operators are on assignment. It's you or no one, Fiddler. Sorry."

Chapter Nine

GRIGORI ANDROV'S CELL PHONE RANG. HE PICKED IT UP and answered with a clipped "You had better have news for me."

The man on the other end was silent for a moment. "We have dogs, sir. They've found the trail—but no sign of the girl or her companion yet."

Grigori gripped the arm of the sofa he was sitting on and squeezed it. Fury hammered through him. If he could reach through the phone and slice the guy's neck, he'd do it just for the pleasurable rush it would bring him.

Incompetent fools. They could have had Sophie when she'd been in that apartment, but they'd gotten stupid and lazy. Grigori *would* have someone's head over that one. He'd sent his right-hand man down there just a couple of hours ago to deal with them. Sergei would make sure the job got done right.

"You will keep looking. You will not stop until you

find them. I want the girl alive—but kill the man. Don't fuck up again."

"Yes, sir."

Grigori ended the call and then went over to the liquor cabinet and poured two fingers of scotch into a glass. He took a fortifying sip of the smoky liquid as he walked over to look at the view from his penthouse apartment. Central Park was a dark island surrounded by the blazing lights of New York City. Traffic moved far below, white and red lights inching through the narrow corridors between tall buildings.

He turned the glass from side to side in his hand, absently, and contemplated what he planned to do to Sophie Nash when he got her back in his possession. He snorted and took another sip of scotch.

In truth, he would do nothing. He couldn't mar her skin, and he damn sure couldn't violate her body. No, she was worth too much the way she was. He had buyers for a girl like her, and he wasn't going to ruin his profit by punishing her—though she deserved it.

He'd taken too much time with her. When she'd caught his eye at the charity event last month, he'd known she would fetch a pretty price. She was a lush beauty with abundant curves, and there were men who would pay a premium for that. If she was a virgin, even better.

She wasn't, as she'd told him haltingly one night when he'd asked, but it didn't really matter because he would market her as a virgin anyway. There were ways to ensure the end buyer believed he'd gotten what he'd purchased.

He should not have lost his temper with her when she'd come to tell him she wanted to stop seeing him for a while. Had he not done that, she would have never run away. And she would not have taken his flash drive.

The mere thought of the theft twisted his gut into knots. It was not the only flash drive with the information stored on it—he'd lost access to nothing—but it still contained critical intelligence. Things he would not want anyone else to know.

It was encrypted, of course. But someone with skill could break it eventually. That was always the way of it. He knew because Zoprava funded a network of hackers in Russia, presumably to test the limits of his software but really to steal credit card numbers and other personal information from people around the world. They then packaged and sold that data to third parties who exploited it for gain. Of which he got a cut, naturally.

If someone like one of his hackers got ahold of the drive, they'd decrypt it in hours. He could not afford to take the chance.

Therefore, he needed Sophie back—and he needed that drive. Once it was secure, he would put her on a plane and send her to his private auction in Monte Carlo where she would be sold to some fat billionaire who would take her home and use her for his pleasure until he was tired of her. Then she would either be put into a brothel or killed. It mattered not to him.

His phone rang again and he answered, hoping it was news to put him in a better mood.

"She visited a shipping facility before she boarded

the train." It was Sergei's voice. "There was a security camera."

"And?"

"She mailed a package and she paid with a credit card. We don't know where she sent the package yet, but Evgeny is trying to hack into the system. As soon as he does, we'll have an address."

Had she mailed the flash drive? Or something else? Whatever it was, he couldn't afford to ignore this piece of information. She'd run from his office, stopped to mail a package, and boarded a train. Odds were good the package was something he wanted.

"How long will this take?"

"Evgeny says the network security is good. It will take some time to break through. A day, no more. He will call me when it is done."

Grigori swore in both Russian and English. "As soon as you know, you will call me. I do not care what time it is."

"Of course, Grigori."

"Where are you now?"

"We've just landed in Baltimore at BWI."

"Find her, Sergei."

"I will."

———

THE SAFE HOUSE was located in a small town on the Eastern Shore of Maryland. It wasn't Waterman's Cove, where Hawk lived with his wife Gina, but it wasn't too far from there either. Tucked on a side street, the house was a small cottage in the older part of town. The street was lined with similar homes—small boxy houses with brick or wooden siding, cars in the yards, chain-link or wooden fences, barking dogs, and the glow of a cigarette coming from a porch or two even though it was late.

Hawk pulled around to the side of the house where there was a carport and a door leading inside. He put the vehicle in park and turned to look at Chase. "I'm sorry I can't take this off your hands, but I just don't have the manpower yet."

"I get it, brother. Thanks for helping us this far."

Hawk nodded. "The house is clear. One of my guys checked it out before we arrived, and everything is set. I'll be back in the morning—with a passport for her," he added, jerking his chin toward the backseat where Sophie appeared to be sound asleep. "I'll need one of yours to make them match."

Chase's gut twisted. "Match how?"

He knew it made sense to pair them up, and he knew what the most likely version was. Shit, he didn't even want to take Sophie with him, but there was no other way. There was no one to protect her while he was gone. It was too dangerous to leave her alone in a safe house, and far too dangerous to have Hawk take her home and stash her in his house with Gina and their kids.

Hawk merely looked at him. "You know how. It'll go much easier if you play a married couple on your way to Paris for a romantic honeymoon."

Jesus.

"Right. Shit."

Hawk thumped him on the shoulder. "Come on, you've had to do worse for the job. Besides, the two of you will figure it out."

"Yeah, we'll figure it out." Chase rummaged in his bag, fished out a passport—he had several, as they all did—and handed it to Hawk. "You think Mendez will have a shit fit?"

Hawk snorted. "Oh hell yeah. But this is personal, just like it was for me when Eli was kidnapped. And we worked that out, right? Y'all had my back, and we got the sonofabitch who took my son and tried to hurt Gina. I'll have your back on this one—and so will everyone else. I'll let them know what we've got going, so don't sweat it."

Chase's chest grew tight. Man, he loved his job. Loved his teammates. They were a brotherhood—and yeah, he included his female teammates in that designation—who stood together through everything. Until he'd joined HOT, his mother was the only family he had. But now his family was big and bad and willing to step up and fight for one of their own even though they didn't share a drop of blood between them.

"Anything you can get on Androv would be good too," he added as he stepped out of the Tahoe and shut the door.

"I'm on it, brother. I'll be back as soon as I can, and we'll get this show on the road."

Chase nodded and reached for the handle to the backseat. He opened the door, his gaze sliding over Sophie's form. She was slumped to one side, her seat belt cutting right between her breasts and showcasing their luscious fullness. She'd taken her jacket off and laid it on the seat. Her arms were bare and the tank top she wore clung to every curve.

He reached out and touched her shoulder and she jerked. He jerked too because, whoa, that was some charge that lanced through him. Probably static electricity, though he hadn't actually heard a pop. Not to mention the air was wet.

Chase frowned. "Sophie," he said, not touching her this time.

She stirred, moaning a little as she did so. The sound went right to his groin and twisted his nuts with need. *Stop. Off-limits.*

"Sophie," he said again, rougher this time. "We're here."

She pushed herself up and shoved a mass of silky hair from her face. Her gaze fastened on him, and she fumbled for the seat belt. "Great. Awesome."

She got it undone and slid from the Tahoe, stumbling as she landed on the concrete pad of the carport. Chase caught her and steadied her. But not before those glorious breasts mashed up against his chest. He sucked in air, set her away from him, grabbed her jacket from the seat and his bag from the floor. Then he shut the door and herded her toward the steps leading up to the house.

"Get some rest," Hawk called from the window he'd rolled down. "I'll text in the morning before I come out."

"Copy," Chase said as he inserted the key into the lock. Hawk waited while he got the door open and punched in the code for the alarm. He turned and gave Hawk a thumbs-up, and the man powered up the window and backed slowly down the driveway.

"Come on," he told Sophie.

She stepped inside and he closed the door behind her, securing it with a dead bolt and resetting the alarm. When he turned, she'd walked into the kitchen and stood there looking at the flowery wallpaper and worn cabinetry.

"Not up to your standards, princess?" He didn't know why he said that, except she looked so out of place there, so shocked at the interior, and it angered him. Because he'd grown up in a house not much different from this one while she'd lived in a Hollywood house with an infinity pool overlooking the LA skyline.

She turned at the sound of his voice, her eyes wide as she wrapped her arms around her body and chafed her upper arms.

"What?" She sounded a bit distracted, and he felt a pinprick of annoyance.

He jerked his chin at the garish wallpaper. Yellow with white daises. Much like the curtains his mother had put up in their kitchen. "A little low-rent for you?"

Her mouth dropped open for a second. Then she closed it and straightened her spine until she seemed to look down at him even though she was much shorter than he was.

"For your information, I was thinking how glad I am to be in a house rather than a tree, and how awesome a shower will feel. But I was also wondering what's in that refrigerator and hoping it's something good."

He refused to feel chastened. Instead, he went over and yanked open the refrigerator. It wasn't packed, but it had food in it.

"Looks good to me," he said. "But you'd better know how to cook because I don't." That wasn't precisely true, but damn if he was cooking for her after everything else.

"I can fix a few things," she said. "But I'm no Rachael Ray."

He let the door close. "Why don't you shower first and then come in here and figure out what you want?"

She chafed her arms again and he handed over her jacket. She took it and draped it over her shoulders. But she didn't leave.

"Are we really safe here?"

Chase nodded. He wasn't going to tell her that even the best preparations sometimes weren't enough, but he was pretty confident they were today. Hawk didn't do anything half-assed, and now he had the money—loads of money thanks to his pop-star wife—to have the best of everything, which included high-tech surveillance equipment and alarms.

"Yeah, we'll be fine. Hawk knows what he's doing."

"Are you just telling me that to make me feel better?"

"Do you really want the answer to that question?"

She nodded, her hair shining in the overhead light, her expression wary and haunted. He wanted to go over and pull her into his arms, hug her tight. No way in hell would he give in to that urge though.

"Yeah, we'll be fine," he said. "Go take a shower and stop worrying."

She looked at him for a long moment before she turned and melted into the darkness of the house.

Chase shoved a hand through his hair as his heart pumped faster than it should and his gut squeezed tight. Jesus, what the hell was wrong with him? Sophie wasn't his type—too soft and pampered—and she damn sure wasn't on the menu.

Chapter Ten

Sophie found the bathroom and turned on the shower to let the water heat. She slipped out of her clothes, intending to hang them to dry when she was finished. There was a fluffy blue robe draped on the door hook, the kind that wrapped you up in a soft hug when you slid it over your skin. She ran her fingers over the terry cloth and nearly shivered in delight.

The bathroom was small and the mirror only provided her with a view of her torso. She studied her nakedness critically, almost compulsively. No, definitely compulsively. It was a habit going back to childhood when friends and family would remark to her mother that she was a little plump and then ask if her mother wanted a guaranteed-to-work diet plan for her.

She was pale with a smattering of freckles marring her skin here and there. Her breasts were full, double *E*s with dusky areolae and nipples that beaded tight as she hefted her breasts and looked in the mirror.

Her waist dipped in where it was supposed to, but it wasn't tiny. And her hips, if she stepped forward and peered downward, curved away from her waist and gave her a classic hourglass shape. Growing up in LA hadn't always been easy, especially with a mom who'd been a Victoria's Secret model. Her mother was tall and lean and toned, even now at the age of forty-six. Sophie was, by comparison, huge.

Not that she was really huge, but standing next to her mother had always made her feel awkward and ugly. It was part of the reason she'd wanted to escape and do her own thing in New York. She snorted softly. A lot of good that had done her.

Steam rose from the shower, and she pushed the curtain back and stepped inside, groaning when the hot water pummeled her back and shoulders. It was almost as good as sex, she decided.

And that was the wrong thing to think of, because sex immediately conjured the image of Chase. Of his naked chest and broad shoulders when he'd opened his door to her. Of the lazy slant of his eyes as he'd taken her in and the heated grin he'd given her before she'd said her name. The man oozed sex appeal. If the circumstances hadn't been what they were, she could well imagine herself falling for that charm. Stripping herself and offering her body up for his pleasure.

Not that she had a ton of experience in that department. She was self-conscious, and that made getting naked with a man a little difficult. Part of the reason she'd been susceptible to Grigori's charm was because he'd told her she was beautiful and desirable. Though he'd never tried to have sex with her, which had made her begin to doubt his sincerity. Why else would he waste time with her? He didn't listen to the blues, had no idea who Tyler was. It wasn't as if he wanted to get close to her to meet her stepdad. Even if he did want to meet Tyler, there were easier ways for someone with his money and connections.

Sophie pushed her face under the spray and let the water wash away her thoughts of Grigori and Chase, at least for a few moments. She was alive and that was a good thing.

She soaped herself all over, washed her hair, and then finished her shower when she figured she was in danger of stealing all the hot water. That would be yet another black mark against her in Chase's book when he stepped into the shower and got hit with cold water.

She dried off, twisted her hair into a towel for a few minutes before combing it out, and then slipped into the robe. Her skin was pink from the hot water, and her face was scrubbed free of makeup. Not that she needed much makeup, but she loved playing with it. If nothing else, she had been fortunate enough to inherit a flawless complexion from her mother.

Which was a good thing because all her makeup was gone, burned up with her purse.

She found Chase in the living room, kicked back on the couch with his feet propped on the coffee table. CNN blared from the television, but he looked up when she walked in. Her heart thumped as his eyes narrowed.

They slipped over her, from her wet hair to the robe and down to her pink toenails before landing on her face again.

"Feel better?"

"Marginally. But I have no clothes to put on."

His face became a thundercloud. "Are you warm enough in that robe?"

She ran her hand down the softness of the fabric. "Yes."

"Then it'll have to do."

"My clothes will be dry by tomorrow—but my boots are ruined."

She knew they would be, but damn, she'd loved those boots. It wasn't easy to get a low heel from Louboutin, or a comfortable one—and those boots had been both.

"We'll get something for you. But if you expect designer names, ain't happening."

She felt herself bristling. Yes, everything she'd been wearing was a brand name, but that didn't mean she *had* to have them. "I don't know what makes you think I won't be happy with a pair of tennis shoes."

"Honey, you look expensive. Those weren't Walmart clothes you had on—and then there's the gold watch on your wrist."

She sniffed. Her watch had been a graduation present from Tyler and her mother—and yes, it was Cartier. "As long as the shoes are dry and comfortable, I don't care who makes them."

Which was essentially true. Maybe if she was in New

York, she'd want to go to Saks and buy whatever her heart desired. She could admit that shopping made her happy. It had been a crutch since she'd been old enough to realize she wasn't ever going to be a Victoria's Secret model herself.

Chase reached into a bag of potato chips sitting by his side and crunched a few. Her stomach rumbled, but she was *not* eating chips.

"There's a washer and dryer behind those folding doors in the hallway," he said without looking at her. "You can wash your stuff and dry it. *If* you know how to use a washer, that is."

"I'll manage," she said tartly. She hadn't realized there was a laundry area in this house, but the thought made her ridiculously happy. So happy that his snottiness wasn't going to get her down.

"Good," he said. "My stuff needs washed too."

She gaped at him. And then she got mad. "Tell you what. I'll fix something to eat better than those"—she nodded at the chips—"and *you* can do the laundry."

His eyes flicked up to hers—and stayed there. The intensity of that gaze—God, she didn't know why it made her heart thunder or her pulse trip. Or her body grow achy and needy.

He pushed himself off the couch, all six foot three inches of him. Then he picked up the chip bag and rolled the top down before tossing it to her. She somehow managed to catch it, but she clutched it to her torso so hard she probably crushed half the chips.

Chase reached behind his back with one hand and tugged his shirt up and over his head in the sexiest maneuver she'd ever seen. Then he smirked at her and balled the shirt in his fist before heading down the hallway.

"Deal," he called behind him. "But the food better be good."

Chapter Eleven

THE FOOD WASN'T BAD. IT WASN'T GOURMET, BUT CHASE finished the grilled cheese sandwich and wished he had another one. Sophie sat across from him at the table in the small living/dining room combo, her eyes on her food as she took slow, deliberate bites.

He'd showered and thrown their clothes into the washer, then returned here to find her fixing grilled cheeses and tomato soup. Hell, he could have done that —except she'd done something to the grilled cheese that tasted better than when he fixed them.

When she'd realized he was in the room, she'd turned to him—and colored immediately. He wouldn't forget the look on her face for a long time. He was wearing a pair of athletic shorts and nothing else because that's what he had in his bag until his stuff was clean.

The look she'd given him had arrowed straight to his balls. He'd seen need on that face. Raw, lustful need— and it knocked him for a loop.

She's not really your sister, dude. You could totally bang her.

Yeah, true—but not helpful. Banging Sophie was a bad idea because he couldn't walk away in the morning. He still had a few days left with her while they tried to get to Paris to find that flash drive before Androv's people did. If he let his guard down and fucked her— which he really wanted to do, God help him—he had no idea how to handle the aftermath.

Typically, he fucked a woman a few times and then they were done. He wasn't a manwhore—well, not totally—but he wasn't looking for a relationship either.

And he was supercareful about birth control too. After the way he'd come into the world and the way his biological father hadn't given a fuck about him, no way was he doing that to a kid.

Not that he didn't have condoms in the bugout bag. He did.

But he was *not* using them.

She looked up then and their gazes clashed. He tried not to let it affect him, but of course it did. The telltale tightening of his groin was a sign that he didn't have nearly the control over his reaction that he wanted.

Fuck, she looked a lot like her mother—but a lusher version of her mother. Yeah, he'd been a horny teenager and more than a bit wowed by the gorgeous model his father had married. Justine DeMontford-Nash had been smokin' in a bikini—and in the bras and panties she modeled in the pages of a Victoria's Secret catalog.

He had a sudden urge to see Sophie in a bikini. She'd have more flesh, more curves—but he would bet anything they were spectacular.

"What did you put in the grilled cheese?" he asked suddenly, trying to shut down that line of thought before he had a frigging tent pole in his shorts.

"Cheese. What else?"

He snorted at her snappy answer. "What kind of cheese, Soph? Doesn't taste like American."

She picked up her sandwich and took a delicate bite. "It's cheddar. I sliced it myself. I also buttered the inside of the bread."

Buttered the inside. Geez, he'd have never thought of that.

"It's good. Best I ever had."

She lifted one perfectly arched eyebrow. Damn but her face was pretty.

"I find that a little hard to believe. It's just cheese and bread."

He shook his head. "No, really. Don't think I've ever had a grilled cheese with anything but American."

She made a face. "Boy, are you missing out."

"Not anymore." He grinned and she quickly dropped her gaze to her plate.

Her hair fell in a reddish-gold curtain over her face and she pushed it back behind her ears before he could give in to the urge to do it for her.

Wouldn't take much to have her on her knees for him…

Stop. No. *Down, boy.*

"I'm glad you like it."

"Yep, it was spectacular. Soup was good too, but that's a can and not you."

She grinned. "Hard to screw up food in a can."

"You'd be surprised." He'd had some pretty basic

meals over the years as a Special Operator, and he knew it was entirely possible to screw up food in a can. Not easy, but possible.

"Can I ask you something?"

He tried not to let himself tense up over that question, but he did anyway. "Sure."

"Why did Hawk call you Fiddler? What's that mean?"

He leaned back in the chair and tapped his fingers on the table. "We work on teams in the military, and we all get team names or call signs. Safer than using our names or ranks when we're in the field. Hawk is a sniper, so you can figure that one out. Fiddler…" He shrugged uncomfortably, remembering the day he'd been christened with that name. He'd been playing guitar and someone asked if he'd ever considered going professional. He'd said he just fiddled around a bit, and it stuck.

"It's from the guitar playing. Fiddles, as in instruments. And then there's the last name. They found it funny."

She looked puzzled. "The last name?"

"Daniels," he said. "Like Charlie Daniels, who most definitely plays the hell out of a fiddle."

"A guitar is not a fiddle."

"Nope, but it doesn't matter. It's whatever sticks. That one stuck."

She shook her head. "I don't get it, but whatever. So you're Fiddler to your team?"

"Yep."

She propped her chin on her hand and stared at

him. Her lips were so pink, so lush. He wanted to suck that lower lip. And then he wanted to slip his cock between her lips and watch her take him in.

"What made you decide to join the military?"

"Freedom."

She blinked. "Freedom?"

"Yep. I fight for freedom. Yours, mine, the next-door neighbor's. Doesn't matter." He hesitated, uncertain if he should go on and then suddenly not giving a shit. "And then there's the freedom I gained when I became my own man. I don't need Tyler for shit. Never will."

"I wish I could fix what was wrong between you."

His gut twisted at the sadness in her voice. Just as quickly, pride and anger filled the gaps. He reached across the table and grabbed her hand. It was an impulsive gesture, and one he thought he might regret as electricity sizzled through him.

"You can't, Sophie. Nor should you have to. Tyler made his bed. He has to lie in it." He let her go and blew out a breath. "You know, I get that he's been good to you and you probably love him. He wasn't good to me, and I just don't see him the same way you do. I don't suppose that makes either of us wrong. Just different."

She blinked at him, and he wondered if she understood how huge an admission that was for him. That Tyler Nash was capable of kindness and warmth, and that Chase could understand why Sophie would care for him.

Her mouth fell open, closed—and then she seemed to make up her mind because her gaze hardened just a little. "Tyler's not bad, but he's not terrific either. He's self-centered. Everything is about Tyler. Everything."

She shook her hair off her shoulders, and Chase gaped at her. Both for the sensuality of the maneuver and for what she was saying.

"He's given me a good life, there's no doubt about that. But you have no idea what it was like to be a child growing up with two people so self-centered as Tyler and my mother. I was an accessory. Something cute and fun and useful, but not necessary, if that makes sense."

She'd stunned him. "I'm sorry," he managed, because he didn't know what else to say.

She sniffed. "Well, and that's more than I've ever said to anyone about my home life. Wow."

She reached for a napkin and dabbed at her eyes. Chase felt like shit.

"I thought you had a perfect life. Everything you wanted whenever you wanted it. Opportunity. Two parents who loved you."

Her head came up, her eyes glittering. "Oh, they love me—or my mom does anyway. But look at me, Chase."

He *was* looking at her and he liked what he saw. But she looked expectant, like she thought he was supposed to find something wrong with her and comment on it.

"You're gorgeous, Sophie," he said, without meaning to.

She bowed her head for a second. "That's sweet of you—but what I was going to say is that I was a bit of a disappointment for two people as beautiful as Tyler and my mom. No matter how I tried, I was always fat. I'm the girl who can't wear a bikini at pool parties, who has to be careful what she eats when guests are over because one bite of the wrong thing and they'll be talking about it to their friends and embarrassing my mom when it gets back to her. I've spent my life wondering why I don't look like her and trying like hell to get there. But I like grilled cheese, dammit. And wings, pizza, burgers—yet even if I ate none of those things, I'd never have a body like hers. I know because I tried."

He didn't know what to say to that. It made him sick to think of her as a little girl trying so desperately to fit in. To be skinny. He hated like hell that her mother had made her feel like she couldn't eat. That her mother had allowed a kid—a *kid*—to worry about what people said about her.

The whole fucking thing infuriated him. And he couldn't let that slide. He couldn't let her think she was anything less than a beautiful woman in her own right.

"Your mother is banging, Soph," he said, and she gave a sad little laugh before he could finish. "Hear me out—so are you. You've got a sweet body, a hot body—a body I'd like to explore if the circumstances were different. I think you're fucking hotter than hell."

Her jaw had dropped a little while he spoke. Maybe he'd said too much, but dammit, he hated to see her fieriness dimming over something so ridiculous. She was fucking gorgeous and she needed to know it. She needed to know that not every man on this planet thought a woman needed to be capable of gracing the pages of *Sports Illustrated* in order to be desirable.

"You're sweet, Chase. Really sweet. I appreciate your saying that."

It took him a minute to figure out that she thought he was just humoring her. Trying to make her feel better.

And that made him mad. Reckless.

"You know, I've been sitting here looking at you in that robe, wondering what's underneath, and fighting a hard-on for the past half hour. I've been telling myself that you're off-limits because you're supposed to be my stepsister, but the truth is that's just an excuse. Because right now, if you dropped that robe, I'd be all over you, Sophie. And then I'd be in you, pounding away until my head exploded. So don't tell me I'm sweet. I'm not fucking sweet. I'm a guy who'd fuck you in a heartbeat if you let me."

Chapter Twelve

HEAT BLOSSOMED ACROSS HER SKIN, MAKING THE ROBE suddenly uncomfortable enough that she seriously considered dropping it to cool off. Her throat went dry at the thought of what might happen then.

He'd said he wanted to be inside her. Pounding away until his head exploded.

Her nipples beaded. An achy heaviness settled in her core. A wild part of her wanted that so much.

The sensible part was terrified. No matter what he said about her being hot or her body being appealing, she knew the minute he saw her he'd notice the rolls and dimples of her flesh. He was tight and toned, beautiful.

She was soft and malleable, like a marshmallow. It wasn't a good combination.

"I, um, wow," she stuttered.

The silence swelled to unbearable proportions. He shoved a hand through his hair and got to his feet to remove his dishes from the table. Her ears grew hot, and her skin itched with his nearness as he moved around behind her, washing his bowl and plate.

She wanted him to turn around and touch her, and she didn't at the same time. What would happen if they crossed that particular bridge? There would certainly be no going back, that's for sure. It would be weird.

Or would it? Chase was the most intensely beautiful man she'd ever seen, and she wanted to experience what it would be like to have sex with someone so pretty. When would she ever get another chance?

If you'd only lose thirty pounds, Sophie, you could be so pretty.

If you want to get a boyfriend, you need to lose weight, Sophie.

Don't you want to get married someday? Then you'll need to lose weight. Men don't like having sex with chubby women…

She kept her gaze on the wall opposite, arguing with herself until he stood by her side and she had to look up at him. She very deliberately kept her eyes off his groin, though she wanted to look. Was he hard? Or had he made that up?

"Finished?" he asked, nodding at the plate and bowl in front of her.

"Um, yes, thank you."

He took the dishes and then he was behind her again, clanking things in the sink. When he was done washing, she still hadn't moved. Her heart pounded and she had no idea what to say.

He came over and stood with his hands on the back of the chair he'd been sitting in and looked at her steadily. "Look, I'm sorry I said that. I was out of line. I just wanted you to know that Tyler and your mom are idiots. You're hotter than fuck, which you should know since we're running from a man who went nuclear because you wanted to break up with him. He clearly hadn't gotten enough of you yet."

She pulled in a breath. "Grigori and I never…"

She couldn't finish the sentence. Her skin flooded with fresh heat. Why had she admitted that? She knew how ridiculous it sounded. How unbelievable. They were two adults who'd gone on a few dates over the course of a month—who doesn't have sex in that time?

Chase's hands appeared to tighten on the chairback as he stared at her in disbelief. "You and Androv never hit the sheets together?"

She shook her head. If she told him Grigori had never even tried to get her into bed, how pitiful would that sound? "We only went on a few dates. He's a busy man."

"Not too busy to attack a hotel maid or send murderous men after you."

Sophie shrugged uncomfortably. "I'm sure we'd have gotten around to it eventually."

"Honey, it's all I can do to keep my hands off you. If Androv wasn't trying to get into your panties on the first date, he's either gay or impotent."

For some reason, that made her laugh. And shiver, because hands. All. Over. Her.

"You know how to make me feel good, Chase."

His eyes gleamed. "You don't even know the half of it. Spread your legs and I'll make you feel better than you've ever felt in your life."

She wanted to be shocked at his boldness, but instead she found herself trying to imagine all the ways in which he could make her feel good. She might not have a ton of experience, but she had a great imagination. And that imagination was conjuring up all kinds of wickedly erotic things right now.

"I thought you didn't like me," she said a touch breathlessly. She had to remember what was going on here. Who they were. Everything had changed so quickly, and she was reeling.

He gave her a lazy grin that awakened fresh heat in her core. "You're growing on me. You'd grow on me even more if you let me see what's under the robe."

She pushed to her feet and pulled the robe tighter around her body, using it like a shield. "I honestly can't tell if you're making fun of me or if you're being serious."

"Which do you want it to be?"

The washer stopped then, as evidenced by the loud buzz. It made Sophie jump, but her gaze stayed locked with Chase's. What the hell was going on here? Why was she so turned on by him, by this situation? And why in the hell was she seriously considering telling him she wanted everything he had to offer?

"Better put those in the dryer," she blurted to stop the words from forming on her lips.

He lifted an eyebrow. "Your call," he said, backing away from her slowly, giving her the chance to stop him.

She didn't.

———

COLONEL JOHN MENDEZ was not a happy man at the moment. He stared at the wall opposite his desk and gripped the receiver in his hand a little more tightly.

"Say that again, Hawk."

Jack "Hawk" Hunter was one of the best damn snipers he'd ever had in HOT. But then the man had married a frigging pop star—a beautiful, smart woman to be sure, but still a detriment for Mendez and HOT—and ended up leaving the military after finishing out his enlistment.

"Fiddler's in the wild, sir." Hawk proceeded to fill him in on the circumstances, and Mendez felt his gut twisting with every word.

Fucking Grigori Androv. The asshole was a criminal. He'd bought Zoprava a year ago in an attempt to look legitimate, but he hadn't given up his other businesses.

He also had powerful friends, which meant he remained largely untouched by the law. Whenever he felt the heat of an investigation or unwanted attention on his activities, he donated a large sum of money to some charity or other and moved the focus there.

Mendez pressed a button to bring his aide into his office. The aide, a crisp first lieutenant from West Point —God, he hated West Pointers sometimes, even though he was one—popped in immediately.

Mendez put his hand over the phone. "There was a fire last night on Ridge Road. Get me the report. And get me the report on Grigori Androv."

"Yes, sir," the man said before executing a perfect about-face and retreating through the door.

"So this girl stole a flash drive from Androv and mailed it to Paris. And Fiddler wants to go get it."

"Yes, sir."

"Jesus H. Christ," Mendez said. He ran a hand through his hair, absently noting that it was time to see the barber, before bringing his mind back to the problem at hand. If Androv wanted this girl dead, then he wasn't going to stop until she was. Putting her in protective custody wouldn't be enough to keep her safe forever.

Fuck, his boys certainly knew how to get into trouble on their own. Give them a few days R & R to get drunk and fuck their brains out, and what did they do?

Some of them ended up as fugitives from Russian megalomaniacs. He should reel Fiddler in hard and put a stop to this—but he wasn't going to. Aside from the fact he wasn't letting an innocent girl's life be put in danger, he also wasn't turning down an opportunity to get something he could use against Androv in the future.

"You're providing mission support?" he asked Hawk.

"Yes, sir."

"That's good. HOT can't officially do anything…."

"I hear a *but*, sir."

Mendez blew out a breath and stared at the wall again. Dammit all to hell. He couldn't send assets in, couldn't officially involve HOT. He had a lot of freedom from typical military bullshit in this organization, something he'd fought long and hard to get. But he still answered to the Pentagon and the president—and he wasn't abusing HOT's autonomy. If he did, he could lose everything he'd gained for HOT over the years.

But he could ask Sam for help.

Samantha Spencer was CIA and she had access to things he didn't—just like he had access to things she did not. Thinking of Sam made his balls ache. Over the past few weeks, he and Sam had renewed their friendship in a way he was definitely enjoying.

Sex with Sam was good—and there were no strings attached, which he liked. She liked it too, and that meant it worked for them both.

"Give me some time to work a connection. Can you continue providing support?"

"Yes, sir—I wouldn't have it any other way."

Mendez couldn't suppress the grin that spread over his face. Special Ops soldiers stuck together in a way civilians could never understand. He loved that about this community, loved being a part of it. Loved taking care of the men and women under his command.

Even though he would chew their asses for getting involved in shit situations every single time.

"You're calling the Strike Team 1 members when we hang up, aren't you?" Because no way would Hawk or Fiddler not let their team know what was happening.

Hawk cleared his throat. "Do you really need to know that, sir?"

"No, probably not." It gave him plausible deniability, though that was just a sham since he knew the truth. He shook his head. God, he loved these guys. And this job. But he was still kicking ass and taking names when he got the opportunity. Damn hotheaded fuckers. "Keep me informed. I'll be in touch soon."

As soon as Hawk clicked off the line, he dialed Sam.

"Johnny," she said in that smooth voice of hers when she picked up. "I was just thinking about you."

He leaned back in his chair and enjoyed the way her purr went to his groin. "Funny, I was thinking about you."

"Business or pleasure?"

He laughed. "Both, if I'm honest."

"Oh, Johnny, I always want you to be honest."

He believed that was true—and it was refreshing. "I need something, Sam. Off the record."

"Hmm, sounds like we should get together and discuss it. Amongst other things."

"Your place or mine?"

"Mine. I'll cook. You bring the wine."

He snorted. "You don't cook, Sammy."

"No, but I can dial up a mean takeout."

He looked at his watch. "I can be there in an hour. Is that enough time?"

"Perfect. I'll see you then."

Chapter Thirteen

CHASE LAY AWAKE ON THE SOFA BED, HIS GUN TUCKED beneath the cushion where he could reach it quickly, and stared up at the ceiling. A quick glance at the clock on the burner phone told him it was shortly after one a.m.

He hadn't slept well. Every time he fell asleep, he pictured Sophie in that damn robe, her eyes round and innocent—and filled with heat. It was a lethal combination, that naïve sexiness and blatant hunger in her gaze.

He'd gone too far though. Telling her he'd make her feel good if she let him. He hadn't meant to do it, but the way she'd said that she couldn't wear a bikini at her parents' pool parties and that she'd had to be careful what she ate—well, that pissed him off. Immensely. And he'd wanted her to know that she was desirable the way she was, that the Southern California environment she'd grown up in had been wrong, not her.

Then there was the revelation that she'd never been intimate with Androv. That had floored him, made a hard stab of need twist in his groin. He couldn't begin to figure out what was wrong with a man who didn't try to get Sophie in bed as quickly as possible.

Gay or impotent. That about covered it.

Chase gave up trying to sleep and sat up. A message pinged onto this phone and he opened it. It could only be from Hawk at this point. His personal cell phone had perished in the apartment, but he'd get a new one and restore it tomorrow. Until then, it was the emergency burner—which he'd also discard and replace tomorrow. Just in case.

MENDEZ NOTIFIED. *Team notified. Be there at 0800.*

CHASE TOOK A DEEP BREATH. They knew now and the wheels were in motion.

Copy, he answered.

He went into the kitchen and rummaged in the refrigerator for a beer. One would be enough to relax him and then maybe he could sleep. He closed the door and popped the top, then went back into the living room —and stopped when Sophie emerged from the bedroom.

She wasn't wearing the robe anymore. She'd found a T-shirt and some shorts in one of the drawers and put those on instead. Her arms crossed defensively over her breasts when she realized he was there.

"I didn't know you were awake." Her voice was raspy.

"Yeah. Couldn't sleep."

"Me neither."

"Want a beer?"

"I think that would be good, yes."

He went back into the kitchen. When he turned around with the beer, she was there.

"Hungry?" he asked.

"I could eat something. You?"

"How about some of those potato chips?"

She was silent for long enough that he thought she was probably warring with herself. But then she shrugged. "Why not? It's been a rough couple of days."

He got the bag off the counter and led the way back to the living room. He settled on the sofa bed and picked up the remote. She stood as still as if a canyon had suddenly opened between her and the bed.

"It's a couch made into a bed, Soph. Sit on the other side and prop your legs up. Think of it like a recliner."

She hesitated, but then she came around and perched on the opposite side of the bed from him. He leaned against the back and crossed his legs before offering the open chip bag to her.

She reached in and took a couple. He noticed that she didn't stuff them in her mouth but rather sat them on her lap and ate one at a time. Slowly. Making it last.

"Did you meet a lot of movie stars?" he asked, unaccountably annoyed at how careful she was with a fucking potato chip.

She swung her gaze to his. "What?"

"Movie stars. Living in LA. Do Tyler and Justine hang out with Brad and Angelina?"

She snorted. "Hardly—but yes, I've met a couple.

Mostly they hang out with other musicians." She shrugged. "LA is like any other big city—you don't know everyone."

He took a sip of his beer and thought back to the few times he'd been there. "That's how my mom talked me into going for a visit. She told me I'd meet movie stars like Pamela Anderson, who I was enjoying regularly in *Baywatch* reruns. Didn't happen though."

Sophie laughed. He liked the sound of her laugh.

"Actually, I think Mom and Pam know each other. Mom was on *Baywatch* once. The Hoff saved her from drowning."

"No kidding."

She nodded. "It's true. Mom wanted to act, but she's not really that good at it. Stick her in a bikini and it doesn't matter though."

"Why do you want to act?"

Her smile faded and she toyed with a chip. He wished she'd eat it instead of playing with it. It was as if she was arguing with herself over every single bite. She hadn't done that with the MRE, probably because it had been nearly twenty-four hours since she'd had anything besides a few crackers. But she had done it with the soup and grilled cheese.

"It's just something I always wanted to do."

He didn't believe her for a second. "There's got to be more to it than that. Come on, Sophie. Spill it."

She leaned her head back against the couch and closed her eyes. "What's it matter?"

He started to reach for her arm to give it a squeeze, but something stopped him. "It matters."

"Fine…" She sighed. "I used to pretend to be someone else when I was growing up. I hated being fat, hated being made fun of—so I pretended I was someone prettier or more interesting. A princess, a movie star, an orphan—didn't matter so long as I wasn't me. It felt good to get lost inside another life, so I decided that's what I wanted to do. I want to pretend to be someone else."

He didn't know what to say. He'd thought her life so fucking perfect. Resented her for it. And here she was tearing his theories apart. Making him feel sorry for her. He could tell her she was perfect as she was, but he'd already done that once. He could tell her that Tyler and her mother were fucking fools for making her feel less than important, but he'd already done that too.

"Are you pretending now?"

She turned her head on the back of the couch and fixed him with those remarkable eyes. "I'm always pretending, Chase. I've been pretending for so long that I don't even know who I am anymore."

"So stop pretending. There's no movie script that can compare to what's going on in your life right now. You're on the run with a handsome and brilliant dude who makes Rambo look like an amateur—that's me if you didn't know—"

She laughed and he kept going, trying to be serious though he wanted to laugh too.

"And there's an evil Russian trying to track us down. We're on the run, desperate, hiding out in a hovel—"

She snorted. "This is not a hovel. It's a very nice little house."

"Fine, hiding out in a very nice little house. Waiting for daybreak. Subsisting on potato chips and beer—anything could happen, anything… But we're the good guys, Sophie, and the good guys always win."

She was smiling as she gazed at him. He liked that. "Do they really?"

He thought of all the mudholes, all the rotten missions in all the war-torn places he'd been, and he knew it wasn't true. Sometimes the good guys didn't win. Sometimes the good guys got killed. He'd seen it happen more than once. Marco and Jim—God, that was a long time ago now, and he still remembered it like it was yesterday. They'd lost Marco and Jim, and they'd gotten Sam "Knight Rider" McKnight and Garrett "Iceman" Spencer in their places. Time moved on, people came and went, and justice didn't always prevail.

He wasn't telling her that, however.

"Yeah," he said softly, holding her gaze. "They do."

"I hope you're right."

"I am. It's my job."

She was silent for a while, watching the TV as he flipped through the channels. There was nothing on, but he kept going. Finally he settled on a hockey game rerun.

"I'm sorry that I made you feel bad when we were kids," she said.

He turned his head to look at her. Her face was in profile, the light from the TV illuminating her skin.

"You didn't know. It's not your fault."

She met his gaze then. "Do you really mean that, or are you just trying to make me feel better?"

He blew out a breath. "No, I mean it. It was easy to blame you for having everything I didn't… but the truth is that Tyler chose to abandon my mom and me. It was nothing to do with you. Hell, he married Justine years after we were both born, so there's that too."

"It had to hurt when you heard he'd adopted me… but Chase, he did it because my mom pushed him. He did it to make her happy. It wasn't because of me. Truthfully, he's always felt like just a guy my mom lives with."

Now he felt like the one who needed to apologize. "Does that bother you?"

She shrugged. "It used to, but no, not anymore. I've had a good life and I've had advantages. I know that. And I'm sorry you feel like those advantages were denied to you."

"When you say it like that, I sound like a fucking whiny asshole."

Her eyes widened. "That's not what I meant—"

"No, I get that. I'm kinda ragging on myself here. But you know why I hate Tyler? It's not because he failed to buy me a car or, hell, every fucking thing I wanted, which is what I thought rich people did. No, I hate him because of what he did to my mother."

He watched as the Bruins scored again, wondering why in hell he was telling her these things. She hadn't said anything, but he knew she was waiting for the rest of the story.

"Tyler and my mother met in Nashville. She was a waitress, and he was just starting to play the clubs. He wasn't famous. Hell, he wasn't even in demand. He was good on a guitar and he had a couple of songs he'd written. But he needed to go to the next level, and he wasn't getting there. He was stuck in a rut. Until he met her. Until they started living together and she listened to him and encouraged him. She wrote lyrics for him and he set them to music. They were a team, and he promised her the world.

"But then she got pregnant, and he got his big break. He left her to play with B.B. King, promising he'd come back when the tour was over. He didn't. He met someone else, and he didn't come back."

"He's an asshole," she said, her voice breaking.

He swung his head to look at her, surprised to see tears on her cheeks. He had a sudden urge to tug her into his arms and hold her close. But he wouldn't do it because he was afraid he wouldn't stop at that.

"She was too proud to ask him for anything. He sent money from time to time—and then one day he decided I should visit him and she agreed. That's when the California trips began. I have no idea why he suddenly wanted me to spend time out there. But when I was sixteen, I told him I wasn't coming back. And I didn't. End of story."

"She should have sued his ass for child support. You deserved that."

She sounded angry, and he swallowed the sudden lump in his throat.

Fuck. This shit was getting too deep. Why had he delved into the depths of his painful childhood? And why did he feel kind of stunned by her vehemence on his behalf?

"Yeah, maybe she should have. But I think she was more afraid he'd try to take me away from her. And maybe he would have out of spite."

Her eyes glittered and her jaw was set in a stubborn line. She was pissed, and it kind of awed him.

"She was probably right. He'd have gotten custody of you and then ignored you while he partied and had a good time. You were better off, even if you didn't have all the things you wanted."

"Did they ignore you, Sophie?"

She snorted. "Let's just say that sometimes the adult in the room was not Tyler or my mom. They would drink until they were falling-down drunk, smoke weed, and fight until they passed out or started ripping each other's clothes off so they could make up. I stayed in my room and pretended my real parents were coming to get me."

"Jesus, I'm sorry."

She shrugged. "We've said that a lot to each other tonight. Maybe we should talk about something else for a while."

He could only stare at her. Her eyes flashed and her cheeks were high with color. She was beautiful, fiery, and he wanted her right now.

But taking her when they were both angry and hurt was not the thing to do. If he hadn't known it before her revelation about Tyler and her mom fighting and fucking, he definitely knew it now.

Instead, he reached for her hand and twined his fingers in hers. She stiffened for a moment—and then she relaxed and squeezed his hand in return.

Chapter Fourteen

SOPHIE SNUGGLED INTO THE COVERS AND FOUGHT THE first currents of wakefulness. She was comfortable, warm, and safe. If she woke up, she didn't know if she'd be any of those things.

The bed was small, narrow, and she was crowded up against the edge on one side and the wall on the other. Definitely a narrow bed. Perilously narrow.

She opened an eye and tried to focus on her surroundings. There was a table and a lamp… and the soft glow of a television. There hadn't been a television in her room—

She gasped and spun over in the bed. The wall she'd been pressed up against was definitely solid. It was also human. She sucked in a breath at his nearness. His utter perfection.

Chase lay on his side, one arm slung across her body, his naked chest a study in ideal human anatomy. She followed the line of dark hair that arrowed down his abdomen, disappearing into his shorts.

Oh, where did anyone on this earth get abs like that? Hard, defined abs that she wanted to trace with her tongue just to see if they tasted as perfect as they looked.

He never opened his eyes as his hand wandered from her waist to the curve of her ass where he tugged her in close. So close that she didn't have to wonder if he was hard or not.

He was. Gloriously, hugely hard. Her gaze shot from his chest to his face. His eyes were still closed, and she swallowed.

Oh fuck, now what? She hadn't intended to fall asleep out here with him, but after they'd spilled their guts and he'd held her hand, she'd felt such a sense of belonging that it had stunned her. They hadn't said another word as the hockey game played on. She'd focused on their hands, on the warmth and rightness that flowed over her. It had been comforting in a way she couldn't ever remember experiencing.

She didn't remember falling asleep, but she was surprised he hadn't wakened her. No, he'd gone to sleep beside her. And now he was *really* beside her.

"Mmm," he said, and her heartbeat quickened.

"Um, Chase. Chase."

"Yeah, baby?" he whispered. "You want it again?"

Again? What the hell?

No, no. Calm down. If they'd had sex, she'd damn well know it. They had not had sex. He was asleep and dreaming. Or something.

"No, I do not want it," she said. "It's me, Chase. It's Sophie. Your, um, stepsister. Kind of."

"Whatever game you want to play, honey," he

106

murmured before spearing his other hand into her hair and pulling her face toward his.

Sophie put her hands on his chest and pushed. "Chase! Wake up!"

His eyes popped open then, and he looked her over in that lazy way he had. "Hi, Sophie."

He had not let go of her ass, she noticed. "Hi, Chase. Can you let me go?"

"You sure about that?"

His erection nestled against her pubic bone, burning into her. Her body responded with a surge of heat and moisture between her legs. Her sex sizzled with electric tingles every time he shifted his hips in the slightest. She wanted to grab his ass and rub herself against all that delicious hardness while pressing her mouth to his chest.

Before she could find her voice, he squeezed her ass one last time. "Much as I'd like to convince you otherwise, we gotta get up. Hawk will be here soon."

He rolled away from her and sat up on the edge of the bed. After grabbing his phone and presumably scrolling through his messages, he stood and stretched, his bones cracking and muscles rippling as he reached skyward.

Then he grabbed his T-shirt and dragged it on over his chest, covering everything she'd been staring at. Her gaze dropped lower, and her heart flipped in her chest at the evidence of his arousal. Wow, that was quite an impressive bulge in his shorts. It lay against his body, pointing toward his heart… and it reached almost to the edge of his waistband.

Holy shit.

"See something you like?"

Her gaze shot to his. He'd arched an eyebrow, staring at her with a smirk on his handsome face. Daring her, she supposed.

She pushed herself up on an elbow and yawned. "Don't be so full of yourself," she said lazily. "I saw tons of hot guys growing up in LA. You're nothing special, Chase."

He snorted. "Liar. You've been staring at me since you walked into my apartment two days ago."

Oh, he was irritating. And confusing as hell. Prickly one minute and sexy the next. Pulling her to him and pushing her away. Being so sweet it hurt and then being angry and defensive.

"That's because I'm not yet convinced you won't get tired of this and ditch me. I'm watching you in case you leave me."

He sobered instantly. "I'm not leaving you, Sophie. I'll protect you with my life. You can count on that."

A knot formed in her throat. After the past two days, she knew it would be no small task to protect her. "Thank you."

He shrugged. "No need to thank me. It's what I do."

She pulled her knees up to her chest and sat back against the couch. "You do this all the time? Run from bad guys and try not to get killed?"

His look was so intense it took her breath. "No, I don't run from the bad guys. If they're smart, they run from me."

"And if they don't?"

"I kill them."

A chill skated down her spine. He was serious. Deadly serious. "What happened to bringing them to justice?"

"What I do is war, Sophie. Innocent lives depend on me and my team. If someone takes Americans hostage, we're not making sure they get due process before we bust in and take the hostages back. It doesn't work that way. Due process is a bullet in the brain of our enemies and no man or woman left behind."

The hair on her arms stood up as another chill rippled through her. Somehow she hadn't understood how deadly he was until that moment. How frightening. "You seem awfully certain."

"I am. Not everyone in this world is kind, and not everyone believes everyone else has a right to live. Some people think killing innocent Americans is justified— well, I'm there to make sure they don't get to do it."

She knew what he did was necessary, and yet it pained her to think of him taking such risks. Making such choices.

His phone rang and he answered. Her heart thumped as she imagined all kinds of bad scenarios. But then he broke out in a big grin and relief coursed through her.

"Yeah, come on. We'll be ready."

———

CHASE OPENED the door to Hawk and Dex "Double Dee" Davidson.

The latter smiled and shook his head, his Kentucky

twang pronounced as he spoke. "Shoo-ee, boy, what kind of trouble did you get into now?"

Chase rolled his eyes in mock disgust. "The kind you can't handle, cowboy."

Hawk and Dex came inside and shut the door behind them. Sophie had gone into the bedroom to get dressed and hadn't yet returned. He was glad for that because he wasn't sure what Hawk would have to tell him. If it was bad, he didn't want Sophie to know.

"How did Mendez take it?" Chase asked.

Hawk snorted. "About as well as you'd expect. He can't provide support, but then we knew that. He may have a connection to work—no promises. He'll probably also take his pound of flesh out of your ass when this is all over. You know that, right?"

"Yeah, I know."

The colonel was a hard man, a scary man in many ways, but there was no doubt he cared about his men. When Ice had been on the run with Grace Campbell, Mendez had put everything he had into helping them reach safety. And then when Gina was kidnapped and Hawk had nearly been killed, he'd sent the team into action to extract Gina and her son even though the mission would take place in the fancy neighborhoods of Northwest DC.

Again and again, Mendez did what it took in support of his warriors. Chase admired that about his colonel—though he also wasn't looking forward to the ass-chewing he was very likely going to get when this situation was over.

"Got some clothes for you both," Hawk said,

handing over a hanging bag. "There's a carry-on in the car with a couple of days' worth too."

"Sophie needs shoes," Chase said. "Hers are ruined."

Dex held up a bag. "Right here."

Chase took everything and laid it on the table. Hawk came forward and pulled an envelope from his jacket. He dropped it on the table as well.

"Passports, plane tickets, and a short-term rental apartment a few blocks from the Eiffel Tower where Mr. and Mrs. Nathan Chandler will be spending their honeymoon. Oh, and plain gold rings to complete the illusion."

Chase picked up the envelope and opened it. He didn't like having to play mister and missus with Sophie, but he was grateful that Hawk had thought of an apartment rather than a hotel. It would make sleeping in separate beds a whole lot easier. And after this morning and the raging hard-on he'd had, sleeping in separate beds was a *very* good idea.

"There's some cash and a couple of credit cards too."

"Thanks, man."

If this were a HOT mission, he'd expect this kind of thing. But it was personal, and his guys were right there with him, giving him everything he needed.

"We called the team," Dex said. "Everyone's out of town, but they're on standby if needed. They wanted to come back, but we told them not to."

Chase's throat constricted. "Why aren't you somewhere, dude? It's R & R."

Dex shrugged, though the corners of his mouth tightened for a second. "Nowhere I wanted to go. Besides, this is more fun."

He grinned and Chase shook his head. "Adrenaline junkie."

"And you aren't? Hell, we all are."

"Yeah, that's the truth."

The door to the bedroom opened and Sophie came out. She was wearing her clothes from last night, though she was shoeless. She hadn't put on her jacket and the tank top molded to her, showcasing her fabulous rack and impressive cleavage. She stopped, her gaze going to his.

Fuck, those were some gorgeous eyes.

Her hair was loose and curly, and he found himself wanting to spear his fingers into it to see if it was as soft as it looked. Wanting to see if her lips were as soft as they looked.

"Whoa," Dex said, and Chase glanced over at him. He was currently staring at Sophie with his eyes bugged out.

For some reason, that raised Chase's hackles. A fierce wave of possession slammed through him. It was all he could do not to go over and shove Sophie behind him, hiding her from Dex's gaze.

"Hi," she said in that sweet voice of hers, and Chase felt a knot form in his gut.

Dex strode over and put his hand out. Sophie took it and smiled.

"I'm Dex Davidson," he said, his voice pitched low and filled with intent.

"I'm Sophie," she replied. She shot a look at Chase, and he gritted his teeth and smiled as she turned back to Dex. "Nice to meet you, Dex."

Her voice was all breathy sexiness, and Chase thought for a minute he wasn't going to be able to suck in any air. If he toppled over right here, what would they think?

Dex lifted her hand to his lips—and that was the end of that.

"Knock it off," Chase growled as he strode over and took Sophie's hand from Dex's grasp.

Dex let his gaze slide between them for a second before he laughed. "Sorry, man. Hawk said it wasn't like that, but I see he's wrong."

Chase dropped Sophie's hand. "He's not wrong—but she's my stepsister. I'm being brotherly here and protecting her from a player like you."

He felt foolish even saying it, especially since he didn't have any brotherly feelings toward Sophie and never had, but shit. What else was he going to say?

The look of amusement didn't leave Dex's face. "You sure about that?"

"I've seen you in action. Hell yeah, I'm sure. Sophie's too sweet for a guy like you."

"Not quite what I meant, Fiddler. But you go on deluding yourself if it helps you."

Chase was ready to throw down over that statement until Sophie rolled her eyes. "If you two don't mind, I think there are more serious issues to discuss than if I'm too sweet for someone or not. Right?"

Chapter Fifteen

THE GUY NAMED DEX WAS SMOKING HOT, BUT HE DIDN'T make Sophie's pulse trip the way Chase did. When he'd flirted and held her hand, she'd felt kind of stunned and then kind of pleased, but she'd never felt a spark of excitement the way she did when Chase touched her.

Which was all kinds of fucked up, she supposed. It didn't matter that they weren't raised together or weren't really a family in any way. The reality was that in the eyes of the world they had a familial relationship. Her adoptive parent was his biological parent. No amount of explaining they weren't raised together would ever make her attraction to him seem less than weird to anyone looking at them from the outside.

But for some crazy reason, that made it even more exciting. Illicit.

Oh God, what was wrong with her?

Chase looked pissed but she wasn't sure if it was at her or Dex. But then he shrugged and sauntered over to the table where he picked up a bag.

"Hawk brought you some shoes," he said, tossing the bag to her.

She caught it and peered inside. A pair of black leather boots with silver buckles and a definite motorcycle vibe sat inside the bag. She took them out and sat down on the couch to put them on. They had that worn-leather look of boots that had been broken in over years. She slid them on and zipped them. They fit perfectly, and they were completely her style.

"Wow," she said, peering at Hawk. "I'm amazed."

He laughed. "You shouldn't be. A few taps of a keyboard and my IT guy pulled up your shopping history off your credit card. Sizes, styles, you name it."

Her mouth dropped open. "Seriously, you hacked my credit card?"

"Yep."

A chill went through her then. She looked at Chase. "I used my credit card to mail the package."

"We saw that," Hawk said before Chase could answer. "The address you sent it to isn't in the credit card file, only the amount and the place you charged it. Androv can get that information, but he'll have to hack the carrier's database to get the address. We'll make that difficult for his people, but they *will* break through eventually."

"There was a tracking number," she said, and the guys exchanged a look.

"Yeah," Hawk said. "That's a bit problematic—but we'll keep him out as long as we can."

"He'll hack the carrier," Chase said. "Depending on how good his guys are, we're living on borrowed time here. We need to get to Paris and intercept that package before they do. They're going to know the address and delivery date soon enough."

"I got you on the first flight out this evening," Hawk said. "Six o'clock, BWI. There's a secure computer in the car."

"A secure computer?" Sophie asked. What the heck was that?

"As soon as we have the flash drive," Chase said, "I'll log on to the computer and send the information to Hawk over a secure connection. He'll get to work decoding it. If we're lucky, there's something incriminating on there. If we're not…"

Sophie swallowed. If they weren't, then there was nothing to stop Grigori from eliminating her. "How do you know you'll need to decode anything? Why wouldn't he just password protect his files?"

The three of them exchanged a look. Chase was the one to speak. "We don't… But Androv has a lot of, uh, businesses besides Zoprava. One of those is Open Sky. Hackers," he added when she didn't say anything. "They broke into an unsecured government system recently and left their calling card—a laughing demon with horns—on the screen. It was on all the news networks."

"I remember hearing about that—I didn't know it had anything to do with Grigori though. I thought his company prevented those kinds of things."

"Technically, yes. But software has to be tested for vulnerabilities, which is what hackers do. Androv's connection to Open Sky is not something widely known outside intelligence circles," Chase said. "But now you can understand why he isn't likely to use a computer or digital storage medium without securing the information. Encryption is one of the ways to secure it—and he's got access to the best."

"Don't worry, Sophie," Hawk said. "We're pretty good at this kind of thing. We'll break the encryption."

Chase was still looking at her with a frown on his face. "You know, this would go faster if I went alone. Dex could stay here with Sophie and keep her safe. I'll be back in a few days."

Her stomach flipped at the thought of him leaving her. Her throat tightened and her eyes stung. Damn him for being so sweet and caring last night, for listening to her and telling her his own secrets, making her like him more than she should. He'd done that and he still wanted to ditch her. It hurt, even though it shouldn't. He owed her nothing. Not only that, but he'd already done more for her in this situation than most men would have.

"I'd like to do that for you," Dex said, looking a little sad and angry at the same time. "Really. But I'm waiting for a Red Cross call. My dad's having emergency open-heart surgery this week. Soon as the Red Cross calls the commander, I'm on my way."

"Man, I'm sorry," Chase said, understanding now why Dex hadn't left town like everyone else. "I hope your dad will be okay."

"Thanks. The doctors say it's pretty routine even though it's critical they do it ASAP. He should recover fully. But just in case... I have to be there."

Sophie offered her well-wishes even while she felt guilty for being relieved that Dex couldn't stay with her. Hawk and Dex talked with Chase a bit more, and then they made for the door, though not before Hawk gave Chase a set of keys.

"Leave it in long-term parking and use it when you get back. We'll be there to back you up if you need it."

"Thanks, Hawk. I can't say it enough, but I appreciate everything."

Chase and Hawk clasped hands. "You'd do it for me. Hell, you have done it for me. Gave up your time off to help me find my son. I won't forget that. Besides, once HOT always HOT. We stick together."

"You're damn straight we do."

———

IT WASN'T YET dark when they left for the airport. Chase glanced over at the woman beside him and felt the same burning in the pit of his stomach he'd felt the minute she walked out of the bathroom with her new hair. It wasn't that he didn't like Sophie with black hair. He liked her too much.

She was gorgeous as a strawberry blonde. She was out of this world as a raven-haired goddess. When he'd handed her the hair dye Hawk had brought, he'd thought she would balk. She hadn't. He'd apologized for making her cover up the red-gold beauty of her hair, but she'd looked him square in the eye and told him that wasn't her natural color either.

"What is your natural color?" He'd thought she had

sort of blondish hair as a kid. Or maybe brown. Hell, he honestly hadn't remembered.

"I'm a dirty blonde," she'd said with a shrug, and that had called up a whole host of thoughts in his head. *Dirty* blonde. Shit. "I like playing with color," she'd continued. "Haven't been black-haired in a while."

And now she was—and she fucking rocked it. She'd made him stop at Walmart on the way out of town so she could grab some makeup. He hadn't wanted to do it, but she'd insisted it was part of the disguise. She'd gotten several things, but it was the cherry-red lipstick she was currently smearing on her lips that had all his attention. Her eyelashes were long, and she'd smudged her eyeliner in that sexy just-got-out-of-bed look he'd admired yesterday. She'd done it all while he was driving too.

The girl was fucking stunning. He just hoped she didn't draw too much attention because he wasn't sure how in hell a bottle of hair dye and some makeup was going to hide her from Grigori Androv's men. In fact, he was pretty sure she would command men's eyes instead of repel them.

"You're going to draw too much attention," he grumbled when she twisted the tube of lipstick and put it away. She turned to look at him, blinking those pretty eyes.

"Short of putting a bag over my head, I don't know what you want me to do. Besides—" She reached into the shopping bag and pulled out a pair of black-rimmed glasses. She ripped the tags off and slid them on, the gold ring on her finger glinting as she did so. "A bag over the head would be even more noticeable than black hair and glasses... don't you think?"

He gripped the wheel and stared straight ahead. Jesus, he'd never thought the naughty librarian look did anything for him, but apparently it did. Big-time.

"Maybe you should lose the red lipstick," he grumbled.

She laughed and then turned and started gathering her hair. He didn't watch what she did, but she rustled in the bag from time to time until she finally said, "There."

He glanced at her. And had to stifle a groan. She'd twisted her hair high up on her head and pinned it, but a few strands still escaped to frame her face. Those cherry lips were wet, glossy, and he wanted to bite them.

It didn't help that she'd come out of Walmart with a men's plaid shirt that she'd put on over her tank top and then tied at her waist. The vee of the open shirt only served to call attention to her cleavage.

Fucking awesome cleavage, he might add.

"You look like a librarian who's hiding a dominatrix underneath her sedate clothing."

Sophie laughed. "Maybe I am," she purred, and his cock jerked in response.

"No the fuck you aren't," he growled. "A dominatrix would have whipped the shit out of Androv and made him beg for more."

He thought he might have hurt her feelings with that one, but she only arched an eyebrow at him. "Do you like being whipped, Chase?"

A lightning bolt of heat shot through him at her suggestive tone. Not that he wanted to be whipped or would tolerate it for even a second—but the idea of her in spiked heels and nothing else, holding a crop and running it between her breasts, was suddenly front and center in his brain.

"No, I don't like to be whipped. Fuck no."

"But you like spanking women, I'll bet."

Jesus H. Christ.

"Never tried it," he drawled. "I might make an exception for you though. You need a good spanking, Sophie."

She laughed. "You and what army? No way."

He couldn't help but snort a laugh. She was funny and sexy and sweet. She was also too trusting, at least where Grigori Androv had been concerned. For that, he did want to spank her. She needed to be more careful who she let into her life.

She propped a booted foot on the dash. "I wish you'd talked to me when you were visiting all those years ago. It would have been nice."

"*I* wasn't nice. I was a moody, pissed-off teenager who wanted to be somewhere else."

"Yeah, I gathered that at the time. But it would have been less lonely for us both if you'd talked to me."

"I'm sorry you were lonely, Sophie."

She shrugged. "I wasn't always. But when I was, it felt like an eternity. Time dragged."

"It dragged for me when I was in LA. I just wanted to go home again."

"I wanted to go with you. Bet you didn't know that."

He shot her a look. "No… but why? I didn't tell you anything about my home. I would have been far too self-conscious about it considering the difference in our circumstances."

She dropped her head and fooled with the buckle on one of the boots. "I heard you talking to your mother sometimes. You put it on speaker, and she had such a lovely accent and sounded so warm and nice. I thought she sounded like what home is supposed to feel like."

And just like that, she socked him in the gut, her words taking the air from his lungs. "You eavesdropped."

But that wasn't the reason her words ripped into him. No, it was the plaintive way in which she said that his mother sounded like home to her.

"I did eavesdrop."

"What else did you hear, Sophie?"

She laughed softly. "You mean the year you had that girlfriend? Jane something. You didn't put her on speaker, but I heard your half of the conversation. I might have learned some new words that summer."

"You really do need a spanking," he growled, and she laughed again.

"Maybe I do."

"I hate to think of everything I said. Jane was the first girl I ever fucked—and believe me, all I wanted to do was get back home and fuck her some more. At that age, a boy's brain cells are all focused on one thing."

"I gathered that. I was fourteen. It was very scandalizing…"

"Hell."

"For the record, I'd say you're still quite fixated on that one topic. I think it's a guy thing."

He *was* fixated on it. And not because he couldn't think of anything else—but right now she had his brain rattled with her black hair, sexy bun, and librarian glasses. He imagined stripping her, turning her around, and fucking her hard while, yeah, spanking her ass. It was a hell of a turn-on—and not what he needed right now.

He needed to be clearheaded, not in a perpetual state of arousal. He was beginning to wish he'd jerked off in the shower last night.

"For the record, you're pushing it, Sophie."

"Pushing it where?" She sounded way too sultry for comfort.

Chase whipped into the exit to the rest area they were about to pass and shot up the ramp before careening the car into a slot and turning to glare at her.

Her eyes widened in surprise. "What are you doing?"

"Don't fucking bait me, Sophie. If you're acting, pretending to be something you're not, then knock it off. And if you're serious, then you'd better be prepared—because I am not tame, or safe—and I won't stay within the lines."

Chapter Sixteen

Sophie's nipples were hard little points scraping against the lace of her bra. Her heart beat hard and her pulse skipped wildly. She was certain he could see it in her throat.

Cars rolled slowly past, pulling into the rest area where people got out and strolled into the facilities. Some people walked dogs, others loitered around the candy and soda machines near the entrance to the building.

She *had* been playing, and he'd called her on it. She hadn't thought much of the act at first when she'd sunk into the character, but now she was thinking too much. Was she really sexy? Sultry? Or was it all a lie?

She licked her lips, tasting the cherry lip gloss she'd slicked over her lipstick as she tried to think of what to say. His gaze narrowed—and then he swore before reaching over and curling a hand behind her neck, tugging her toward him.

"I think you like playing with matches, Sophie," he said, his lips a whisper away.

And then his mouth came down on hers.

It wasn't the hard meeting she'd expected, but rather it was hot, tender, sweet. He sucked at her mouth, nipped her lips softly, and devastated her with how gentle he could be. As if he knew she didn't have a ton of experience. As if he knew she needed to be stoked and teased before she burst into flame.

Oh dear heaven, it felt good. Somewhere in the back of her brain, a voice whispered that this was wrong, that it was illicit and forbidden, but she didn't care. She wasn't thinking about forever here. She was thinking about naked bodies and heated pleasure. About explosions of sensation and satisfaction so intense it stole her breath.

Her body ached for more. She wanted him to touch her, wanted him to cup her breasts and tease her taut nipples. And then she wanted him to free her breasts, lick them, suck them...

Oh...

He pushed her away suddenly but gently and leaned back in his seat, raking a hand through his hair.

"I shouldn't have done that."

"No, I... I liked it."

He turned his head on the seat back to look at her. His mouth was red from her lipstick, and that made her stomach corkscrew. *Mine, mine, mine...*

"You're too sweet, Sophie. You deserve something more than a quick fuck in the backseat of a car—and make no mistake, that's where this was headed."

Her heart thumped. "Maybe that's what I want."

He laughed, but there was no humor in it. "No, you definitely don't. You want romance. You want to be swept off your feet and wowed, not stripped and used hard and fast."

Sophie's stomach fell to her feet. She tugged in a deep breath even as anger twisted in her belly. "What makes you think you know what I want better than I do? You don't know me!"

His eyes were too perceptive. "I think I know you better than most after last night and today. You've said far too much for me to ever believe you don't need an emotional connection."

"We *have* an emotional connection, Chase. You just proved that with what you said. You know me. I know you. Nobody said it had to be love."

He stared at her for a long moment—and then he swore. He jerked the car into gear and reversed out of the parking spot before jamming the gas and heading back onto the highway.

They rode in silence the rest of the way to the airport. She stared out the window, her eyes and throat burning as she tried to process what had just happened between them. He'd kissed her. Kissed her so sweetly she'd wanted to cry.

And she'd wanted more. She thought he did too. But clearly there were more important things at work here. Grigori wasn't going away because she wished him to. He hung over her head like a malevolent cloud, threatening and malicious.

The highway grew more crowded with traffic the

closer they got to BWI. Finally Chase pulled into long-term parking and shut off the engine. They got the bags and started toward the terminal.

"Hold on," Sophie said and Chase stopped. "You've got, uh, red lipstick…"

"Shit." He wiped the back of his hand across his mouth. It came away red.

"Here, I have wipes."

She rummaged in the purse she'd bought at Walmart and came up with the pack of makeup removal wipes. He was glaring at her, but she ripped one from the package and handed it to him. He scrubbed it over his mouth and then looked at her in question.

"You got it all," she said.

He wiped the back of his hand and then started walking again, tossing the wipe in a trash can as they passed. They found the Delta counter, checked in, and then passed through security. Her heart beat hard the whole time. She didn't have any problem remembering that her name was Beth Chandler or that Chase was supposed to be her new husband Nathan.

But she worried that Grigori's men were around every corner. They'd found her so quickly when she'd gone to Chase's house that she kept expecting them to pop up at any moment. She told herself she looked different with dark hair, fashion glasses, and the cherry-red lips she'd fixed after Chase kissed her lipstick off.

And oh, remembering that moment was pretty much all she could do. The heat and passion, the fury and fire. He'd kissed her sweetly but hungrily. She'd wanted more. So much more.

She glanced at Chase as they walked through the terminal. He was huge, muscular, and intense. Her heart flipped at the sight of him—and at the way women looked at him as he sauntered along with a backpack over one shoulder and a gorgeous nonchalance to his gait.

But she knew he wasn't nonchalant. He was alert, wary, and ready to spring into action.

He walked right to the gate area and found a seat. She sank down beside him and then glanced around nervously. Chase put in a pair of earbuds and laid his head back against the seat, closing his eyes.

Well, hell.

Sophie sat for a few minutes until she was too bored to be still. There was a bookstore nearby, and she started to get up and go browse.

Chase's hand shot out and grabbed her wrist, searing into her and stopping her from moving at the same time. His eyes were open now. She forced a smile as a lady looked over at them, her eyes moving between them with interest.

"I was simply going to the bookstore, darling," she said lightly.

Chase's eyes narrowed as he tugged her back and put an arm around her. His lips were at her ear.

"What the fuck are you doing? Your passport is American."

It took her a moment to realize what he was talking about. She'd spoken with a British accent. She hadn't consciously thought about it, but it seemed right. Another layer to the disguise.

She lowered her voice for his ears only. "I don't see how that matters. The only people who'll ask for it now are the immigration control personnel in France. Besides, it's another way to hide from Grigori."

His eyes flashed hot—and then he released her, but not before sliding his fingers along her cheek and down her throat. She knew he did it for the woman watching them, but she liked it anyway. A shiver slid down her spine and into her toes.

"All right, honey. If that's what you want. We'll go look at the books."

"You don't have to go with me. You can see the store from here."

He stood and shouldered the backpack before taking her hand and pulling her up. "Doesn't work that way, babe. I'm on you like superglue until this thing is over."

She tried not to think about all the ways she'd like him to be on her as they strolled to the bookshop. He held her hand casually, lightly, and all she could think of was the way his skin burned into hers. What would it be like if there was nothing at all between them but skin? How would his skin sizzle into her then?

And, oh my, how would it feel to have him inside her?

Sophie shivered as they entered the store and he dropped her hand. His fingers settled against her spine, right in the small of her back, as he let her lead the way through the store. She walked over to the romance novels and stared at the covers.

Chase stood behind her, his presence solid and reassuring—and nerve-racking at the same time.

"That one looks good," he murmured in her ear, reaching past her to point to a book with a cover that featured a fully clothed man who had a woman up against a wall, her legs wrapped around him.

Her pulse skipped a couple of beats, both at the cover and at the gold ring on his finger. "You can't base your decision solely on the cover," she said, trying desperately not to step backward and into the solid heat of his body.

"Then pick it up and skip around for the dirty parts. I'll read them to you on the plane."

Sophie laughed, but it was nervous laughter. Because holy cow, Chase reading the dirty parts to her? That thought made her nipples tighten and her pussy throb with heat.

"Maybe not," she said, reaching for a nice, tame book with a woman in a flowing dress on the cover. Something about becoming a duchess. She turned it over and tried to read the back, but Chase bent over her until his cheek was beside hers.

"Maybe there are some dirty parts in that one," he murmured.

She couldn't focus on the cover copy. She put the book back and picked up another one. Chase reached out and picked up the first one he'd mentioned.

"I'm getting this one," he said when she put back the one she'd just picked up and snatched another one.

She turned and took a step backward, putting distance between them. He confused her and intrigued her—and his nearness was driving her insane.

"You can't be serious."

He shrugged. "Why not? I might learn something."

Then he gave her that grin she was beginning to learn was filled with wicked intent.

"Fine." She flipped over the book in her hand and read it. Something about a billionaire and a virgin. "I'm getting this one."

She strode over to the magazines and picked up *InStyle* and *People StyleWatch*. Chase grabbed a *Popular Science* and a guitar magazine.

"Done?" he asked.

"Yes."

He took the magazines and book from her and went to the register. It bothered her that she couldn't pay for her own stuff, but she had no cash. No credit cards. Everything had burned up in the fire, and she'd had no time to try to replace it just yet.

When she'd gone into Walmart, he'd had to go with her and pay for everything there too. At least he hadn't asked why she'd needed or wanted something. He'd just stood at the register and peeled off the bills when the purchases were totaled.

The cashier was eyeing Chase from beneath her lashes as she rang up the books and magazines. Sophie felt a hard, hot feeling twist into her heart. She stepped up to Chase's side and put her right arm around his waist and her left on his chest before she could think better of it.

"I can't wait to get to Paris and start our honeymoon, sweetheart," she said on a sigh.

Chase, bless him, played right along. "You'd better

use the flight to rest, honey," he said, "because I'm taking advantage of you the minute we get there."

The cashier stopped smiling and finished the transaction. Chase took the change, handed her the bag, and they walked out of the bookstore together, his arm around her shoulders. She felt warm and happy, even if they'd been pretending. That cashier hadn't considered that she could be with a man like Chase until she'd pressed the point.

A fake point, but so what. He'd played it perfectly.

But all her happiness drained and she stumbled to a stop as her gaze landed on the man sitting in one of the chairs they'd vacated earlier. Chase kept his arm firmly around her, but his body tensed in readiness.

"What is it?"

"That man," she whispered, her heart thundering. "I recognize him."

Chapter Seventeen

"Who is he?" Chase asked, as Sophie stiffened beside him.

Sophie clutched the bag of books to her chest as if they were a shield. "I've seen him with Grigori. I don't know his name."

The man was sitting in the chair and scrolling through something on his phone. He glanced up from time to time, but gave no indication of recognizing Sophie.

Which was a good thing, but who knew how long it might last?

"Come on." Chase started to push Sophie toward the guy and she pushed back, resisting his efforts to make her move. He was much stronger than she was and could do it forcibly, but that would be too obvious.

"He's already looked at us. He has no idea who you are. If you act like you're afraid, you'll draw attention. Now walk."

She moved, but reluctantly. Her body trembled as he held her close against his side.

He bent his head to her ear. "I told you I wouldn't let anyone hurt you. Trust me."

She relaxed marginally as he led her past the man and then to a seat a couple of rows over where they could see any moves this guy might make.

Chase tugged her down and tucked her against him. She still clutched the magazines and her chest rose and fell a little too quickly. He reached over, took the bag, and set it down on the seat beside him. Then he tipped her chin up so she could look at him—and instead of telling her to calm down, he let his gaze slide to her mouth.

Those red, plump, cherry lips that had tempted him earlier. That he hadn't stopped thinking about since he'd kissed her at the rest stop. Every thought he'd had about keeping his hands off her evaporated.

He wanted her. Wanted to strip her slowly, discover all her delicious secrets, and eat her up from head to toe. It didn't matter that he shouldn't do it, that she was his stepsister, that any involvement with her could bring his father back into his life. And what about his mother? Would she be hurt if he got involved with Tyler's step-daughter? She'd never said a negative word about either Justine or Sophie, but then she'd never been forced to endure their presence in her life either.

Guilt ripped through him even as desire followed hard on its heels. Chase glanced up at the people in the surrounding gate area and then did what he wanted so badly to do.

The instant his lips met Sophie's, she moaned. It was a small sound, but it pounded through him like a summer squall on the Chesapeake. Her mouth slipped open and he thrust his tongue inside, stroking hers. She stroked back, and his cock took notice.

He knew he was getting that damned lipstick all over him again, but he didn't much care. It wiped off. The cherry flavor of her lip gloss was sweet as he moved his mouth against hers.

Her hands came up and slid around his neck. He tugged her in closer, almost on his lap, and bent her backward, kissing her with the kind of desperate passion he'd held in check earlier.

"Get a room," a male voice said.

It was precisely what he needed to hear. He gentled the kiss and carefully extracted himself before things got any more out of control than they already were.

Sophie looked up at him with wide eyes. Her lips were wet, and her lipstick was smeared. He knew it was smeared on him too. For some reason, that made him grin.

Sophie grinned back. "You look like a clown."

"And you look delicious." She hadn't dropped the British accent at all. It turned him on more than it should.

"I'd better get out the wipes again."

"Yep."

She didn't bother looking at the man sitting with his back to them, but he knew she hadn't forgotten he was there. She fished in her purse, handed him a wipe, and then took out a mirror and her lipstick.

"You're gonna go through that tube mighty fast," he grumbled. "And the wipes."

"Not if you'd give me warning first, darling."

"Hard to warn you when I don't know I'm going to do it until I do."

She finished slicking on the red lipstick and put everything back in her purse.

"Feeling better?" he asked as he finished wiping the stain off his mouth.

She glanced toward the man and then smiled. "A little bit, yes."

"You're pretty fucking sexy, Beth Chandler," he said, and she dropped her gaze as if she were embarrassed.

He put a finger under her chin and tipped it up until she had to look him in the eye. "That's the honest truth, baby. No lie."

She swallowed. "Thank you. That's very nice of you."

He leaned toward her so only she could hear what he said. "I'm not being nice. It's the truth—and if we were still in that house, I'd sink into you and not come up for hours."

Her breath hitched and her skin flushed a pretty pink. "Then I wish we were still there."

He leaned back against the chair and pulled her into the curve of his arm. He told himself it was because they were supposed to be on their honeymoon and they needed to look the part, but in truth he liked having her there.

She sighed and settled in, her hand drifting up to twine with his where it hung over her shoulder.

"Why do you think he's here on this particular flight?" she whispered after a few minutes.

Chase didn't take his eyes off the man. His back was still turned and he still seemed oblivious to their presence. Chase's instincts told him there was no way the dude knew Sophie was here.

"I think he's here because Androv figured out he needed to send someone to Paris. No sense calling him back to New York first."

"Do you think he's figured out the address?"

"Yeah. Even if he didn't get it from the credit card information, he'll have figured it out by investigating your background. You have a connection to Paris, and he'll explore that first."

"If he has the tracking number, he'll know when the package is delivered."

"True. Nothing we can do about it but get there first."

"I should have kept the flash drive. We could be analyzing it now."

"You did the best you knew how to do. And if he'd caught you, you'd be dead and he'd have his information back. So, no, you shouldn't have kept it."

Chase took his personal cell phone that he'd replaced earlier from his pocket and sent a text to Hawk. "Stay here," he told Sophie as he got up and sauntered over to the other side of the lounge. He picked up a bottle of water from a vendor, paid, and then turned and snapped a pic of the area with his phone. He snapped a couple of more pics as if he were a tourist taking photos of the airport and then sauntered back to

Sophie's side where he sent the photo of the man to Hawk.

She'd taken a magazine from the bag and was currently flipping through it. He saw clothes, purses, and makeup, and zoned out. Whatever.

"You okay?" he asked.

She glanced up at him. "Mostly. I just wish we were on our way already."

"Me too."

Because he didn't like waiting for the go order. He liked it when they were busting balls to get to the drop zone, when everything was critical and actions mattered. He liked the rush of exploding onto a scene with his team and taking care of business.

The only team he had on this one was Sophie, however, and the mission was not to explode onto the scene so much as to tiptoe in and out again like thieves in the night.

For Sophie's sake, he hoped that's exactly how it went down. In, out, and back to DC with the kind of valuable information that meant they could put Grigori Androv behind bars for a long time. Only then would Sophie be safe.

Chapter Eighteen

THEY ARRIVED IN PARIS EARLY IN THE MORNING. SOPHIE was bleary-eyed as they got off the plane. They'd been in economy class and Grigori's man had been in first. He'd walked right past her when he'd presumably been stretching his legs. His gaze had slipped over to her, but the recognition she'd feared she might see wasn't there. She'd kept her expression carefully blank, and he'd walked down the aisle and then up the other side while her heart hammered the whole time.

But what could he do on a plane? Not much, though she feared that someone would be waiting for her and Chase as they exited the airport. Even if they were, Chase had that covered, it seemed. He took her hand and tugged her through the terminal. They did not go to baggage claim, instead exiting in a different area and heading for the parking lot.

Of course Hawk had a car for them, an Audi turbo that was sleek and dark and promised to be fast. Chase slung their bags in the backseat and retrieved another bag from the trunk. Sophie tried not to gasp when he opened it to reveal an arsenal of guns, but she couldn't quite stop herself.

Chase looked up at her as he grabbed a pistol, checked it, and tucked it into the side pocket of the door. He zipped the bag and tossed it in the back with the rest of their stuff.

"I didn't think guns were easy to get here."

"They are when you know where to go. Hawk has connections."

Sophie belted herself in and tried not to let everything feel so surreal. She was in France with her smoking-hot stepbrother, and danger was on her heels. It was so far removed from her life thus far that she sometimes thought she must be dreaming.

But then Chase growled at her or kissed her or just took her hand and held it like they really were Nathan and Beth Chandler, honeymooners, and every cell in her body went on red alert.

No, she definitely wasn't dreaming.

He started the car and zipped through the parking lot. Soon they were on their way, speeding out of Paris's Charles de Gaulle Airport and toward the city. Sophie turned to look behind them, but the traffic was so heavy she'd never know if anyone was following or not.

"His name is Sergei Turov," Chase said matter-of-factly, and Sophie's head swung around. She knew he'd sent a picture to Hawk—and apparently he'd gotten an answer. "Not a nice guy, but then none of Androv's associates are known to be nice. Turov's specialty seems to be human trafficking."

Sophie's heart froze. "Human trafficking?"

Chase glanced at her, his hands tightening on the wheel. "He buys and sells women, Sophie. Poor women from Russia and China who believe they're going to a better life in the US. They end up in the sex trade mostly."

Sophie put her hand over her mouth. "Oh my God. But Grigori isn't part of that, right?"

He didn't say anything, and the horror spread within her heart. *My God.*

"I had no idea," she whispered. "Really."

She'd trusted Grigori. If she'd been someone else, someone poor and alone and unfortunate… God, it didn't bear thinking about. How could he? How could anyone?

She shuddered, tears pricking her eyes, and Chase reached over to squeeze her hand. "It's not the kind of thing he'd mention, I'm sure. And he's hidden his tracks well, because this is the first Hawk or I have heard of it. Not to say that it wasn't known higher up the chain, but it's apparently not common knowledge."

Fury clogged her throat at the sheer evilness of what Chase was saying. "How could I not have known what a vile man Grigori is? How could I have ever thought he was decent?"

"Because he presented himself that way. It's not your fault."

"And yet there's the maid." She'd heard the story and dismissed it when Grigori told her it was a lie. Because he was rich and the maid was poor, and it made sense that she'd want to sue him and possibly gain more money than she ever would as a maid.

"He gave you good reason to think it was a setup from someone wanting money."

Sophie snorted as she looked over at him. Traffic whizzed past, but she barely registered it. "You're defending me now? I thought you believed I was an idiot for getting involved with Grigori in the first place."

"I did think that… but that's before I spent time with you. You've got a good heart, Sophie. You aren't judgmental and you're trusting. Those are admirable traits."

She would have laughed if the subject weren't so serious. "I may just fall out on the floor from all this praise. And then I want to know where Chase is, because I don't know this alien who stole his body."

"No aliens. I just realized you were easily duped."

"And there he is after all—stupid is what you meant to say. You called me that when I was in your apartment."

He sighed. "There's a difference between being willfully stupid and being manipulated by a master liar. I could wish you'd been more suspicious, but you weren't. Now we deal with the aftermath."

Sophie yawned and shook her head. Maybe he was tired too and that's what was causing all this niceness. "I just want to go to sleep for a few hours."

"Usually I'd say that was a bad idea, but since we aren't really tourists and we're only staying as long as it takes to get that file, I don't think it matters whether or not your body acclimates to Paris time."

Sophie closed her eyes as they sped along the

autoroute. And then she opened them again and speared him with a look. "You're trying to get rid of me. You intend to stash me away, let me sleep, and go looking for the package." She yawned so hard her jaw cracked. "No way, no how, buddy."

"You aren't going with me to Tyler's apartment. You're staying in the rental until I return. Besides, it's not due to be delivered for another day. I'll go tomorrow —and you'll stay put while I do."

"You won't be able to get into the building."

"Do you honestly believe that after the past few days? I have the address. I have a lockpick. I know how this is done."

Panic blossomed in her belly at the idea. "Grigori's men will be watching."

"Which is why you aren't going."

Sophie bit her lip. "Madame Renard collects any mail that comes for Tyler. The postman delivers it to her box when he's not in residence. You need me to go with you. She won't give it to you."

Chase gripped the wheel harder and swore. "You could have told me that a couple of days ago, Sophie. What was the point in hiding that information?"

He was furious, and rightly so. But she hadn't told him originally because she thought he might not think the situation so dire. That he might not help her. If all she needed to do was call Madame Renard and ask her to forward the package, why go to Paris at all?

And yet the longer the package was out there, the more fearful she became. She didn't need to wait days for it to arrive—she needed it *now*. She needed to know if there was anything on that flash drive that could stop Grigori from hurting anyone else. From hurting her.

"I thought you wouldn't help me."

He took an exit and they found themselves in bumper-to-bumper traffic. He turned to her, his brows two slashes on his handsome face.

"From the moment those assholes set my apartment on fire, I was on your side, Sophie."

Shame crawled around in her belly. "I didn't know that. I thought you'd dump me at the first opportunity. You were so angry…"

He shoved a hand through his hair. His eyes were red rimmed from lack of sleep, but that didn't make him any less sexy.

"I was angry. I *am* angry. But I wouldn't leave you to face this alone. That's not who I am."

"I know that now."

"Then why didn't you tell me sooner that this Madame Renard gets the mail?"

She closed her eyes and leaned her head back. "I don't know. Everything has been so stressful and unpredictable—and I guess I thought you might find a way to leave me behind if you knew."

"You just said she would only give the mail to you."

"Yes, but given enough time, you'd have charmed her. Or you could have gotten Tyler to call her or something."

"Fuck me, Sophie," he said—and her core reacted in ways that sent a delicious tingle through her. What was it about the way he said those words? "I can't follow your logic half the time."

"I also thought you might want me to call and have her forward the mail."

He shook his head. "Definitely not. The sooner we get the fucking thing, the better. She's in danger too so long as this thing is out there."

Sophie's chest ached suddenly. "But they can't know she's getting his mail. It goes to her apartment, not his—and I didn't require a signature."

He shook his head. "They'll figure it out. Maybe not right away, but when there's no mail at all, they're going to know it's being redirected. And they're going to find out who's getting it, especially when the tracking number shows that the package was delivered."

Guilt speared her. "We can't let that happen. Madame Renard is a sweet old woman. She doesn't deserve that."

"I'm not going to let it happen, Sophie. But swear to fucking God, you had better not keep anything else from me. You got that?"

It hurt to have him growl at her, but she understood why. She swallowed the lump in her throat. "I'm not keeping anything else from you, I promise."

"Good."

Traffic suddenly started moving and he pressed the gas, whipping between a couple of slower cars and accelerating to the next snarl and then the next. It took over an hour to reach the street in the seventh arrondissement where their rental property was, partly because of traffic and partly because Chase didn't go directly to the rental. He took side roads, backtracked, and circled before finally sliding into a space around the corner from their building. The building was old in a charming way—but the elevator was out of service so they had to walk up four flights to the garret on the top floor.

The property agent met them at the door. She was very French, elegant and refined, and so terribly excited they were on their honeymoon.

"We have champagne for you, monsieur and madame," she said, leading them into the tiny kitchen with a window from which they could see the top of the Eiffel Tower. But that wasn't the best part. The best was a small balcony off one of the bedrooms with a view of the tower.

"*Merci*," Sophie said. "We are delighted, madame."

The property agent spent another twenty minutes showing them every conceivable thing about the apartment before she suggested they make dinner reservations at a bistro down the street. Or, she mentioned, she could do it for them.

"Thank you," Chase said, "but I'm not sure we'll go anywhere tonight." He put his arm around Sophie then and squeezed her to him. "It's been a long night of travel, and I'm ready to be alone with my wife."

The woman smiled knowingly. "But of course. I will bid you adieu now."

And she disappeared with a wave and a smile, the door closing firmly behind her.

Chase blew out a breath as he let Sophie go and walked over to the bag of guns and ammunition. She knew he'd slipped the other gun into his waistband beneath his jacket.

"Do you really think you're going to need those?"

He was busy stacking ammo boxes and laying out weapons. "Never know. Best to be prepared."

She watched as he peeled off his jacket and his muscles bunched and rippled while he worked. It was mesmerizing in a way.

He paused in his stacking and looked up at her. "You should get some sleep."

She hugged herself as she leaned back against the small dining room table. "And what will you be doing while I sleep?"

"I won't leave you alone if that's what you're worried about."

She swallowed. "I kind of am, yes. You left me in the tree stand."

"That was different. This is a city and I don't need to scout the perimeter. Besides, I told you what I was doing when I left."

Sophie rubbed a hand over her eyes tiredly. "Fine. Which bedroom do you want?"

"The one nearest the door."

For some reason, that answer disappointed her. As if he'd been going to say *Whichever one you're in.*

She'd kind of hoped he would, especially after what he'd said about sinking into her if they were still in the safe house in Maryland. But clearly he was beyond that now. If he'd ever meant it in the first place.

He confused her and she didn't like it. She didn't like herself much at the moment for caring what he meant either. She knew better than to put much stock in what people said, and yet she sometimes did.

Sophie grabbed the carry-on suitcase that had her clothing and rolled it to the bedroom where she shut the door and stood weary and unhappy even though she had the room with the charming view. She wanted a shower, and yet she wanted sleep even more. She walked over to the bed, pulled the covers back, and took off her clothes before dropping onto the sheets in her bra and panties.

Chapter Nineteen

MENDEZ LOVED THE FEEL OF SAM'S LEGS WRAPPED around his waist. She gripped him hard as he pumped into her body, her skin slick with sweat, her moans punctuating the air around them. Sex with Sam was still fucking hot, even after so much history between them.

"Yes, Johnny—oh God, just like that," she said as he lifted her ass higher and plunged into her harder and faster than before.

And then she screamed as he found her G-spot, her body shaking apart in his arms as he thrust hard and deep before groaning his own release.

He rolled off her and went to take care of the condom. When he came back, she was sitting up and looking very pleased with herself. Hell, he was pleased too—he didn't much care if she seemed a bit smug.

He reached for his uniform pants and started to tug them on again. Sam thrust out her lip. "Aw, leaving so soon, baby?"

"Have to get back to the office. Shit going down."

"Shit is always going down," she said, reaching for her electronic cigarette and taking a puff. She lay back against the pillows, her naked form lush and lovely.

She looked decadent lying there with vapor curling above her head and her legs spread wide enough for him to see the slick pinkness he'd just been enjoying. She lifted a hand and slid it over one nipple. His cock started swelling again.

"You're a bad girl, Sam."

She arched an eyebrow. "Maybe you'd like to spank me?"

He tugged his T-shirt on and followed it with the camouflage shirt, buttoning it quickly before sitting down to lace up his boots. And, yeah, his cock was about to tent his pants.

"I'd love to spank you—but it'll have to be later."

When he stood again, she got to her knees and came over to the side of the bed where she put her palms on his chest and ran them up to his shoulders before hooking them around his neck. "You are so damn hot, Johnny. Still amazing in bed. And still so damned difficult to understand."

He kissed her, his hands cupping her breasts, teasing her nipples into stiff peaks. "What is this? I thought you wanted a fuck buddy, not a potential life partner."

She arched her back and thrust her breasts into his hands. "You have a way of messing with a woman's head. And maybe I sometimes regret what could have been."

"No regrets. That's what you said at the beginning of this, remember?"

"I remember." She sighed and let him go, leaning back on the bed with her legs open. So tempting. "I wish I'd married you instead of Dan. You were much more exciting."

He picked up his hat and keys. A memory flashed through him, bringing with it remembered bitterness. "Too exciting, I believe. Or so you told me at the time."

She shrugged. "You were always dashing off somewhere, not calling for weeks at a time, returning with that wild look in your eyes. It was too much for me back then."

He snorted. "And then you left the Army and joined the CIA to become a field officer. Pretty exciting stuff on its own, don't you think?"

"What choice did I have when the Army wouldn't let me try out for the Rangers, much less the Green Berets or Delta?"

That much was true, but the Army had come a long way in the past twenty years. Women were trying out for Special Forces now—and getting in. Still, that wasn't what they were really talking about here. "We wouldn't have lasted, and you know it. We were always like oil and water—except in bed."

"You asked me to marry you."

"And you said no." He didn't think he was bitter over that anymore, but maybe he was. And not necessarily because of her. If he'd married Sam, maybe he could have avoided the resounding heartbreak that came later. The woman who had come later and who had been taken away when his feelings for her were still so new and overwhelming.

Sam blew out another cloud of vapor. "I did. My bad."

Mendez couldn't help but laugh. "You aren't in the least bit broken up about it either."

She grinned. "No, I guess not. I'm just pissed off at all the great sex I could have been having if I'd said yes."

He leaned down and kissed her, then licked a nipple while she gasped. "Look at it this way—if you'd said yes and we'd gotten married, we'd have ended up divorced and not speaking to each other. And we definitely wouldn't be fucking now, would we?"

"No, we wouldn't." She brought her foot up and rubbed it over his crotch when he straightened, laughing as she discovered his hard-on. "We could go another round before you leave."

He sighed. "Wish I could, but I got to get back."

"You're still worried about your operator, aren't you? Daniels, right?"

"Yeah." He knew Fiddler and the girl had made it to Paris and that Hawk had set them up with everything they needed. But he didn't know what Androv was up to other than the typical intel he had on the man. He couldn't send assets into the mix right now, and it was killing him not to be able to do so.

He'd asked Sam, but she'd been uncertain she could do anything from her end. She grabbed her robe from the bed and stood up, putting it on and belting it. Her eyes were sympathetic as she gazed up at him. "This thing with Congressman DeWitt has really got you wound around the axle, hasn't it?"

DeWitt shouldn't be anyone important as a junior member of the House Armed Services Committee, yet he seemed to have made it his personal mission to turn a critical eye onto everything HOT. He'd been busy whipping up interest in Congress for an investigation into HOT's operational scope. One wrong move right now and DeWitt would have all the ammunition he needed.

Not to mention that Mendez hadn't forgotten what Ian Black had said to him once. *DeWitt... watch him closely.*

"It happens with every administration," he told Sam. "Remember when the president and the joint chiefs kept the NRO a secret from Congress back in the seventies? Now they're paranoid about everything the Pentagon does."

She set down her e-cigarette, put her arms around him, and hugged him tight for a second. "Let me try again, okay? I'll see what assets we have in Paris that can help."

He pushed her hair back from her cheek. "What do you know about Ian Black?"

She seemed to hesitate for a second, but then she frowned. "He was disavowed a few years ago. He's gone rogue from what I understand. But how do you know him?"

Every instinct he had told him to be cautious here. If Sam didn't know that Black was still with the agency, it wasn't his place to tell her. "I ran into him in Qu'rim. He's an interesting character."

"He's a traitor."

"So I've heard."

"You sound as if you don't believe it."

He didn't say anything for a long moment. "You know as well as I do that nothing is as simple as it seems in this business."

"If the agency tells me he's a traitor, then he is." She picked up her e-cigarette and put it to her lips. But her fingers trembled slightly as she did so. It surprised him and puzzled him.

But he didn't mention it. He'd learned as a Special Operator that some of the smallest things were often some of the most important. Instead, he smacked her on the ass and grinned.

"Good-bye, Sam."

She returned his smile. "Bye, Johnny. I'll call you if I have any news."

———

IT WAS dark when Sophie woke. It surprised her that she'd slept so long, but she didn't remember getting up even once. She went and took a quick shower, then put on the robe hanging on the back of the door. When she opened the bedroom door, she fully expected to find Chase watching television or cleaning guns.

But the room was dark and empty. She moved toward the bedroom he'd said he would take. The door stood open. She peered into the darkness, trying to make out a shape in the bed or hear the sound of his breathing.

But there was no sound, no movement. Sophie spun

with a cry and rushed back into the living room. The apartment was empty. Just empty.

Bastard.

She clenched her fists at her sides and sucked in air. He'd lied to her. He'd said he wouldn't leave her alone, but he had. He'd gone to Tyler's apartment, gone to see the lay of the land and figure out if any of Grigori's people had been there. He'd left her here alone with no phone and no way of communicating with him.

Fury rolled through her—

Something rattled the door and her heart hammered harder. What if it was Grigori's men? What if they were breaking in, coming for her?

She spun, heading for her room and the balcony that overlooked the courtyard and the rooftops. She could go out there, climb over to the next roof maybe—

The lock turned and the door swung inward, freezing her in place. Chase came inside and closed the door behind him, locking it.

She stalked toward him, and he looked up as he saw her move in the light coming from outside the windows. She didn't stop, and he dropped something before catching her arms and locking them at her sides. That's when she realized she'd raised them as if she were going to strike him.

Or maybe she'd just been planning to wrap her arms around his neck and not let go.

"What the fuck, Sophie?"

She twisted, trying to break free, but he was too strong. "You left," she panted. "You promised."

Tears sprang to her eyes. Angry tears. Helpless tears.

"I'm sorry," he said and she turned her head, lowering her chin. She didn't want to look at him, didn't want to see the casual disregard in his eyes.

"Let. Me. Go."

He did and she stumbled back, swiping at her eyes and cursing herself for letting him see how upset she was.

He retrieved whatever he'd dropped—and she smelled food. He flipped on a light switch and the room flooded with soft light. She blinked as she looked at the bag he held up.

"I went to get dinner. I was gone for twenty minutes."

And just like that, he made her feel like a crazy bitch. Food. They needed that, didn't they?

"You could have left a note. Or you could have woke me."

She knew she sounded ungrateful, but he'd scared her. God, she hated that they had to wait to get the package. It was making her lose her shit. She just wanted to get it and go—but it had to arrive first.

"I was gone twenty minutes. I didn't think of it."

She went over to the kitchen and searched the cabinets for plates like a normal person would—a normal person with trembling hands. "You should have. I bet you don't disappear on your teammates, do you?"

He set the bag on the table and shrugged out of his leather jacket. "No, I don't."

She turned with plates in hand and set them down. "Then don't do it to me either, okay?"

"Okay."

She looked up at him, surprised he'd agreed. His voice had been soft as he said it, almost regretful.

"Do you mean that?"

"Yeah, Sophie, I mean it. I should have lit a firecracker under your ass and woke you up just so I could tell you I'd be back in twenty minutes."

"You should have."

He shook his head as he removed the food containers from the bag. Sophie gaped at what he pulled out and then couldn't help but laugh in spite of her determination to hold on to her anger a bit longer.

"You're in the greatest city in the world for food and you got Chinese takeout?"

He frowned at her. "It was fast and I know what I'm getting."

She grabbed the chopsticks that had been shoved in the bag and started opening containers. They sat down and she broke the wooden chopsticks and rubbed them together to get rid of splinters. Then she carefully took a little bit from a couple of cartons before setting them down again.

When she looked up, Chase was watching her.

"You hardly took anything," he said, and she felt herself color.

"I have enough."

"Do you?"

"Yes, I do."

He dumped out a bunch of orange chicken and some noodles onto his plate. Then he picked up an egg roll and tore into it with his teeth. "You know what I think?" he said after he swallowed the bite.

"I have a feeling you're about to tell me."

He pointed at her plate with his chopsticks. "I think you need to stop worrying about what everyone else thinks. You said that starving yourself wouldn't make you look like your mother. Well, you know what? You look better than she does. Ten times better. Healthy and gorgeous—so eat the fucking food and stop thinking about your weight."

She grabbed a piece of chicken with her chopsticks and ate it. The flavors melted on her tongue, and her stomach rumbled anew.

"I *am* eating, asshole."

He picked up some noodles with his chopsticks and held them out to her. "You didn't take any noodles."

"Noodles are starchy."

"Try them, Sophie. For me."

She snorted. "Don't tell me you're one of those guys who like to stuff a girl full and watch her get fat."

His eyes gleamed. "Oh, I like to stuff a girl full all right, but it's not food I'm using when I do it."

Chapter Twenty

She was sitting there in that fucking robe—the second time she'd worn a robe in his presence—staring at him with her mouth hanging open. Her hair was messy and piled on her head, and she didn't have on any makeup.

But it was the gaping vee of the robe that had most of his attention. He could see the curve of a breast, the creamy swell of flesh and the lacy edge of her bra. He wanted to put his face there, smell her skin, and lick his way to her nipple.

He'd gone to check on her after he'd wakened earlier. She'd been lying on her stomach in that bed, covers thrown back, one leg kicked up, her ass cheeks peeking through the lace of her panties. Fucking lace panties with no lining. Just lace and skin and a pretty pink bow at the waistband. He'd wanted to turn her over and see if the lace was see-through on that side too. If there was another bow.

If he could see the soft triangle of her curls and the pink lips of her pussy.

He'd stood there above her, fighting the urge to wake her gently with his mouth on hers, his hands filling with her curves, and frantically thought that going to get food was a damn good idea.

He'd desperately needed the cooling-off time that going around the corner for Chinese would give him.

He wanted to fuck her. Badly. And every time he decided that was acceptable, it wasn't the place or the time. So by the time he found himself with ample opportunity, he'd had time to talk himself out of it. To think of all the reasons it was a bad idea.

First, there was Grigori Androv and their mission to consider. He had to keep a clear head over that. Second, she was Tyler's stepdaughter, and that brought with it a whole level of complication he didn't need. Third... he'd forgotten what was third.

"You always say stuff like that," she finally said, recovering her equilibrium, "and I have yet to see evidence of it. I'm beginning to think you make it all up, Chase."

He still held the chopsticks out, and she finally leaned forward and took the bite of noodles. He couldn't say why that gratified him, but it did.

"Mmm," she said, closing her eyes for a second.

And Christ, he wanted to kiss her. His cock hardened and sweat broke out over his body. When was the last time he'd been so intrigued by a woman that he'd felt this kind of anguished need for her?

Or maybe that was just the situation. Who they were. The forbidden aspect of his desire.

She opened her eyes again, and he picked up more noodles, held them out. She took them without hesitation. The next bite went into his mouth.

She offered him some of her orange chicken and he took it. Somehow they ended up feeding each other off their own plates, trading bites in silence, their eyes locked together in some sort of sensual duel.

It was, without doubt, the most erotic meal he'd ever had in his life—and that was counting the time he'd eaten dessert off a woman's body. She'd been a chef and the entire meal had been spectacular, ending with an amazing array of chocolate, strawberries, and fresh whipped cream placed strategically over her naked form.

Yet somehow that didn't compare to trading bites of Frenchified Chinese food with Sophie. She curled her tongue around the chopsticks, moaned at every bite, and chewed slowly and deliberately.

Finally, when he couldn't take it anymore, he took the chopsticks from her and laid them on the table. Then he dropped to his knees on the floor and spread her legs open, running his palms up her calves, the insides of her knees, her thighs. She trembled beneath his touch, her breath shortening the higher he got.

"What is this, Chase?" she asked as he pulled her ass forward on the chair. "What are you doing?"

He looked up at her in disbelief. "You can't figure it out?"

She sucked her lower lip between her teeth and an

arrow of need lanced into him. "I keep thinking I'm going to wake up. Or you're going to say never mind, this is a bad idea."

"It is a bad idea. But a hard-on has no conscience, Sophie—and I've been hard for you for days."

Her hands went to the tie of the robe and she undid it. He didn't miss the trembling in her fingers as she unknotted the belt. But she pulled the robe open and his breath caught in his lungs.

"Jesus," he said softly.

His eyes slid over her body, the lacy white bra pushing her breasts—big, beautiful, creamy breasts—into soft mounds of flesh. Her belly wasn't flat, but he didn't care. It was soft and curvy, her waist was defined, and her hips flared out into killer curves. A tiny scrap of panty covered her pussy. It wasn't lacy, however. Judging by the strings on the sides, it was definitely a thong.

Holy shit, she'd changed from sexy panty to off-the-fucking-chain panty.

His mouth went dry. His throat ached. Sophie's beautiful eyes glittered in challenge, but he knew she was putting on a brave front because he'd dared her to.

"Not quite what you expected?" she said, her chin thrust upward even as she leaned back in the chair with her ass on the edge.

"Better than I expected."

And that was the fucking truth.

Her chin quivered and he changed his plan to eat her pussy first thing, instead leaning in to her and curving his hand around the back of her neck before taking her mouth in a hard, passionate kiss.

Her lips opened and his tongue slipped inside, stroking hers. She moaned into his mouth and his balls tightened. Her arms went around his neck, her hands spearing into his hair. Her touch was sensual, sizzling. It shocked him how much she affected him with that simple gesture.

Hell, had he ever been this excited in his life? This ready to explode?

He lifted her up as she gasped, then walked her the few steps to the counter, setting her on it. But he didn't stop kissing her, didn't stop devouring her mouth even as he pushed the robe off her shoulders and went for the catch of her bra. He felt it snap free, and then he filled his hands with her tits. Her nipples were already hard points, but he intended to suck them into harder ones.

Just as soon as he managed to stop kissing her.

It took a lot longer than he expected. In the meantime, he thumbed her nipples until she squirmed, and then he tugged her forward on the counter until their groins fit together. He was very aware of the fact he had too many clothes on when her legs wrapped around his ass and her hips shifted, pressing her pussy against his cock.

But then her hands went to the waistband of his jeans and she started tugging his T-shirt out of his pants. When she had it free, she lifted it up until he had to break the kiss to let her pull it over his head. He took it from her and dropped it before claiming her mouth again.

Her palms were on his skin, leaving fire wherever she touched. He thrust his fingers into her hair and found the clip she'd used to pile it on her head. Then he released it and practically groaned when the silken strands fell against his skin.

He wound his hand into its length and tugged her head backward until he had to break the kiss with her. Then he let his mouth trail down her throat.

"My God, Sophie, you are so fucking hot."

"Chase," she moaned as he fastened his mouth over a nipple.

He sucked it between his teeth, softly nibbled the tip, and then slid his tongue around it. Her fingers curled into his shoulders and her body squirmed on the counter. Her legs were still wrapped around him, and he wished he was buried inside her while doing this.

All in good time. Because he wasn't stopping until he'd gotten everything he wanted—and given everything he had.

Chapter Twenty-One

Sophie thought she might come simply from his mouth on her nipples. Chase spent so much time there, licking, sucking, biting, until her pussy was soaked and she could barely form a coherent thought.

But then his hands settled on her hips and his thumbs hooked into her thong. Her heart slammed into her throat as she anticipated what would come next. She'd had sex a few times, but she wouldn't call it the best experience of her life. It was usually done in a dark room with a man who didn't spend nearly enough time making her comfortable before he was grinding away on top of her and saying things like *"Oh baby, yeah, that's it, baby."*

Chase started tugging her panties down her hips, and everything she'd been thinking hit her at once.

"Wait," she gasped and he looked up, his eyes glazed. "The lights."

His brows lowered. "What? Fuck the lights. I want to see you."

She was actually touched by that because she believed he meant it. He said it with too much conviction not to. "The neighbors can see. Or worse," she told him as she thought about Sergei Turov at the airport.

Chase's expression eased. "Honey, we're safe. No one's finding us here. But I gotta agree that the neighbors don't need to see what's going on."

He reached for the switch and they were plunged into darkness. But it wouldn't take long for the light from outside to illuminate him for her. Behind him, the top of the Eiffel Tower shone over the rooftops and her heart felt light and free, at least for now.

Who didn't want a romantic evening in Paris with a hot guy, even if that wasn't the real purpose of this visit?

Chase reached for her thong again, and she levered herself up so he could slide it from beneath her. Her bare ass was cold when it hit the counter, but she was too excited to care.

Chase was about to fuck her—and she was certain it would be good, at least for a little while. Until he got off and she pretended she had too. Until reality came crashing down.

But then he pushed her back on the counter until her ass was right on the edge. When he pressed an open-mouthed kiss to her belly, she wasn't sure what was happening—until he slid his tongue around her belly button and down, down, down into the wet seam of her sex.

"Oh God," she gasped as he pushed her open with his fingers and sucked her clit.

"*Oh Chase* will do," he said, his voice muffled, his breath hot against her slick pussy.

He pushed a finger into her, slowly and carefully, his mouth never stopping the magic it was doing to her. When he started fucking her with his finger, she moaned at the sensations wreaking havoc on her body. He added a second finger, fucking her slowly and deliberately while he licked her hard and soft, fast and slow.

Sophie's body tightened quickly, spiraling inward until she was on the verge of an orgasm so intense she thought she might scream when it happened.

"Chase, please… please," she panted.

She was so close and so afraid it wouldn't happen, that he would stop for some reason, that she'd never reach that peak she was straining for.

But he didn't stop. He spread her wide and devoured her with a skill and intensity that sent her over the edge so hard she saw stars. She didn't scream—she couldn't make a sound at first, couldn't breathe, couldn't move…

And then the spell snapped and she dragged in a breath, her body trembling and tingling as if she'd been hit by lightning. Chase stood in front of her now, looming over her, his height blocking the view of the tower in the background.

"You okay, baby?"

"Okay? I think I'm shattered beyond repair."

He chuckled. And then he gathered her up and lifted her against him.

"You'll hurt yourself," she protested, but he only laughed as he started walking toward the bedroom.

"I outweigh you by at least seventy pounds. And I've

had to carry men my size through battlefields, so don't you even start that shit with me. Carrying you is easy compared to a full ruck and an injured teammate."

She believed him, especially considering the ease with which he navigated the room. He kicked open her bedroom door and carried her in, depositing her on the bed and coming down on top of her.

Then he reached up and the light snapped on as he found the lamp.

She turned her head and closed her eyes. "What are you doing?"

"Looking at you."

"I gathered that. Why?"

He laughed, a low, deep, almost menacing sound in his throat. "Because I want to watch your face as I sink my cock into you. And the next time you come, I want to see it happen."

She knew she was blushing, but she made herself open her eyes and turn her head so she could look up at him. And, heaven help her, he was beautiful. All hot, hard, perfect muscle hovering over her. He rippled when he moved, and it was a sight to behold.

He let his gaze drift down between them, over her curves and pale flesh, slowly taking her in. And, for once, she felt beautiful instead of nervous. He made her feel like that with the way he looked at her.

It hit her that he really meant it when he said she was beautiful. Oh, she knew she had a face that made men turn and stare sometimes, thanks to her mother— but she didn't have the body, and she knew that too.

Until now. Now she believed what she saw on

Chase's face. He was into her. This wasn't a chore to him. A task. The boy who would never talk to her when they were teenagers was now looking at her like he could eat her up with a spoon.

And that thought made her blush because he had eaten her up. Eaten her up and made her fall apart spectacularly with his fingers buried inside her and his tongue sliding over her clit again and again.

"What's on that pretty mind of yours?" he asked.

"I think you know."

He skimmed his fingers between her legs, against her clit, and her back bowed. "This."

"Yes…"

"You want more?"

His fingers moved back and forth, barely touching her but eliciting a response nevertheless.

"Yes."

He dropped his head and licked her nipple. "You're going to have to be more explicit than that. Tell me what you want, Sophie."

She moaned, grasping his head to her breast. "You're evil, you know that?"

"Consider it payback for that shit you pulled when we were driving to the airport." He lifted his head and looked down at her, his expression serious. "You were pretending and I know that. But don't pretend now. Tell me what you want, Soph. What you *really* want… and I'll give it to you better than you've ever had it."

He made her shiver. "Arrogance isn't attractive, Chase."

He snorted. "Hell yes, it is. Especially when it

involves sex. I'm good and I know it. That should make you happy, not annoyed."

She reached for the button fly of his jeans. He was right. "I want to feel you inside me. I want to come that way—and I never have before, so now you know the challenge you face."

She could feel fresh heat wash over her skin as she said it, but what the hell? He needed to know, though maybe that was a mistake too, because what if it was bad after all and he didn't want to stop until she came—and she couldn't?

Like he could be bad after what he'd just done to her.

He lifted himself until she could finish unbuttoning his jeans, and then he kicked them off and his cock sprang free, standing up straight and tall—and intimidating. Yep, that was the word.

It was huge and veined and, hell, would she survive being impaled by that thing?

She very much wanted to find out.

He picked up his jeans and pulled a condom from the pocket. She watched him tear it open and roll it on, every move sensual and hot. In fact, she could watch him stroke himself until he came, his head rolling back and his eyes closing as he shot semen onto her belly.

Maybe she'd tell him she wanted that the next time. *The next time.*

She didn't know if there would even be a next time, but this time she spread her legs as he settled between them, his hand still gripping his cock, his eyes hot as he slid the head of his penis against her pussy, wetting it before he pressed into her entrance.

"Oh," she moaned, her back arching as he slid all the way inside her. She felt full, almost too full, but it was a good feeling. An amazing feeling as he stretched her wide, creating tension against sensitive nerve endings.

"Holy shit," he said when he was deep within her, their bodies quivering with energy and sizzling with heat. "You feel incredible."

If she could've talked at that moment, she'd have said the same thing.

Sophie wrapped a hand around his neck and dragged him down to her, thrusting her tongue into his mouth. It was either do that or lose her mind and start saying shit she wouldn't remember the next day. She'd never in her life needed what she needed right then.

"Fuck me, Chase," she whispered against his mouth. "Make it good."

Chapter Twenty-Two

"You are certain it was her?"

Grigori Androv stood in his Manhattan office, staring at the view of the Hudson River. He'd been on edge for the past few days, angry that his men couldn't seem to find Sophie Nash and recover his flash drive.

But they'd gotten a break yesterday when Open Sky hacked the shipper's database and found where Sophie had sent the package. He'd immediately ordered Sergei onto a plane bound for France. Once there, Sergei would use men from the Paris operations to watch the apartment and intercept the package that was due tomorrow.

And now they'd gotten another lucky break, because it seemed as if Sophie was planning to show up personally to collect it. When she did, his men would grab her. Then Grigori would send her to the auction in Monte Carlo where she would fetch a nice price.

Small compensation for all the trouble she'd caused.

He didn't care that her parents were wealthy or that

her father was a famous musician. They would never find her, nor would they connect him to her. Open Sky would make certain of that. When they were finished, Sophie would have a checkered past involving drug abuse and illicit sex. No one would be surprised that she'd disappeared.

It was risky, but he got off on risk. Lived for risk. Risk made him hard.

"It was her," Sergei said. "It took me a while to figure it out. I knew she seemed familiar when I saw her in the terminal—but she has black hair, and she was wearing glasses and speaking with a British accent. It wasn't until I got close enough to see her eyes that I knew."

It was a stroke of good fortune that Sergei had gotten on the same plane as Sophie. If Grigori had made him return to New York first, that would not have happened.

"And she's with a man?"

"Yes—and they were very affectionate with each other."

Grigori gritted his teeth. "Presumably this is the man she went to see in Maryland."

"I think so, yes."

They knew next to nothing about the man Sophie had gone to. Grigori had the usual people looking in the usual places—but there was very little to find other than the man's name, which was Chase Daniels, and that he was in the United States Army.

It was highly disturbing that Sophie had gone to see this Chase Daniels. In all of Grigori's time with her, she'd never mentioned a potential boyfriend or ex-boyfriend. Part of what Grigori did was find out everything he could about a girl's situation—her parents, her connections, who would miss her, who would look for her—and Sophie had never once talked about a man in her life. She'd mentioned her parents, but he'd gathered that her relationship with them was troubled. A definite plus for him.

Chase Daniels was not a plus. He was an unknown element.

"And the building where she sent the package?"

"It's in the seventh arrondissement. It's entirely residential, an apartment on the fifth floor. Sophie Nash and the soldier have not appeared there yet, but we are watching."

"I want her alive, do you understand? I want the package and I want her unharmed. No marks, or she will not bring as high a price. Do what you need to do with her companion."

"Of course. Have I ever failed you?"

Sergei had been with Grigori from the beginning. They'd grown up together in the orphanage and they had a bond few shared. They were brothers, but without the blood tie. "No."

"And I won't start now. I will get the girl and the package. You will have them both very soon."

———

THIS WAS NOT what he was supposed to be doing, and yet there was no way he could do anything different right now. Chase's balls were so tight it hurt, and he wanted nothing more than to fuck Sophie hard and fast until he lost his load and his balls stopped hurting.

But shit, he wasn't going to do it quite like that. No, he was going to make this last because it might be the only night he ever had with her.

He started to move as she kissed him hard, her teeth mashing against his, her moans feeding into his throat. He fucking loved it the way she moved beneath him. It was almost as if she didn't quite know what to do, but she was quickly learning.

The bed rocked against the wall as he upped the pace, pounding into her like a crazed animal. And he was crazed because he'd never felt quite like this before. He'd fucked a lot of women, and some of them had been pretty freaky in bed. Sophie was plain vanilla in comparison—and for some reason that turned him on at a whole new level.

She was soft and sweet and hot, her moans and gasps like a drug to his senses. Everything he did was to elicit another sound out of her.

His name—that's what he really wanted. His name drawn out long and low, like a dying word. A gasp of surprise. Of necessity.

He'd never much cared what a woman said when he was fucking her, though he expected to hear his name. Now he *needed* to hear it.

"Sophie," he groaned into her neck as he tore his mouth from hers, needing air. Her flesh was damp and sweet, and he sucked the skin of her throat. He didn't care if he left a mark. Hell, he wanted to leave a mark.

He wanted to brand her as his for as long as he felt like this.

However long that might be.

He put a hand beneath her ass and lifted her higher, changing the angle, fucking her harder. She arched her back, lifting her hips to meet him.

He couldn't take it. He couldn't get close enough like this. He got to his knees and lifted her legs, putting her ankles against his shoulders. She looked up at him with so much trust, so much belief, that he wanted to fulfill every fantasy she'd ever had.

She'd said she'd never come like this, but he was damn certain she would. He wouldn't let himself go until she did. And he was perilously close.

He lifted her higher and stroked into her harder, pounding against her as he drilled deep. Her eyes closed and she bit her lip.

"More," she gasped, and he pushed her legs wider, until he was deeper inside her than he'd ever been.

Part of him wanted to stop and just feel this connection with her. But he couldn't do it, not when every nerve ending he had was demanding release.

"Come for me, Sophie," he growled.

Her lips parted and her back bowed, and Chase thought he'd never seen anything so beautiful. She was fucking stunning. And she belonged to him right now. He was the one making her come, owning her body, owning her response…

"Chase," she gasped. "Oh…"

For good measure, he slipped his fingers over her clit and stroked her.

She came apart beneath him, her body shuddering, her eyes closing as she moaned hard. And then she said his name, a long, beautiful sound that dug beneath his skin and rushed into his veins. It was like a drug, and it shattered all his control. He came hard, pumping into her with no finesse, his body spent as he gave her everything he had.

His blood roared in his ears and his heart pounded as he somehow got to his feet and went into the bathroom to deal with the condom. When he returned, Sophie hadn't moved. She was still sprawled on the bed, her legs spread, her head turned to the side and her eyes closed.

She looked like a satiated goddess reclining against the cushions of her throne. When she turned her head and their eyes met, a fresh jolt of electricity rocketed through him.

For a moment he considered grabbing his clothes and returning to his own room, but everything within him said no way in hell to that choice. So he strode back over to the bed and got in beside her, turning on his side and propping his head on his fist as he let his gaze trace over her body.

"How did that work out for you, Soph?"

"Mmm," she said, and he skimmed his fingers over a nipple.

It began to peak beneath his touch. He couldn't help but dip down and slide his tongue over her sweet flesh.

She gasped and he tugged her nipple into his mouth, sucking it deep before letting it pop free. The peak was tight, high, and wet. Not to mention fucking beautiful.

She brought her hand up and traced it along his jaw. It was a tender gesture, but it hit him somewhere in the vicinity of his chest like a heavy punch.

"That was pretty amazing," she said.

Yeah, that made him preen like a damn peacock. "Of course it was."

She tweaked his chin as if he were a child. "Learn to accept praise humbly or no one will ever give it."

She was grinning though, and he couldn't help but laugh. "I'll be humble about anything else you want. But not that, Sophie. I fucking rocked your world just now."

A shadow passed over her face, and he wished he could call the words back—but then the shadow cleared and she seemed fine. "I'll give you that. You did things I had no idea could be done."

"Seriously, who have you been fucking? Because that's pretty much Sex 101 right there."

"Apparently not the right people."

"People? You into girls too? Because I could totally get into that—you and another hot babe kissing—"

She put her hand over his mouth, her cheeks red. He wanted to laugh. Hell, he didn't want to share her with anyone really, but he couldn't help but tease her.

"Not *people*. Men. I like men, not women, and I am not kissing another woman just to trip your trigger."

He licked her palm. "Too bad," he said when she snatched it away.

She yawned and stretched. "You know, I'm kind of hungry now."

Unbelievable. "So basically, if I want you to eat more, I have to fuck you first?"

She grinned. "Works for me."

Worked for him too. In fact, it worked right now. He rolled on top of her, his dick already hard and ready to go again. He licked her bottom lip, then sucked it into his mouth.

"Once more unto the breach," he whispered.

She gripped his hair and pulled his head back. Her eyes were suspicious. "I thought you hated Shakespeare."

"I said *Julius Caesar* was a bore. You assumed the rest."

"You didn't know who the Bard of Avon was. You said so."

"A white lie," he murmured. "You just seemed so prissy about it that I couldn't help but go along with it to shock you."

"You're bad, Chase. Very, very bad."

He snorted. "Oh honey, you have no idea. But I aim to show you…"

Chapter Twenty-Three

SHE WAS TOTALLY GOING TO HELL. SOPHIE STOOD AT THE window in the kitchen, looking at the Eiffel Tower in the soft light of afternoon. She was pleasantly sore between her thighs, and she had love bites on her neck. She was also completely addicted to Chase.

Her stepbrother.

Oh, my…

It was so wrong, but thinking of him like that gave her a thrill. As if they were doing something unspeakably illicit, something that would get them thrown out of polite society. They weren't, of course. They'd never been part of a family unit together, never lived with each other day in and day out, never gone to the same schools or known the same people.

Their only connection was Tyler, and that was a tenuous one as far as Chase was concerned. Tyler had never been a father figure to him. And he hadn't been much of one to her, quite honestly.

She could only imagine what her mother and Tyler

would say if they knew. Then again, why would they care? They hadn't much cared about anything she'd ever done, except not be skinny enough.

Well, that was her mother, not Tyler. He didn't even care about that. Why would they care that she was fucking Chase?

Fucking a man who was technically her stepbrother.

And there was that thrill again. She remembered Chase as a gorgeous, moody teenager, remembered when she'd started thinking about sex and how he'd figured into some of her masturbatory fantasies. She'd touched herself and thought of the boy in the room down the hall—and now the boy was a man, and he touched her better than she'd ever touched herself.

She heard the bedroom door open—her bedroom door because he hadn't left her alone the way she'd thought he might when they were finished—and she turned. Her heart flipped and then pounded faster.

He was dressed in jeans and a long-sleeved gray Henley with the top two buttons undone. There was a mark on his neck, right above his collar, and heat pooled between her thighs at the sight. She'd done that. She'd marked him the way he'd marked her.

God help her, she wanted to do it again.

His dark hair was still damp after his shower, but his eyes smoldered as he looked at her across the room. They simply stared at each other, and she wondered what was going through his mind. Was it regret? Desire? Disgust?

"How are you feeling?" he asked.

How was she feeling? Uptight. Jumpy. Needy. Angry

because she wasn't here to have fantastic sex with a gorgeous man but rather because some asshole was threatening her life.

And then there was the tenderness between her legs, the delicious little hurts of the love bites on her skin, and the tingling in her nipples even now as she stared at him. How could she quantify any of that into words?

"I feel fine," she said. It was a lame response, and his eyes narrowed.

"Fine." He stalked toward her and her pulse fluttered. When he stopped in front of her, he didn't touch her. But he was close enough that his body heat enveloped her. "What's that mean, Sophie?"

She swallowed as she stared up at him. "It means I feel fine. I'm not hurt or upset or anything."

His gaze dropped to the vee of her sweater. Bless whoever had picked out clothes for her, because they'd managed to get things that flattered her body instead of making her look and feel fat. She knew they'd hacked her credit card records, but there were things in there she'd bought that she didn't like. Thankfully they hadn't chosen those styles.

"How do you feel about what we did last night?"

Wow, that was blunt. She could feel the heat blossom in her cheeks. "How do *you* feel?"

He snorted and pushed a hand through his hair. "You want me to answer before you do. I get it."

He took a step closer to her and put a hand on her hip, drawing her into him. She didn't resist because what kind of crazy woman would?

"I feel like I want to do everything we did last night

again," he said. "I feel like I'd fucking kill for the chance to taste you right now—and yeah, I feel guilty too."

That shocked her. He was such a hard, dangerous man that she hadn't thought he could feel guilty about any of this. She'd thought he might be angry with her, or with himself, for what they'd done. She'd thought he'd be pissed because of the connection to his father. She'd never thought guilt would enter into it.

"But why? Why are *you* feeling guilty?"

"Because you're sweet and inexperienced. Because this can't end well for us, no matter how hot we are together. There's no future here, Sophie, and you need to know it. I should have told you before—but I didn't."

Her heart ached at his words even though she knew they were true. "I didn't ask you for a future, did I?"

"No."

"I'm not stupid, Chase. I know why we can't be together, assuming we'd even want to be after this. It's sex, nothing more."

Surprisingly, it hurt to say that. There was something about being with Chase that made her feel things she'd never felt in her life. It wasn't love or anything like that—how could it be?—but it was something more than just sex.

For her anyway.

He threaded his fingers into her hair and cupped her head in his hand. "You haven't had a lot of experience," he said softly, and her stomach hitched.

"What makes you think that?"

His smile was tender. "Honey, a man knows."

"So now you're telling me I suck? Geez, Chase, way to make a girl feel grand."

He snorted. "You definitely don't suck. You're pretty damn hot in bed, in fact. But you haven't fucked a lot of men. It's not a criticism. In fact, I find it to be a bit of a turn-on."

"That's because you're lecherous."

"Show me a man who isn't."

He had her there. She put her hand on his wrist, held him lightly. She loved that she could do that. That she had the right to do it, at least for now.

"So I haven't been with a lot of men. So what? It doesn't mean I don't know what this is, okay?"

His gaze settled on her mouth. "I'm not sure I know what this is."

She squeezed his wrist. "Yes, you do. It's not just sex —it's the connection between us, the one that says we shouldn't be doing this. It turns you on. It turns me on. Because it's not wrong, but it kind of feels like it should be. Your father is my stepfather. What if we'd been doing this as teenagers in Tyler's house? That would have been crossing a line, and I think we both think about it when we're together. It's naughty, right? And naughty feels good."

His grin was all kinds of sinful. "Yeah, naughty feels damn good. I've got a few naughty things I'd like to do to you, but we've got a mission and time is not on our side." His grin faded. "This isn't wrong, Sophie. There's nothing to be ashamed of. The only connection we have is on paper—your adoption certificate and my birth certificate. And if I heard you right, he wasn't much more of a father to you than he was to me."

She frowned. "You didn't hear me wrong. Tyler and my mother... Well, it's a good thing they never had kids of their own. They aren't abusive or anything, but they just aren't equipped for dealing with others' needs."

"I hate to tell you this, baby, but neglecting a child *is* abuse. It might not seem like it, but it is. They should have put you first."

She sucked in a breath. She could feel her chin quivering, feel herself on the verge of losing her shit. He cupped her cheeks in both hands and kissed her, staving off the breakdown. It was such a tender, sweet kiss that her heart clenched tight in her chest as other feelings assailed her.

No one had ever treated her like her feelings were important. Part of that was her fault because she hid them so well—but not with Chase. He had a way of digging deep, of forcing her to show her vulnerability.

"You okay?" he whispered against her lips.

She pulled back and looked into his green eyes, her stomach flipping at the intensity and tenderness she saw there. She wanted more of that. Wanted to wake up and see that look on a man's face every day of her life.

Sophie nodded, but he didn't remove his hands from her face. "So what happens next?" she asked, needing to escape the feelings swirling in her heart. "When are we going to get the flash drive?"

He ran his fingers down her throat, dropped his hands. "You're going to call Madame Renard, and you're going to tell her I'm coming to get the package."

She started to protest, but he anticipated her.

His hand covered her mouth. His eyes flashed hot. "This is not up for debate, Sophie. I'm going alone. Sergei Turov is almost certainly watching Tyler's building, and he won't be doing it alone."

She pulled his hand away, determined to have her say. "He didn't recognize me. How will he know it's me if I go with you?"

"He saw us in Baltimore, and he can put two and two together. We can't take that chance."

Sophie's stomach churned. She wanted to argue with him, but she knew he was right. There was no reason for her to go. They'd come this far and that was enough. Far safer to let him go on his own.

"When are you going?"

He let out a breath, as if he'd expected more argument from her and was surprised she didn't offer it. "I had a text from Hawk earlier. The package should be delivered anytime after two tomorrow afternoon. That's as specific as the carrier gets."

"What about the tracking number? Doesn't that help?"

"Not much, which is probably good considering Androv has access to the same information. The location scans aren't showing up immediately in the system. By the time they do, the package has moved on. The most specific the information will be is when the package is loaded on the van for delivery. Turov could intercept the van, but that's not easy to do when there are hundreds of delivery vans in the city. He won't know which one is the correct one until it pulls up in front of

Tyler's building. He could guess before that moment—but if he's wrong, it's risky to storm random delivery vans and demand packages."

Sophie dragged in a frustrated breath and turned away from him. God, it was all so complicated. "Why did I mail it? Why didn't I just take it with me and hand it over when I reached you?"

His hands were on her shoulders. She liked it much too much.

"You were scared. Getting the flash drive out of your possession wasn't a bad thing to do."

"But now all we can do is wait for it to show up—and hope Turov doesn't get it first."

"No plan is without flaws." He pushed her hair aside and put his mouth to her neck. Softly. Gently. His tongue caressed the love bites, and a shiver slipped down her spine. "If we have to wait, I can think of a few things we can do."

Warmth flooded her core. And a wave of tenderness swept through her heart. "Do you want to be naughty, Chase?"

"Oh, hell yeah."

"We just got dressed," she said as his fingers slipped beneath her sweater.

"Is that a problem?"

He found her nipple, tweaked it. Sophie bit her lip to stop the moan in her throat.

"Definitely not."

"Good, because I want to strip you naked and bend you over. Then I'm going to fuck you from behind until you scream my name." He licked her neck and she shuddered hard, her pussy tingling with anticipation. "How does that sound?"

"Like something I'm going to enjoy."

"Fuck yeah, it does." He straightened and turned her toward him. "But first, call Madame Renard."

He held out his cell phone and she took it with shaking fingers. "I have to call Tyler to get the number. It was in my phone, but I don't remember it."

Chase's expression went carefully blank. "Then call him."

"Do you want to talk to him?"

The corners of his mouth tightened. She wanted to kiss that tension away, but she didn't move. Her fingers were sweaty where she gripped the phone and her heart throbbed.

But Chase didn't get angry—or if he did, he didn't show it.

"No, I don't want to talk to him."

She started to punch in the number, but he reached out and touched her hand.

"Don't stay on the line, Sophie. Any tracking attempts will be jammed by the system, but the longer you talk, the more information you give away. Just ask for the number and get off the line."

She blinked at him. "I'll do my best."

"Do better than your best, babe. Our lives depend on it."

Chapter Twenty-Four

SHE'D GOTTEN THE PHONE NUMBER WHILE CHASE STOOD there and listened to the call, gritting his teeth and trying not to snatch the phone away and tell Tyler what a motherfucking asshole he was. And not just because of how he'd treated Chase's mom.

Now he added Sophie to that mix. She was a tender, sweet, lonely girl who'd deserved better from the asswipes who'd raised her. He'd thought she'd grown up with everything she'd ever wanted, but he understood now that the things she'd wanted couldn't be bought.

She'd managed Tyler well enough, getting the number and getting him off the phone quickly, and then she'd called Madame Renard. She'd spoken in French, and he'd stared at her as if she'd turned into an alien. She hadn't spoken French at the airport, nor with the estate agent—though there was that one moment when she'd said *merci.* But anyone could do that. He'd thought nothing of it, but damn if she didn't speak French.

And it was sexy as all fuck.

When she got off the phone, she shook her head. Chase's gut churned at the look on her face.

"Madame says there have been men in and out of the building all day. She won't give Tyler's mail to a strange man she doesn't know."

Chase wanted to punch something. Instead, he focused on the obvious while he worked to control his temper. "You speak French. You didn't tell me that."

"And you quote Shakespeare."

"Fucking to be or not to be, baby. That is the question. Whether 'tis nobler in the mind to suffer the slings and arrows, blah, blah, blah."

"Damn, Chase, listen to you rock Hamlet old-school."

"I'm a man of many talents."

Sophie handed him the phone and then shoved her hands into her pockets. "So I guess I have to go with you after all."

A flash of anger sizzled into him. "How do I know you even suggested she give me the package without you there?"

Because she spoke fucking French. For all he knew, she'd been discussing the weather with Madame Renard.

Her eyes widened. And then her brows slanted down. "You think I would do that?"

"I don't know," he growled. "Maybe. You didn't tell me about Madame Renard until we hit Paris—not to mention how determined you were to come with me in the first place."

Her cheeks were red, but not with embarrassment.

With anger, he decided as her eyes flashed. "I'm not stupid, Chase. Yes, I wanted to come to Paris because it's *my* life in danger, and no, I didn't tell you about Madame Renard at first. I already told you why."

"Will she give the package to you?"

"I think so. I told her that Tyler would call her and give her permission to do so."

"Fucking hell. So now you have to call that asshole back."

"Yes, I do. But not right now."

"This blows, Sophie. You going anywhere near that fucking building is *not* safe. Turov and his men will be all over it tomorrow, waiting for the package to arrive. We're going to have to change the plan. We'll have to hit the carrier before he gets to the building."

She swiped her tongue over her lower lip and heat arrowed into his cock. *Not right now.*

"How are we going to do that?"

He took out his phone. "Going to call Hawk and see what information he can get. Then we're going shopping."

"Shopping?"

"You aren't disguised enough, baby. Not for getting anywhere near Tyler's place. We're going to fix that."

She cocked her head. "You aren't worried they'll spot me tonight while we're out, but I need to be more disguised tomorrow?"

"That's exactly right."

Her sudden smile did things to him that he didn't understand. Her expression was happy, and that made him happy for some reason, in spite of all the turmoil. Damn, what was that all about?

"Okay, let's do it," she said. "I don't get it, but let's do it."

He called Hawk and explained the change in plan. It would necessitate moving to another safe house afterward, but that was doable. And then there was the matter of getting the carrier's movements in real time. That wasn't going to be easy, but Hawk was on it. If that failed, then yeah, they were going into Madame Renard's with guns blazing—well, maybe not literally, but close.

After the call, they prepared to go out. Chase tucked guns into the holsters beneath his jacket and at his ankle. He armed himself with a knife too, just in case. Sophie watched him with a worried expression.

"I don't expect trouble tonight, but I can't go out unprepared," he said.

It was dark and they were wearing jackets. Sophie had a scarf around her neck and over her hair. She didn't look anything like the Sophie Nash that Androv's people knew. Tonight they were Nathan and Beth Chandler, newlyweds.

She nodded. "I didn't stop to think how dangerous your job must be if you always have to be armed."

"I'm a soldier, Sophie. I fight wars you'll never know about. This is nothing."

"I'm beginning to understand that. It's frightening."

He frowned. "Do you want to stay here? I'll go pick up some things and you can order takeout for us. When

I get back, we'll spend the night inside. You can translate French TV for me."

She laughed, but her arms came up and she hugged herself. Her eyes seemed a little shiny. "No, I want to go out. I just… I don't want anything to happen to you, Chase."

"I don't either." He went over and put his hands on her shoulders. Why did he need to touch her like this? He didn't know, but damn if he could stop himself. "Hey, I've been in the Army for nearly eight years. I've been in Spec Ops for four of those years. I'm good at my job and it saves lives."

She looked up at him with such softness in her gaze that his heart thumped hard in his chest. "Okay. I'll stop worrying then."

"Sure you will."

She slipped her arms around him and stepped in until she could put her cheek on his chest. He liked that. He slid a hand up and into her hair. If he wasn't careful, he could strip her naked and take her to bed without ever setting foot outside tonight.

"You're sweet, Sophie. I take back everything I ever said about not liking you."

He felt her chuckle. She pushed back, her eyes shining and bright. "Apparently, sex is the ticket into your good graces. Before that, I was just a woman who'd brought a whole lot of trouble to town with me."

"Sex doesn't hurt. I can forgive a lot when the sex is as smoking as it is with you."

He loved that she blushed. And he knew part of the reason she did was because she didn't believe he meant what he said. She thought he was exaggerating to make her feel better.

He tipped her chin up and made her look at him. "I lied about Shakespeare, okay? I know who he is, and yeah, I even know some lines. But this is too important to lie about. You're hot as hell, Sophie, and I never lie about how good the sex is. If I tell you it's smoking, I mean it."

She sniffed and twisted her fingers in the open edge of his jacket. "Tell me another line from Shakespeare."

"You're killing me, Soph." He sucked in a breath. "Okay, fine. 'O for a Muse of fire, that would ascend / The brightest heaven of invention, / A kingdom for a stage, princes to act / And monarchs to behold the swelling scene!'"

"Holy cow, you know *Henry V*."

"Well, I did quote you the 'once more unto the breach' line. Why are you surprised?"

"I thought maybe you'd picked up that line from TV or something. What the hell were you doing that you learned *Henry V*?"

He sighed. Fucking hell. "Drama club, okay? I went through a nerdy phase."

Her mouth hung open. And then she snapped it shut and started to laugh.

"What?" he asked sullenly.

"It was the girlfriend, wasn't it? *Jane.* Sixteen, getting a piece of pussy—you did whatever she wanted, didn't you?"

Why did he feel heat creeping up his neck? "Go ahead and laugh—yeah, I did whatever she wanted.

When it's your first taste of sex, you pretty much do whatever you have to in order to get more. Jane had a hard-on for Shakespeare. Therefore, I had a hard-on for Shakespeare. The more I quoted those damn lines to her, the hornier she got."

Sophie started to giggle. She slapped a hand over her mouth, but she didn't stop. Then she stepped backward and bent over, laughing and hugging her middle. He wanted to be stern and dignified, but hell, she laughed so cutely. And it *was* kinda funny.

Okay, maybe a lot funny.

He tried to keep a straight face, but it wasn't easy. Pretty soon he was laughing too, though he'd stop every once in a while and try to be stern with her.

"Sophie."

She kept laughing, and then he laughed. Fuck.

He steered her over to the couch and let her collapse on it. Then he stood over her and told himself to stop fucking laughing. Didn't do much good though, and he fell onto the couch too, laughing with her.

Hell, he hadn't laughed like this in, well, forever. Other than laughing with the guys at Buddy's Bar, he couldn't remember the last time he'd had so much damned fun with a woman—a civilian—that he lost his shit.

"I'm glad you're amused," he told her seriously.

More giggles. She peered up at him, tears rolling down her cheeks, and he thought, *Fucking hell, she's amazing.*

Which was not what he needed to be thinking about Miss Sophie Nash. But he couldn't help it because, dammit, she was pretty spectacular. Once you got past the smoke and mirrors and into the heart of the girl, she was someone you wanted to know more about. Someone you felt like you could trust.

Finally she sucked in a breath and worked on calming herself. He was still laughing too, but not as hard as she was. Together they sort of ran out of steam until all they were doing was smiling and lying back on the couch. They turned their heads to look at each other.

"Finished laughing at me?" he asked.

She giggled, but it didn't last. "I think so. Sorry."

"You aren't."

Her smile was electric. "No, not really. You had me going, Chase. All that macho Shakespeare-hate bullshit —and all the time, you could quote lines like the worst theater geek. Not because you admire the Bard, but because you wanted to get laid. I admire that level of dedication."

He snorted softly. "Yeah, well, teenage boys will do anything for sex. Guess that proves it."

"Oh please. As good-looking as you are, Jane wasn't the only one willing, I bet."

"Maybe not, but once I got her panties off, it was easier to learn some fricking lines of Shakespeare than to start over with another girl who might or might not be willing to put out. Jane was willing to put out with a frequency that made a teenage boy's dreams come true. She was also the prettiest girl in my town, which didn't hurt."

Her expression softened, took on a wistful cast.

"Probably blond. Head cheerleader, the most popular girl in school—all that stuff."

By all that stuff, he was pretty sure she meant skinny. "Pretty much what you'd imagine, yeah. She also ended up having an affair with a married man who left his wife for her. It was quite the scandal."

Sophie's eyes widened. "Not when you were in high school though, right?"

"No. But she was only nineteen when it happened. He might have been fucking her when she was under-age, but nobody knows for sure."

"So your heart wasn't broken, I assume?"

"Nope. By then I'd realized that other girls didn't need Shakespeare to get them hot."

"Poor Shakespeare."

"I'm sure he's unaffected by my betrayal."

Sophie sighed. "Well, for your information, quoting lines to me will likely result in a loss of panties—but only the right lines."

"Such as 'Being your slave, what should I do but tend / Upon the hours and times of your desire'?"

Her jaw dropped. Yeah, all that study of Shakespeare hadn't been in vain after all. Who knew?

"Oh, Chase—what a cruel and wonderful girl this Jane was. I should write her a thank-you note."

"No way in hell. She's probably forgotten every line she ever knew, yet I can't get rid of it."

"That's not a flaw. In fact, it's kinda hot."

He took her hand and pulled her up. Any more talk of being hot and sexy, and he'd bury his face between her legs and not come out until she'd screamed his name a few times.

"Come on, Sophie. Let's go for a walk. We can stand under the Eiffel Tower, and I'll conjure up some more lines. You'll be mightily impressed, and then we'll come back here and spend the night naked and sweaty. You'll be willing to do anything for me, which will make me fucking happier than hell."

She got to her feet and he caught her, kissed her quickly lest he give in to the temptation to strip her and fuck her here and now. She was warm and soft, and he loved the way she felt in his arms.

"You ready?"

"Yes," she breathed. "I'm ready for anything."

He hoped that was true.

Chapter Twenty-Five

"Sir, the new deputy commander is here. Should I show him in?"

Mendez got to his feet. "Send him in, Lieutenant Connor."

Connor executed a perfect about-face and went out the door. Another moment and the door opened again. This time it was a different man who entered.

"Alex," Mendez said, holding out his hand.

The other man took it, grinning as he did so. "Sir, it's great to have the chance to work with you again."

Mendez snorted. "You didn't really want to leave that cushy assignment down at SOCOM did you? From palm trees and sandy beaches to the Beltway—what a letdown."

Alex "Ghost" Bishop laughed. "Cushy my ass, and you know it. But yeah, I'm thrilled to be back at HOT. Thrilled to be your deputy commander."

Mendez went over and took a seat behind his desk, indicating for Alex to sit across from him. He'd been going over Alex's record right before he came in, though he knew most of it anyway. The Special Ops community wasn't huge, and besides, they'd worked together before.

Lieutenant Colonel Alexander Cameron Bishop. Sixteen years in the Army, twelve as a Special Operator. Alex had been a Green Beret, recruited to Delta—and then he'd come to HOT where he'd transitioned into supervising operations rather than leading them. He brought a hell of a lot of experience with him, along with a Purple Heart, a Bronze Star, and countless commendations—though no doubt fewer than he deserved.

The truth of being a part of an outfit like HOT or Delta was that you didn't have nearly as many medals as your regular Army counterparts—nor did you care. This wasn't a profession for people who needed accolades. And Alex wasn't the kind of man who wanted them.

In short, he was a good choice to be second-in-command of HOT. He was young enough at thirty-eight to have a lot of time left in his career but not so young as to lack the experience to lead. He wouldn't make full bird for a while yet, but he had put on light colonel slightly quicker than the average. In short, Alex Bishop was just what HOT needed right now—provided Mendez could trust him.

These days he didn't trust anyone, especially with Congressman DeWitt calling for investigations and inspections. Trust took time to build—but time was the one thing they had so little of.

Still, Alex was his deputy now, and this organization had to have a smooth and efficient chain of command in order to run the way it was supposed to. The mission was far more important than any one man or woman in the organization.

"We've got a lot to go over," Mendez said. "It's going to be like drinking from a firehose for a while. Operations have expanded and so has our mission. We're bigger than the last time you were with us."

Alex's expression was serious and determined. "I'm looking forward to learning everything, sir. HOT is exactly what I want to do at this point in my career— and you're who I want to learn from. I asked for this assignment. I'm ready for whatever you throw my way."

Mendez grinned. "Then you'd better get ready, Alex, because the shit is about to hit the fan."

They spent the next half hour discussing various missions and operational details. Alex asked good questions and had interesting suggestions a couple of times. He was the kind of man Mendez wanted to hand HOT over to someday—with Matt Girard as Alex's deputy if he had his way—though that someday was far in the future. Mendez had no intentions of retiring and giving up HOT anytime soon.

He wouldn't know what the fuck to do with himself if he did. Sam flickered through his mind, but she didn't stay. Hell, Sam was as dedicated to her career as he was to his. It was no longer a job but a lifestyle—for both of them.

What the hell would they do anyway? Get married? Kids were out for more than one reason. He was too old to deal with toddlers—and too impatient to handle them. Sam was in her forties too, and she'd never indicated a desire to have children. So what did that leave?

Buying an RV and driving to Florida? Touring the national parks? Sitting on a beach and losing track of time because he had nowhere to be?

Mendez tried not to shudder, but fuck, he shuddered anyway. No. Just no. Slowing down wasn't for him. He'd die in this job if he could. Preferably not in this chair, but who the fuck knew what could happen?

When they'd talked about everything they could in the allotted time slot and Alex was sufficiently both briefed and overwhelmed at once, they shook hands and Alex left to take care of some of the details to do with his move to DC. He'd be in the office the next day for his first full day shadowing the outgoing deputy, and they'd go from there.

Mendez stared at the phone, then reached over and picked it up, dialing Sam before he could change his mind.

"Johnny," she said when she answered, and her voice was warm like honey.

"How are you today, Sam?"

"Busy. You?"

"Same. Hey, anything for me in Paris?"

Sam laughed softly. "Not even pretending to butter me up first?"

"I'll butter you up later," he said with a smile. "Literally, if you like."

"Oh, kinky. I might like that a lot." She blew out a breath. "I've got nothing available in Paris right now.

I've tried, but everyone is tied up with other assignments."

Mendez ground his teeth and then stopped when his jaw ached. "Thanks for trying."

"Is everything okay over there?"

He sighed. "So far as I know. I'm not involved, remember?"

"I know. And I know how upset you are about it."

"Yeah." Upset was a mild description of what he was feeling, but there wasn't much he could do about it. Pissed off and frustrated was more like it. "If that flash drive has something on it we could use…*fuck*."

"You can't take the risk, Johnny. You can't use military assets to assist one of your soldiers in a personal matter."

"I know." He'd done it before, when push came to shove, but people had been on the verge of dying then. He hated that he had to wait for that kind of moment, but he wasn't the dictator of his own military organization here. There were rules, and he believed in them.

He just hated when they interfered with what he needed to do.

"Why don't you come over tonight? Let me ease your pain."

"Can't tonight, babe. Have to work late."

She sighed. "Take care, Johnny. Don't let the stress get you."

"Roger that."

But when he hung up, he stared at the wall opposite for a good long while, weighing his options. And then he took out his personal cell phone and made a call.

Ian Black picked up on the first ring. "What a surprise, Colonel."

"Need your help, Black."

"I'm all ears."

———

IF IT WAS possible to have an almost perfect evening while being on the run for your life, then Sophie was having it. Chase held her hand as they walked down the Champs-Élysées. She'd been to Paris before, more than once, but she'd never enjoyed it quite so much.

Because she'd never come to the City of Love with a man before. And though she wasn't in love—*they* weren't in love—they were certainly in lust and having a great time of it. Lust in the City of Love was perfectly fine with her.

Chase steered her into a store where he forced her to try on the ugliest flowered tent dress she'd ever seen in her life. Then he added insult to injury by handing her a pair of clogs.

"No," she said. "Not happening."

So he found her a pair of black ballet flats instead. Not quite as bad, though nothing was fixing the ugliness of the dress.

"You can't look like you," Chase said by way of apology. "I'm sorry."

Eventually they left the store with their bags and walked down the chilly street. They didn't speak for a long while. Chase kept her close, tucked into the curve of his arm. The cool air kissed her cheeks, made her sniffle, and he stopped and turned her toward him.

"Look, I'm sorry about the dress. I know it's hideous. But it's best that way."

"I know." She sniffed again. "It's okay."

"Then why are you crying?"

She blinked. "I'm not crying. The cold air makes my nose run."

He rubbed his hands over her arms, as if that would warm her up. It didn't, but it felt nice.

"We should eat," he told her. "We can pick up something on the way back or find a restaurant."

"How about an out-of-the-way bistro near Notre Dame?"

"You know such a place?"

"*Mais oui.*"

He shook his head. "You amaze me, Sophie. Fucking French."

"I had a lot of time to study as a child. And I had a tutor. Mom thought it would make me more marketable."

"Marketable." He said it flatly, not a question at all, and she knew he understood.

"Well, I was going to be a big girl, so I needed skills if I was going to attract a man."

He growled—and then he pulled her into his arms, crushing his mouth down on hers. He kissed her hard and deep. It was a hot, wet, arousing kiss. When he pulled away, she clung to him. She was wet now, of course. If they could find a dark corner somewhere, he could slip inside her and make her come within moments.

She almost suggested it, but she bit her lip and kept the words inside.

"Fuck your mother," he said.

Sophie giggled. "I'd rather you didn't."

His eyes widened and then he laughed too. "That's not what I meant."

"Good… because I'd probably get stabby if you did. Mom's gorgeous at forty-six—more gorgeous than I'll ever be—but she already has everything she needs. She is not getting you too."

His face was so beautiful in the lights reflecting all around them. He had a hard, harsh beauty to him. He wore a day's growth of beard, and his eyes flashed in the glow of the city lights.

"You aren't gorgeous like your mother," he said. "You're gorgeous in your own way. And it's better—far better, if you ask me."

She cocked an eyebrow at him. "Are you or are you not the man who memorized whole passages of Shakespeare in order to get laid?"

He laughed suddenly. "All right, yeah. I did—but I'm not blowing smoke up your ass, Sophie. I don't need to do that to get laid by you or any woman."

"Arrogant," she chided softly.

He stuck out his tongue and flicked it up and down quickly. "Confident," he said after a second.

Sophie's stomach flipped. Wetness flooded her panties.

"Keep that up and we aren't going to dinner."

He stepped in closer to her, his body big and over-whelming in her space. And so, so comforting.

"All I need to eat is you, babe," he whispered.

If words could make a woman come, those would do it. Sophie swallowed. "Food, Chase. We're going for food first. Then we're going back to the apartment and getting naked—and I get to eat you first."

His eyes widened as he started. "Holy fuck. Warn a guy before you say shit like that."

Sophie laughed. "Why, did you come in your jeans?"

"Not quite." He wrapped an arm around her and tugged her away from the rail. "Come on, let's get dinner so we can go home and get naked."

Chapter Twenty-Six

Dinner was terrific, but dessert was even better. Sophie was naked on the bed, the curtains wide-open so they could see the Eiffel Tower against the night sky, and her legs were on his shoulders. He held her open with his thumbs and licked her pussy while she writhed and moaned.

She tasted sharp and sweet, and her response drove him fucking insane. He spread her wider and increased the pressure of his tongue against her clit. She arched her back and he slipped down the wet seam of her sex, thrust his tongue inside her while she whimpered and begged him to let her come.

"Chase, please, Chase…"

He loved that sound, the rawness of her voice, the little jerks of her hips as she rode his face. He was a good lover, always cared about pleasing the woman he was with—but pleasing Sophie was something of an obsession. He'd fucked her for the first time yesterday, but it felt as if he'd been with her forever.

Maybe it was the shared history, even if it was brief. Maybe it was the illicitness of doing something naughty, as she'd said, even if it was only an illusion.

Though it couldn't be that because God knew he'd been naughty before. Seriously naughty. He was single and good-looking, and women threw themselves at him. If more than one woman wanted him at a time, he was willing. Had been willing, anyway.

Right now he didn't want anything more than this. Licking Sophie's sweet pussy and listening to her whimpers. Until he teased her too much and she reached down and grabbed his hair, tugging his head up until he had to look her in the eye.

"If you don't let me come, Chase, I'm going to fucking scream. And then I'm going to get up, go into the bathroom, and finish myself off with my fingers. You won't ever get up in this business again, you hear me?"

"Yes, mistress," he said meekly. He would have gotten away with it if not for the humor in his voice.

"Asshole," she hissed, and he laughed again.

But he did what she wanted. He lowered his head and devoured her until she screamed his name, her body shaking apart beneath him. He held her hard to him, licked her while she squirmed and begged him to stop—

And then she begged him to keep going, to please, please, please keep going.

So he did. When she came that time, she sagged into the mattress and he could hear her panting in the aftermath. He crawled up her body, licking his way up over the delta of her soft belly, the gorgeous peaks of her tits, the lush plains of her collarbone, and on up to the mysterious delights of her mouth.

He sank his tongue into her, and she met him with an arched back and her arms around his neck. He didn't know how long he kissed her before he pulled away and rose above her.

"Fucking beautiful," he said as he reached for the condom and tore the package. After he rolled it on, he sank into her, groaning as he slid home. He'd planned to get her on her knees, fuck her from behind, but that wasn't what he wanted right now. He wanted her softness, the sweetness and connection he felt when they were face-to-face.

He rocked into her again and again, and she lifted her legs to put them around his waist.

"You feel so amazing, Sophie," he whispered, his voice harsh and soft at once. "I could do this forever."

That admission shocked him, confused him. What the ever-loving hell?

"I wish you would," she said in his ear, her breath warm and sensual against his skin. "I never want to be anywhere but right here with you. Like this."

His heart beat faster then. Where the hell was this going? What was he saying? What was *she* saying?

And yet he couldn't think beyond what was happening right this second. The way his body fit into hers, the tightness of her pussy around his cock, the way the hair on the back of his neck stood up as he tunneled into her body again and again.

He had to do something to shake this up, shake

himself up. He pulled out of her and got to his knees. She looked up at him, her eyes glazed and puzzled.

"On all fours, sweetheart," he said, and she obeyed him.

At the last second, he pushed her head down to the pillow so that her ass was in the air—and then he thrust into her, certain this angle would distance him. Distance them.

But it didn't feel as anonymous as he wanted it to feel. It was still Sophie, still her sweet body he slammed himself into again and again.

She gripped the pillow in her fists and thrust back against him, and he knew he'd changed nothing. If anything, he'd made it worse, because she was so hot like this, her back arched, her sweet ass in the air, her body thrusting backward against his as he pushed into her.

He wasn't going to last like this. He'd thought he might, but he could feel the impending crisis. So he fingered her clit and felt a surge of triumph when she gasped and rocked into him harder. That was all he needed to lose it.

Which he did. Spectacularly. He came so hard black spots swam in his vision.

When it was over, Sophie sank to the bed and he sank down with her, still deep inside her but unable to move.

"My God," she said, her voice muffled in the pillow. "I think I'm going to need a bigger vibrator when this is over. Or a gigolo."

Chase frowned. Had she just said…?

Somehow, he rolled to the side and she rolled the other way, until she was facing him.

"A gigolo?" he croaked. "What the fuck?"

She scooted over and kissed him. It was tender and sweet but his cock still jumped in response.

"Well, this is pretty much over when we get the flash drive—and a girl has to satisfy her needs, Chase. Don't tell me you won't be satisfying yours with the next available waitress."

He wanted to tell her there was no way he'd be doing that. But what the fuck was he thinking? Of course he would. Because Sophie would go back to her life in New York or California and he would go back to his. There would be no more of this. No more Sophie in his bed, in his mouth…

Which was good, because he didn't want her there anyway.

Liar.

"Of course I will," he said. "I love waitresses."

"I know you do. And they love you."

He didn't know what they were saying. What the hell was happening. All he knew was that he felt like shit inside. But he wouldn't let her know it. He couldn't. He climbed from the bed and went to take care of the condom.

When he returned, he got into bed beside her and pulled her into his arms. She snuggled close, throwing a leg over his and wrapping her arm around his waist.

They fell asleep like that, entwined like two vines growing together.

"IT'S GO TIME," Chase said, his expression somber as he pulled on a baseball cap. He had a pair of dark sunglasses tucked into his jacket and a gun beneath it.

Sophie adjusted the ugly dress even though there was nothing to adjust. It hung off her like a sack, though it clung to her breasts in a very unflattering way. She looked like a granny. She slipped on the glasses she'd bought at Walmart. She'd put her hair in a tight bun at the base of her neck, and she'd gone minimal on the makeup. She wrapped a pink scarf around her head and tied it beneath her chin Grace Kelly-style.

She didn't look like Grace Kelly. More like Grace's maiden aunt. She frowned at her reflection, but Chase only nodded his approval.

"Looking very unattractive, Soph. Excellent job."

"Thanks. I think."

His green eyes were very serious. "You ready for this?"

"Yes."

"You're staying in the car, you got it? I'm getting the package from the carrier before he ever gets to Tyler's building, but you're along just in case I don't intercept it in time. We'll go to Madame Renard if we have to—but the plan is not to let it get that far."

"Won't Sergei Turov have the same plan?"

"Maybe. Which is why we have to get to it first."

Sophie's heart tripped along like a skier on a downhill run. She was nervous about the plan, sure. But she was also nervous because when they got the flash drive, this thing between them—whatever this thing was—was over.

It hit her that she'd yet to get him in her mouth. He'd managed to make her so incoherent with pleasure last night that she'd fallen asleep after he'd made her come—over and over—but she'd never explored him the way she'd wanted.

And now she might never get to. That thought made her heart ache and her belly tighten.

There was so much more she wanted to say, much of it nonsensical and confusing. She had this crazy feeling that if something happened to him, she'd never recover. That she would mourn him for the rest of her life.

She caught the lapels of his jacket and held him hard. "Chase, I—"

"What, baby?" he asked softly, running the back of a finger over her cheek.

"I don't know," she said truthfully. "I just know I want more of you—"

"I want more of you too."

"But when this is over, when we have the flash drive —" She couldn't say it.

"We'll figure it out, Sophie."

She didn't know what else to say. She'd already said too much. It was crazy to feel so strongly, but she had a connection with him, and she didn't want it to end. She wanted more of the insanity of being with Chase. More of the excitement. More of him.

He squeezed her hand. "We have to go now. We have work to do."

She nodded. He shouldered the gun bag, and she

rolled the suitcases out the door. But he wouldn't let her carry anything downstairs. He took both suitcases, carried them down, and then she rolled them outside and along the sidewalk until they reached the car. He shoved them in the trunk and stowed the guns behind her seat before helping her into the car as if she really were a helpless old granny.

He got into the driver's seat and started the engine. Then he turned to her. "You do everything I tell you, got it?"

Her heart thumped. "Yes."

"If I tell you to drive away, if I'm bleeding in the road and six guys are standing over me with guns drawn, you drive away. Got it?"

She swallowed. "Yes."

"You sure?"

No. "Yes."

He nodded. "Good. Then let's get rolling."

Chapter Twenty-Seven

CHASE FUCKING HATED THAT HE HAD TO TAKE SOPHIE along with him. More than anything, he wanted to leave her locked up tight in the apartment. Safe. But if he couldn't get to the package on the van, then he had to take her to see Madame Renard, in which case there would be no time to turn around and go back for her. If he had to get the package from Madame, it had to happen very fast.

Unfortunately, there was every chance that Turov had the same plan he did, which was to intercept the driver—but it was a risky plan as plans went. Far easier to wait for the package to be delivered and snatch it then. Except Chase couldn't count on Turov caring about the risk, which meant that Sophie was in danger every step of the way on this mission.

He checked that his earpiece was working and then dialed Hawk at his offices in Annapolis. He picked up right away.

"You on the move?"

"Affirmative," Chase answered. "You got the coordinates for where we need to go after the mission?"

"Yeah, shooting the address over to you now."

Chase's phone pinged. He glanced at the address as he navigated traffic. "Montmartre."

"That's it. Trying to charter a jet to get you out of there, but everyone wants twenty-four hours' notice. It's fucking ridiculous."

Chase could hear the frustration in Hawk's voice. "This isn't a HOT mission, Hawk. I don't expect miracles."

The other man grumbled. "Yeah, well, I do. And I'm not ready to give up yet, so don't get too cozy in Montmartre."

"So do we know where the delivery van is?"

"I've got Billy the Kid on it."

Chase nearly sighed in relief. Billy "the Kid" Blake was a fricking computer genius. "Jesus, that's awesome he's there."

"The other guys are on their way. They all want to help. Dex's dad came through surgery so he has to stay in Kentucky, but he's with you in spirit."

Chase didn't typically get choked up, but the fact his teammates were rushing back from R & R and joining Hawk was enough to make his throat tight.

"Putting you on speaker," Hawk said, and then Chase heard Billy's voice.

"Heya, Fiddler. Hear you got into some trouble."

Chase glanced over at Sophie. She was staring straight ahead, her fingers curled together over her midsection. The dress she wore was awful and unflattering to her figure, but her profile was still the loveliest thing he'd ever seen. She must have felt him looking at her, because she turned her head and their gazes met for the briefest of moments before he had to put his eyes back on the road.

"A little bit," he said. "But you're going to help me out of it, I hope."

"I'm working it, man. I've got the package's last scan —and I've managed to break into the carrier's network, so I can see where the van is."

"Damn, dude, you're the best."

"Can't guarantee that Androv's people haven't done the same thing, though I've added a script that should make it a little more difficult for them. They can hack it, but it should give us a few extra minutes."

Chase didn't understand anything about computers. "How do you know they didn't get there first and add a script to slow *you* down?"

Billy laughed. "Trust me, I'd know. You worry about getting the package, and I'll worry about Open Sky."

Chase had worked with Billy long enough to believe him. "Where am I going and what am I looking for then?"

"There's an office building two stops before Nash's apartment. Sending over the coordinates now." Chase heard keys tapping and then his phone dinged. "The driver has to go inside and up to the third and fourth floors for deliveries. The van will be unattended for several minutes. You'll have to pick the lock to the bulk-head door. It's a simple cylinder lock. You get the coordinates?"

"Yes."

"Good. The package is at location 1045. That's inside the bulkhead door, to the left, top shelf."

"Copy that. What's the van's ETA to the store?"

"Twenty minutes approximately. Traffic could change that."

Chase checked the GPS. "We're ten minutes away. Should be able to get into position and wait."

"I'll stay on the line and give you updates."

"Man, I wish you guys were here."

"Me too. But we'll get you through this. Soon as you send me the info from the flash drive, I'll get to work cracking it. We'll have Androv's balls in a vise by tomorrow afternoon, promise."

"Think I love you right now, man."

"Course you do. I'm fucking awesome."

Chase laughed. "Watch it, or Olivia will cut that ego down to size for you."

"Dude, she's my number one fan."

"If this is successful, I'll be your number one fan. Olivia's going to have to move over and let me love you for a while."

Billy snorted. "In your dreams, Fiddler. In your dreams. Now go get that fucking package and let's bury Androv."

"Copy that."

———

"WHAT DO you want me to do?" Sophie said when Chase finally slowed the car and slotted it into a spot on the divided boulevard where the office building was. A spot, she noted, that had a No Parking sign in front of it because it blocked a driveway.

The boulevard wasn't very wide, but it was two lanes of traffic on each side that turned into one lane when people parked their cars. A landscaped median with benches divided the boulevard. There was a bus stop in the median and a Métro entrance across the street.

"I want you to stay in the car," Chase said, glancing at her.

"That's it? Shouldn't I drive or something?"

He snorted. "You ever take a defensive driving course?"

She swallowed. "No."

"I'll do the driving."

Her heart thumped. She didn't like the idea of waiting in the car while he went and stole a package. She also didn't like the idea that Sergei Turov was out there, watching and waiting. What if he had the same idea Chase had? What if his guys were planning to intercept the van before it reached Tyler's building?

But why would they do that? They didn't know she was here, or that Chase was with her—unless maybe they did. It was certainly possible by now, even if Turov hadn't recognized her on the plane.

Sophie shuddered as she thought of the way his gaze had met hers. So cold. So cruel. She would hate to be at his mercy.

Sophie scanned the traffic, the people on the sidewalks, inside the cars that passed, and her blood rushed through her veins. She kept expecting to see something out of the ordinary, something that indicated they'd been found, but there was nothing. It was a normal day in a busy city, and everyone had somewhere to go.

There was also no sign of the delivery van as the minutes passed.

"Talk to me, Kid," Chase said, the sudden growl of his voice making her jump. "Where's the vehicle?"

His fingers curled around the wheel as he listened to whatever the man on the other end was saying. "Fuck, that's not good. ... Yeah, nothing to do but wait."

"What?" she asked, her pulse throbbing.

He gave her a look. "Accident on the route. The van's delayed."

"Can we go find it?"

He shook his head. "Too risky. We could get caught in traffic and our escape route cut off. Not to mention I'd have to physically restrain the driver—that would get us noticed, and not in a good way. The reason we're here is because this is the best stop to obtain the package undetected."

Sophie nibbled her lip. "I hate this," she said after another minute went by. "I hate being so close and not knowing if we'll succeed. What if Sergei Turov has the same plan? He'll be somewhere nearby, waiting like we are."

"Yeah, he will. This is the best spot to take the package from before it gets delivered." He tapped the steering wheel. "The vehicle's ten minutes behind schedule. Shit, this is not good. Any sign that Open Sky is in the database, Kid?"

The man on the phone must have replied because

Chase raked a hand through his hair. "Yeah, I understand. Let's just hope that if they are, the script keeps them busy."

A car suddenly appeared on the passenger side, headlights flashing as the driver warned them they were blocking his driveway. Sophie jumped and Chase swore, but he put the car in gear and moved out of the spot. The other car—a Peugeot—whipped into traffic and accelerated past them at a wide spot in the road, but not before the driver laid on the horn.

"Yeah, yeah, buddy. I get it." Chase nodded toward a glass-and-steel structure as they passed. "That's the office building."

It was across from a block of residential buildings, but none of it was familiar. That was a good thing because it meant they weren't too close to Tyler's apartment. Chase went up the boulevard, then turned and circled back.

"Thanks, Kid," he said to the guy on the phone. Then he glanced at her. "Van's on the move again. Ten more minutes."

It took a few more minutes, but Chase found another spot for the car, this time beyond the office building. He left the engine running and unclipped his seat belt as he turned to her.

"I'm going to walk back toward the office. The van will be here soon. I'll get the package and be right back. Don't do anything. Don't move. Don't scream. Don't get out of the fucking car. If something goes wrong, climb over the seat and drive. Don't stop until you reach the airport."

He took another phone out of his pocket, a burner he'd picked up for France. "There's a number programmed in here. Call it when you reach the airport and Hawk will answer. He'll get you home."

She suddenly wanted to kiss him, but she didn't dare. Instead, she took the phone and squeezed his hand. "Be safe, Chase."

It wasn't quite what she wanted to say, but she was very aware of the man on the other end of the line.

He gave her a grin, then leaned forward and kissed her cheek. It was brief, but it sizzled into her like he'd touched her much more intimately.

"It'll be okay, babe. This thing is almost over."

———

THE WEIGHT of the pistol tucked into the shoulder holster was reassuring, as was the weight of the ankle holster and the knife at his belt. Chase didn't want to use any of them, but he was prepared if he needed to. He picked up a freebie city paper from a stand near the office building entrance and continued down the street before taking a seat on a bench and opening the paper.

The van rolled up the street toward him, the carrier logo emblazoned on its sides. Chase scanned his surroundings, looking for anything out of the ordinary. There were people on the sidewalks, but no one seemed to be loitering. Cars moved along the road, brakes squealing and horns honking to signal the displeasure of the drivers.

Across the boulevard, a white car rolled two wheels

up onto the median and parked, obviously too frustrated to find another—a legal—spot. The metal posts spaced at regular intervals meant that no car could get into the median, but there was clearly enough room for this guy to get out of traffic and piss off a whole lot of others while he did so.

The van passed Chase's spot, gears grinding as the driver slowed to pull into the loading zone in front of the building. Across the street, the doors to the white car opened and two men got out.

One of them was Sergei Turov.

"Son of a bitch," Chase said into his earpiece as he stood and started for the van. "Company's here."

"Goddammit," Billy said. "The accident gave them time to defeat the script."

Inside the van, Chase could hear the bulkhead door rolling up as the driver prepared to grab the packages he needed. Chase would have preferred to let the driver enter the building, but that wasn't going to happen now. He had to get the package before Turov and his companion managed to cross the street.

Thankfully, traffic was zipping along because the light at the intersection up ahead was green. Turov and the other guy couldn't just run across the street without risking being hit, so they hung at the edge of the median, waiting to sprint across as soon as possible.

Chase dropped the paper as he reached the open door of the vehicle. He put his hand on the inside of his jacket and took the steps up into the van. The driver was inside the cargo area with a dolly, putting packages on it and checking his handheld scanner. He looked up in surprise when Chase appeared.

There was no time to lose. The man broke into a stream of French, but Chase drew his weapon and the words ceased as the driver's hands shot skyward.

"Sorry, dude," Chase said. "I just need one thing. I'm not going to hurt you."

He advanced into the cargo area. The 1000 shelf was to the left just like Billy had said. A quick scan along that shelf and he spotted a small padded envelope addressed to Tyler Nash. He grabbed it and sprinted off the van just as Turov and the other man came around the back.

The Audi wasn't far, but he had to get to it, get onto the driver's side, which was the traffic side, and get into his seat without getting hit by the cars rushing by. Then he had to whip the car into traffic. It was a lot to do before Turov and the other man caught up. His other choice was to keep running, to lead them away from Sophie and escape through the alleys and side streets.

But that would mean leaving Sophie vulnerable. Sending her to the airport to call Hawk was a last resort, not without risks of its own. It might be her best chance, however.

He had almost decided that was the best option when the Audi's passenger door flew open. His heart nearly dropped to his toes. If she got out now—

But the car lurched suddenly, backing into the car behind it and then moving forward again, its nose inching out into traffic.

Fuck!

Chase put on a last burst of speed. He threw himself into the passenger seat, turning to fire behind him as Turov and the other man approached. He didn't aim to kill, not here in the open with so many people, but he did intend to disable.

His shot must have winged the companion because he stumbled and fell to the ground, his palms coming out in an attempt to save himself. He rolled, screaming in pain, as Turov ducked into the protection of a doorway.

"Go!" Chase yelled at Sophie as she worked the car out of the slot.

"There's too much traffic!"

"I don't fucking care! Floor it!"

He yanked the passenger door closed just as something thunked into it. Turov peered around the corner and fired again. Chase ducked just in time as the bullet shattered the glass and then passed out through the windshield, leaving a round hole.

"Go!" he yelled again, firing back at Turov. The man on the sidewalk was crawling toward the door where Turov hid. Police sirens sounded in the distance and Chase's blood chilled. They had to get out of there before the police arrived. Before Turov succeeded in hitting one of them.

Turov ducked out of the door again, raising his weapon. Chase took aim, intending to drop the son of a bitch—but he was thrown back into the seat when Sophie careened into traffic suddenly. Brakes squealed and horns sounded, but she hit the pedal and the car picked up speed, accelerating away from the scene.

Chase looked back to see Turov running out into the street. The bastard wanted a clear shot so he could take out the driver—

"Turn, now," Chase ordered as Turov's arm came up.

"It's a one-way street—"

"Turn, goddammit it!"

Chapter Twenty-Eight

SOPHIE'S HEART FELT LIKE IT WAS GOING TO BURST FROM her chest, but she whipped the car into oncoming traffic and prayed they didn't crash. Drivers laid on horns, but they swerved out of the way. She kept going down the street, saying, "Sorry, so sorry, oh my God," the whole way.

"Turn here," Chase ordered.

She cranked the wheel, turning the car to the right and onto a street where they were now going in the right direction. Her heart still hadn't slowed, however. The window beside his head was shattered, a big gaping hole with jagged glass hanging from it.

And then there was the bullet hole in the windshield. It had come in at an angle and passed low, but it was almost perfectly in front of her. If that had hit her... Oh God.

"Pull over."

"Are you crazy? We have to keep going."

"Turov is on foot, the police are coming, and even if

he did get to his car, he's facing the opposite direction. It won't take long for us to switch places."

Sophie swallowed the knot in her throat. Her hands were shaking and her heart thrumming—maybe it was better if she let him drive. She found a spot and pulled over. Her legs were rubber as she got out of the car and ran around to get in the passenger seat.

"Watch the glass," Chase ordered as she pulled the door closed.

She snatched at the seat belt, buckling it in place while Chase did the same. And then they were accelerating down the street, whipping through traffic at a breakneck pace. They hit a roundabout, spinning through it and out the other side while Sophie clung to the door handle.

"We have to get rid of the car," Chase said.

"Okay." As if she would argue that.

He glanced at her, and she realized he was talking to his guy on the other end of the line. "Can Hawk get me something else? Or do I need to borrow a car?"

She didn't like the way he said *borrow*. Clearly it was a loose term meaning he would have to steal a car. She hoped he didn't. It was bad enough she'd performed a hit-and-run on someone else's bumper. Crossing over into grand theft auto was just a bit much.

Sophie spied the padded envelope on the floor and snatched it up. When she turned it over, relief coursed through her at the familiar handwriting. Chase shot her a grin as she clutched it to her chest.

"Told you," he mouthed.

"Thanks," she mouthed back.

He'd done it. He'd gotten her to Paris, retrieved the package, and they were still in one piece. But it wasn't over yet. She knew that much. First they had to get to the safe house, and then they had to hope there was information they could use on the flash drive. Information that would stop Grigori from harming anyone else.

"Copy that," Chase said. "Heading for the rendezvous point now. Will send over the information as soon as we reach shelter."

———

IT TOOK ABOUT two hours to reach the safe house in Montmartre. First, they had to ditch the car, which they'd done in a garage in the financial district. The garage attendant hadn't even blinked an eye when they'd driven inside. Obviously on Hawk's payroll, or at least paid well enough to turn a blind eye when the time came.

A BMW had been waiting for them. Chase transferred all their gear to it in a flash, wiped down the Audi for prints, and then jumped into the Bimmer and took off. He'd taken a circuitous route across Paris, always looking in the rearview for pursuers. But there were none, and he'd finally started to relax. He found the new building, parked the car on the street because that's all that was available, and then he and Sophie took everything into the building.

This apartment was on the top floor too, but there was no elevator, only five floors of narrow stairs. This place was smaller than the last, mustier, which meant it wasn't used often. It was a studio with a kitchenette, a small bed, and a balcony. Unlike the last place, it lacked an exciting view even though it was on a quiet street.

Chase took out the secure laptop and booted it up. Then he took the package from Sophie and ripped it open. The flash drive was in a little Bubble Wrap pouch. He unfolded it and took it out. It was a black cylinder, perfectly ordinary looking.

Sophie twisted her fingers together as he inserted the drive into the USB port. Then he opened up the file manager to reveal the files on the drive.

"They're in Russian," Sophie said. He could hear the disappointment in her voice, the fear.

He tapped some keys. "We expected this. The software on this computer can copy the contents, including hidden folders, and then I'll send everything to Hawk. Kid will decrypt it."

"How long will it take?" she asked.

"Hours maybe. Or days. Open Sky isn't a group of amateurs. Their code is pretty sophisticated."

"Days?"

He looked up at her, at the worried expression she wore, and his heart kicked. "We have the information now, Sophie. That's a step in the right direction—and the Kid is good at what he does, honest. If the delivery van hadn't been delayed back there, Turov wouldn't have caught up to us. He'd have come along after we left and found nothing."

"It was close, Chase."

"It was. But we're here and we have the flash drive."

He picked up his phone, dialed Hawk, and informed him the files were on the way.

"I've got you on a private jet," Hawk said. "I'll text over the details, but the flight's at four a.m. Leave the car with the weapons in the trunk. Long-term parking."

"Copy," Chase said, rubbing his temples. Not quite twelve hours away. They talked for a few more minutes and then he hung up. For the first time in hours, he felt like he could breathe again. He'd gotten the flash drive, Sophie was safe, and they were on their way home soon.

He ejected the flash drive from the USB port and pocketed it, then stood and shrugged out of his jacket. He unstrapped the weapons and laid them on the table. When he took in the haunted look in Sophie's gaze, he dragged her into his arms, squeezing her tight.

She squeezed him back.

"Sorry for the scare today," he told her, his lips against her hair.

"Are you mad because I disobeyed you?"

He tilted her head back until he could look into her eyes. "I'm not happy about it. But you reacted to the situation and got us out of there. It's over now."

"I saw you jump out of the van, and then I saw Turov coming after you—I almost stayed in my seat, but it occurred to me that for you to go around the car and try to get inside with oncoming traffic would give them the chance to catch up."

"Yeah, it would have."

"So I threw open the door and climbed over the console. I knew you'd be mad, but I had no choice."

"I'm pissed you risked it—but it worked, so I'm going to get over it. But Sophie…"

"Yes?"

"You got lucky. Next time, do exactly as I tell you. I wasn't going to lead Turov to you. I would have kept going, and you could have safely driven away."

Her eyes widened, her fingers curling in his shirt. "You would have left me there alone?"

"It was the safest option. Yeah, I would have left you there alone. You would have driven to the airport like I told you and called Hawk. He'd have gotten you out."

She clung to him tighter. "Then I'm glad I didn't do what you said. I'm glad we're here together."

Jesus, she did something to him. Something that twisted his guts into knots and made his heart ache. He dipped his head and kissed her. He only meant to kiss her, but of course it didn't end there. Touching Sophie was like touching a match to gasoline. The flame was inevitable.

He stripped her quickly, and then he was inside her, moving hard and fast and taking them both to the edge of pleasure. When it was over, when she was limp and sated on the bed, her eyes drowsy with slumber, he got up and dragged on his jeans.

Her gaze instantly sharpened. "What are you doing?"

"Protecting you, Sophie. Go to sleep. I'll keep watch."

Chapter Twenty-Nine

CHASE AWOKE WITH A START, STRAINING HIS EYES IN THE darkness to make out where he was. He heard traffic below and remembered they were in Montmartre. Sophie slept beside him, her naked body lush and warm. He sat up, stretching.

He'd stayed awake earlier, watching over Sophie until she'd awakened and they'd ordered takeout. They'd eaten and talked, and then Sophie had dropped to her knees and shown him another side of pleasure with her. It was the first time she'd sucked him, and he'd loved the sight of it.

Sophie on her knees with his dick in her mouth was just about the most exciting thing he'd ever seen in his life. She gripped him with both hands, licked and sucked him like he was made of chocolate, and he thought the top of his head might blow off if she kept it up.

So he'd pulled her up, bent her over the bed, and slammed into her from behind. Damn, but her pussy was addictive.

Then he'd set an alarm and lain down in bed with her. Now he stood and pulled on his jeans—not the easiest of tasks when just thinking about Sophie made him hard—then walked to the glass door and peered outside. Nothing looked out of place. He turned and went back over to the bed. Sophie lay on her side, curled under the covers, and he wondered for a few moments how many more times he would see her like this.

One more time? Twice? Never?

That thought sat like a stone in his gut. He told himself it didn't matter, that he'd be banging some new chick by this time next week and her pussy would be every bit as wonderful. It was just the circumstances making this so exciting.

That and the way they talked about anything and everything. Now that he'd miss.

Chase swore softly, then checked his phone in case he had any texts from Hawk. There was nothing.

"What time is it?" Sophie asked, her voice gravelly with sleep.

"Not quite midnight yet."

She sat up and pushed her hair out of her face. She yawned; then she got up from the bed. She was completely naked, her skin gleaming like pearls in the evening light. Her body was lush, full-figured. Her breasts swayed as she bent to retrieve her jeans from where she'd dragged them out of the suitcase and set them earlier. She didn't try to hide her body as she began to get dressed. He knew that was a big deal, just as he knew if he were anyone else, she probably would have hidden herself from him.

The fact that she didn't hit him in the gut and sucked away some of his air. Then she pushed her hair away from her face and he was hit again, this time by how beautiful and amazing she was. No self-consciousness there. Only a sultry kind of beauty and the satisfied look of a woman who'd had great orgasms.

Jesus, he was a lucky bastard that she'd shared all that beauty and sexiness with him.

"Hungry again?" she asked.

"Yeah." Only he didn't think she meant hungry for sex, which he definitely was—but he was also the other kind of hungry. It had been a few hours since they'd eaten, after all. "You?"

"Oh yes. Sex with you is like running ten miles on the treadmill. A month with you and I could totally rock a bikini."

He knew she was joking, but the fact she was putting herself down pricked him anyway. "You could rock a bikini now. In fact, I'd like to see you in one. For my eyes only, of course."

"Come to LA this summer and maybe I'll wear one for you."

He crossed his arms and regarded her. "Not going back to New York?"

She frowned. "I kind of want to go somewhere far away from New York right now."

"I thought you had an audition next week."

Her chin lifted. "I do… but it doesn't matter. I'll find something in LA when I'm ready."

He hated that she felt like she had to run away, but he understood it. Doing what he did, he often saw the effects of posttraumatic stress on people. What Sophie had gone through could certainly cause a need for retreat and safety in familiar surroundings.

"They film television shows in DC and Baltimore."

She stared at him for a long minute. Her throat moved as she swallowed. He cursed himself then because what the fuck was he doing? He couldn't encourage this. Getting involved with Sophie would be bad. They'd have to hide their relationship—their familial relationship on paper, that is—and he'd have to lie to his mother.

It wasn't worth it. But that thought made his chest constrict. *Why not? Why isn't this worth it?*

"I can't go to DC, Chase."

He shrugged even though there was an ache in the pit of his stomach. "It was just a thought."

He tugged on a shirt. He wouldn't sleep again before it was time to leave for the airport. He'd rested when it was safe to do so, but the closer they got to go-time, the less safe he felt. It was typical mission adrenaline. Once they were back in DC, he'd feel better about the whole thing.

A car's brakes squealed to a stop outside and then doors slammed shut. He didn't think much of it until the sound of multiple footsteps began to echo up the stairwell. He listened hard. It could be anything. It could be nothing. There was no way that Turov had found them. How could he?

But Chase's instincts wouldn't let him ignore it. He grabbed his jacket and then shouldered the bag with the weapons and ammo as he turned to Sophie. She was standing frozen near the bed, her head cocked as if she was listening too.

The footsteps grew louder. Too much purpose in them, too certain of their destination.

"Get your shoes and jacket on. *NOW!*" he told her.

She grabbed the motorcycle boots and pulled them on, zipping them up quickly. Chase went over and threw open the sliding door to the balcony. The night air was cool, but he wasn't since adrenaline rushed in his veins.

"What's going on?" Sophie asked as she hurried to his side.

"We're leaving," he ground out as he pushed her onto the balcony and shut the door.

Behind him, everything was quiet—until the sound of splintering wood cracked into the night.

Sophie gasped, her head turning toward the room they'd just left.

"No time," he told her. "Climb over the edge and down onto the roof next door."

"Are you crazy? It's a six-foot drop, at least. And if I miss—"

"You won't miss. It's wide and flat—go, Sophie, for fuck's sake!"

She did as he said. The roof next door *was* a drop, but there was no space between the buildings. All she had to do was land and wait for him.

He heard her hit and then he went over the edge and joined her. Above them, he could hear the balcony door slide open. Russian voices came to them from the balcony. Someone peered over the edge, spotting them just as Chase dragged Sophie behind a concrete casement on the roof.

She trembled as the Russians shouted, her eyes wide, her chest rising and falling rapidly as she worked to control her breathing. She was terrified, and that made him angry. Angry with himself and with these fucking Russians.

Goddammit, the flash drive must have had a tracking program enabled when he plugged it in. But he hadn't transmitted over an open connection. He'd had a secure satellite link.

Which meant the transmitter was programmed to seek out any open Wi-Fi source and transmit that way. It would explain why it had taken hours for the Russians to find them. They'd been narrowing down the signal, trying to pinpoint the exact location it had come from. They hadn't wanted to make a mistake, so they'd bided their time.

Fuck.

"Stay low," he said as he dragged her toward the rooftop door that hopefully led down into the building.

There was a thunk and a vibration beneath his feet, and he knew the Russians had jumped onto the roof.

Chase grabbed the door handle and twisted. It opened, and he rushed Sophie through, closing it behind him and turning the lock.

"It won't hold them for long, but we don't need long," he told her as he started down the stairs, Sophie on his heels.

"How did they find us?" she panted behind him.

"The flash drive. It must have a locater program on it."

"Shit."

An understatement.

They thudded down the stairs, flight after flight, and Chase listened for the sounds of pursuit. The door was metal, so the Russians wouldn't shoot it, but they could break it in given enough leverage. Which they would do, but he hoped it would take them a little bit of time.

It was possible there were more than the three of them he'd gotten a glimpse of, which meant there could be men outside this building waiting for them. But he had to take the chance, because what other choice did he have?

He could barricade them into an apartment and shoot anyone who tried to take them, but that would be dangerous for the residents—and it would bring the *gendarme*. If Androv had even half the influence in Paris that he seemed to have in New York, then what were the chances Chase and Sophie would last the night in police custody?

He didn't know, and he wasn't taking that chance. When they reached the bottom landing, Chase stopped and held Sophie back with an arm.

"What now?" she whispered.

The door upstairs burst open with a loud *whomp* sounding against the wall, and Sophie jumped, looking up with round eyes.

He grasped her shoulders and forced her to look at him. "If they're out there, they expect two people to walk out of this building. We have to split up." He shoved the key fob at her. "Go and get the car. Calmly, as if you have every right to be here."

She clasped the key fob in her hand. "And then what?"

"Drive away."

"What? No, I'm not leaving you!"

He gripped her harder. "This time you have to. If you wait, if you swing back around for me, they'll know."

"And if they catch me anyway?"

He kissed her quickly, frantically, while the sound of boots echoed down the stairwell, bringing the Russians closer. "Don't think like that. Just go. You're an actress, Sophie—so fucking act. Don't let them suspect it's you. It's dark and they don't know what they're looking for— other than a man and a woman. They'll watch you, but if you don't look suspicious, they won't bother you."

He gave her the burner phone he'd tucked into his jacket after they'd gotten to the safe house, closed it in her hand. "Go to the airport. Call Hawk. I'll meet you there if I can."

She tugged him back down and kissed him hard. "You better be there, Chase." She sucked in a breath and a little sob escaped her. "Damn you."

Then she turned and strode toward the door, and Chase prayed like hell he was right and that she would get away.

Chapter Thirty

SOPHIE TOOK A DEEP BREATH, SHOOK HER HEAD TO clear it, then walked out into the night with her head high. She twirled the key fob around her finger and sang a song in French, as if she'd just come from a hot night of passion with her lover but had to leave for some reason. She strutted down the sidewalk, toward the BMW parked there, and prayed the Russians weren't watching for her.

Closer, closer.

The Bimmer grew bigger, but she didn't punch the button to unlock it. If Sergei Turov was out here and knew she and Chase had a BMW now, she didn't want to give it away until the last minute. She couldn't give it away, because she had to get into the car and drive past the building no matter what Chase said. She had to give him a fighting chance to run to the car.

She strained her ears to listen for the sound of footsteps on pavement, following her, but she heard nothing.

Her heart hammered and every instinct she had told

her to turn around and go back to Chase. How could she leave him? It physically hurt to walk way. To kiss him like that and imagine it could be the last time.

What would she do if it *was* the last time? How would she recover from it?

She just had to get the Bimmer and drive past the door, let him see that he could run to her. She reached the car, but fear spiked in her belly and she didn't stop. Instead, she walked a little farther down the street, just a couple of cars, but then she crossed to the outside and walked back to the driver's side. She held her breath as she pressed the button, then she yanked open the door and climbed in.

She nearly melted in relief that she was inside, that no one had stopped her. She reached for the ignition button—but the passenger door jerked open and a man dropped into the seat beside her. The breath stopped in her lungs. She couldn't manage a proper scream, but when she thought her chest might burst from lack of air, her lungs suddenly worked and she sucked in a breath, letting it out in a sort of half yell.

She punched the ignition, thinking if she blasted away from the curb he'd lose his balance and fall out before he could shut the door. But no such luck since he slammed the door and turned to her.

"Drive, Sophie. And do it quickly."

Except she couldn't move, couldn't manage to perform the tasks necessary to get the car moving. She gaped at the man. He hadn't spoken with a Russian accent, which was a good thing—but she didn't know him. He could still work for Grigori.

"Who are you?"

He reached over and pressed the start button—she hadn't pressed it at all, which she now realized as the engine roared to life. "I'm someone who's here to help you—and I can't do that if you don't get this car moving."

"What about Chase?"

"He'll be fine. He's highly trained and deadly. Without you to distract him, he'll get the job done. Now please fucking drive."

Sophie shoved the car in gear and managed to ease out of the spot without hitting anything, which was a miracle considering the way her hands shook.

"You didn't tell me who you are," she squeaked, heart pounding furiously in her chest. Chase hadn't mentioned anyone who might help them. Whoever this guy was, Chase hadn't known he was here. He'd told her to call Hawk. This man was not Hawk.

"Call me Ian," he said, glancing over at her before looking behind them, presumably for signs of pursuit.

"Ian. Are you on Chase's team?"

He laughed as he turned back to her. "Hardly. But he knows me."

Traffic wasn't exactly light this time of night, but it was better than during the day. Though Sophie had never driven in Paris, she could at least read the signs.

"We need to help Chase," she said as she turned onto a wide boulevard.

"He doesn't need our help. Now pull over up there and I'll drive."

She gripped the wheel. Hard. "I'm not letting you

drive. Chase didn't mention anyone named Ian. For all I know, you work for Grigori."

His smile was pleasant, but something about it chilled her nonetheless. "It's good that you're suspicious, Sophie."

"How do you know my name? How did you know where to find us?"

Chase had mentioned a tracking device on the flash drive. This guy could be one of Grigori's men and just toying with her. For the first time, she wished Chase had given her a gun.

"I know your name because Mendez told me. I knew where to find you because he told me that too."

Mendez. She'd heard Chase mention that name, and not in a bad way. "Who else do you know?"

"Hawk is the one who set this trip up for you. Jack 'Hawk' Hunter. He's married to Gina Domenico— beautiful woman and beautiful children."

Gina Domenico? Hawk's wife was the pop star? Holy shit. Maybe, just maybe, this guy was on her side after all. He knew things she didn't think anyone working for Grigori would know. Her hands relaxed on the wheel a little bit.

"So you know Hawk and Mendez. But why are you here now? Where were you before those men found us?"

"Sorry, had a job in the south of France. I got here as quickly as I could."

"I want to call Hawk." Because Chase had told her to. Because until she did, how would she know she could really trust this man?

"Go ahead. I'll wait."

She fumbled the phone from her pocket and tried to dial. It was impossible while driving. Finally, she eased the car over to the side of the road and managed to find the right button to connect her to Hawk.

He answered on the first ring. "Fiddler, what's up?"

"It's not Ch-Chase," she said, glancing over at Ian.

"Sophie—what's wrong? Where are you?"

"I'm with someone named Ian. He says you know him. The Russians found us… Chase… I don't know how he is. He was fine when I left him—"

Her throat was tight. Her pulse tripped and sweat broke out on her skin. If something happened to Chase…

Oh God, she couldn't think it.

"Fucking hell." Hawk sounded concerned and a little pissed, but he didn't sound like he thought she was about to be murdered. "Can you give the phone to Ian?"

She held the phone out without a word. Ian took it and put it to his ear.

"Your boy's got backup," he said. "One of my guys is there to help mop up the Russians." He put an elbow against the window and shoved a hand into his hair. "Yeah, I know you aren't happy. Take it up with Mendez. It's not my fault you bitches don't talk. … You know, this isn't where I wanted to fucking be, Hunter. I've got a business to run, and this kind of shit takes valuable time. … Yeah, love you too, baby. Here's Sophie."

He shoved the phone at her and she pressed it to her ear. "Hawk?"

"Do what Ian tells you, Sophie. He's on our side. And don't worry about Chase. He knows what he's doing."

———

CHASE COULDN'T WATCH as Sophie went out the door and headed for the car. He hoped like hell she made it. It was a calculated risk, and one that it killed him to take. But he had to. The men coming down the stairs were moving fast. They'd be in the lobby soon—and he didn't want Sophie anywhere near him when they arrived.

He had to let her drive off on her own. If he tried to go with her, any Russians watching outside would realize who they were. He couldn't take that chance. If he had her circle around and pick him up, she'd still be in the vicinity and they'd have an opportunity to intercept her.

No, he wanted her gone. On her way to the airport while he created a diversion and bought her some time.

He took out the Sig and retreated into the shadows of the stairwell. Waiting. Above him, the footsteps grew louder. A door in the building opened and someone yelled in French, no doubt angry at the late-night disruption. He was surprised there weren't more doors opening.

Though there probably would be quite soon. In fact, they'd be dialing the *gendarme* before this was over.

Chase cleared his mind, focused on the noise of the men approaching. Three guys, no more. The feet pounded together, but he'd had enough experience to separate out the sounds. They echoed in the stairwell, along with the angry French.

He could wait, take out the first man, but the next two would know he was there. They would turn, fire.

He had to do it. Had to protect Sophie. He'd heard nothing outside, no sounds of struggle or surprise.

The door to the outside opened, and he wedged himself farther into the shadows. A man entered, and Chase swore silently. The last thing he needed was a resident getting into the middle of a firefight.

But then the first Russian hit the top of the landing, and the man who'd just walked in raised a pistol and fired. The Russian dropped.

Chase didn't have time to be surprised. He bolted into action as the other two Russians opened fire over the side of the stairwell. He darted out, fired up, darted back.

The man who'd shot the first Russian fell back into the shadows opposite him.

"Who the fuck are you?" Chase demanded.

Eyes flashed in the darkness. "Ian Black sent me."

Fucking Ian Black. Jesus, that dude had a way of showing up at both the best and worst times. Right now counted for one of the best.

"Sophie?"

"Last I saw, Ian got in the car with her. She's protected."

Thank God for that. The relief coursing through him was strong—and calming. He knew his job and he could do it under pressure. But the news that Sophie was safe with Ian Black gave him the kind of eerie calm that sometimes settled in when the battle was raging and he ceased thinking about his own death. It was when he didn't care anymore that he did some of his best work.

Sirens sounded in the distance, and he knew they were headed for them. He didn't want to be here when they arrived. Chase signaled the other guy, who nodded. They both stayed in the shadows, waiting, keeping quiet.

The Russians crept down the stairs, thinking they'd left. It wasn't until they were in the entry that Chase and his companion struck. He didn't see what the other guy did, but he wrapped his arm around the neck of one of the Russians and popped his chin with the other, breaking his neck and dropping him to the ground. When he looked over at Ian Black's man, he'd done something similar.

Chase held out a hand. The man was Special Forces, or had been. Typical of Ian Black's mercenaries. They weren't misfits, which was what Chase and his team-mates had thought when they'd first encountered them in Qu'rim.

No, they were guys with backgrounds similar to the HOT soldiers, but they'd decided they liked hiring out their skills and not answering to a governmental authority the way the men of HOT did. The US Army owned Chase's ass. Nobody owned this guy's.

"Chase Daniels."

"Brett Wheeler."

Chase took a breath and wiped the sweat from his face. "Think we better get the fuck out of here, Brett."

"Couldn't agree more."

They stepped outside and started down the street as lights popped on in the building behind them.

"You got a car?"

"Around the corner."

Chase glanced back over his shoulder, but nobody followed them. He patted his jacket pocket, feeling the outline of the flash drive. Must be some fucked-up shit on this thing if Androv was so desperate to get it back.

He just prayed that Billy Blake could bust the encryption. If not, Sophie would never be safe. And that was a thought he couldn't bear.

Chapter Thirty-One

Mendez was at work when his personal cell phone rang. "Hawk. What do you have for me?"

"Androv's people found Fiddler and Sophie, but they got away. Three Russians eliminated. Ian Black assisted… I wish you'd told me that might happen, sir."

Mendez ran a hand through his hair. Hawk wasn't active duty anymore. He could cuss out his former commander if he wanted to, but he didn't. He kept the military protocol in place because it was ingrained in him.

"I couldn't, Hawk. If he didn't show, then his name didn't need to be mentioned. Black walks a dangerous tightrope of his own. I can't compromise that."

"Yes, sir."

"You're pissed."

"Yes, sir."

Mendez laughed. "Goddamn, boy, you aren't in the Army anymore. Tell me to fuck off if it makes you feel better."

"No, sir, not doing that. But next time, tell me. I'll treat the information with the care it deserves."

Mendez leaned back in his chair and stared at the ceiling. He'd kept so many things to himself for so long that it was almost impossible to trust anyone. Or endanger anyone. The more things he shared, the more likely it was that someone would get hauled before a House committee if the time ever came. He didn't fucking need that. Couldn't do that to those who depended on him.

"Where are Fiddler and Sophie now?"

"En route to Charles de Gaulle."

Hawk didn't have to tell him they weren't out of the woods yet. They'd both been in this business long enough to know that was understood.

"Any progress on the files?"

"Still locked tight. But it's only been a few hours."

"We've got to get them open." He wanted HOT working on those files, but the best he'd been able to do was send Hawk's former teammate Billy Blake to help. If anyone could crack it, the Kid could.

"Working on it, sir… That's all you need to know, by the way."

"Yeah, copy that," Mendez said. He didn't need knowledge of what was going on until they had something worth knowing. It was all about the deniability. "Let me know when you have something. And let me know when Fiddler and the girl are back safely."

He clicked off the line and looked up at the television screen. He'd muted it, but he grabbed the remote and put the sound back on.

Grigori Androv was on the screen, smiling wide. The headline was definitely attention-getting.

Zoprava CEO Donates 20 Million to Refugee Relief

Mendez watched the report. He'd seen Androv before, but this time he paid attention to the details. Grigori Androv appeared soft, nerdy. He was tall, thin, wore glasses, and he smiled like he owned the world. It wasn't a nice smile. It was the smile of a man without morals or limits. An arrogant smile.

Mendez understood that kind of man well. He'd encountered them all too often in his life. A side effect of the job, no doubt.

He was about to snap the sound off again when the footage cut to a charity banquet. And there, right there on his screen, Androv stood beside a man whose hand he was clasping in a handshake. As if they'd just cut a deal.

Congressman DeWitt smiled as he said something to Androv. His other hand came up and clasped the man's shoulder. A spontaneous move, familiar. A chill shot through Mendez, settled like a rock in his belly.

There was nothing out of place about that shot. Nothing that suggested any impropriety whatsoever. DeWitt was a congressman, and a refugee relief event was a perfectly legitimate place for him to be. There was no evidence he knew Androv, no evidence they'd ever spoken before that event.

But it caused the hair on Mendez's neck to prickle anyway. His senses twitched. There was just something about DeWitt and Androv in the same frame that didn't sit right with him. Something that said there was more to the story than he'd ever guessed.

Now he really wanted to know what was in those fucking files of Androv's. And he was willing to risk a lot to find out.

———

IAN BLACK CHECKED them into a small suite at the airport. It was after midnight but still a few hours until Sophie's flight out. She was happy he'd done that instead of forcing her to sit in an airport lounge all night, though she didn't relish being in a room with a stranger.

She glanced over at him as he paced the room, his attention on the phone screen in front of him. Black was tall with dark hair. He was, appropriately she supposed, dressed in black from head to toe, and his expression was hard and businesslike. He might not be Chase's teammate, but he was like Chase. Cut from the same cloth. The badass-military-man cloth.

She hadn't been around that kind of man long, but she pretty much thought she could recognize them now. There was something about them. Something strong, something deadly. Something honorable, at least in Chase's case. And Hawk's.

She didn't know about Ian Black.

"Any news?" she asked when she thought she might go crazy from the silence and her thoughts.

He glanced up. "I told you an hour ago he was safe."

"Yes, but where is he?"

She'd nearly melted in relief when Ian had gotten a call earlier and then told her that Chase and another man were on their way.

"Is he okay?" she'd asked.

"Yes."

That was all she'd needed. Until now, when she kept expecting him to walk into the room at any moment. She was going just a little bit crazy waiting to lay eyes on him again. It shocked her just how much she needed to see him. How necessary he'd become.

Except that she had to put an end to those kinds of thoughts because he wasn't necessary at all. He couldn't be. This thing between them was ending, whether tonight or when they landed in DC. Over. Done. Had to be.

He didn't want her in his life. He wanted the sex, but he didn't want her. Too complicated.

"They're on the way. Traffic is a bitch in this city, you know."

She did know. She turned away and went over to the windows, gazing out at the lights. Planes took off and landed at regular intervals. She didn't know how long she'd been standing like that when there was a knock at the door.

Ian went over and looked through the peephole. Then he swung it open and Chase and another man stood on the other side.

She couldn't help her reaction even though she'd told herself to be cool. Calm.

She was neither of those things. With a little cry, she ran toward the door as Chase walked in. He caught her as she threw her arms around him and hugged him tight.

She was shaking, but she didn't cry. She swallowed the lump in her throat. Dear God, don't let her cry. He was strong—all these men were strong—and she wasn't going to be the one who fucking cried.

Chase held her close, a hand sifting up into her hair, pressing her to his chest. He smelled good, a little like the night, a little smoky, a little spicy.

"It's okay, babe," he said into her ear. "You're okay."

She couldn't stop the shaking, nor could she manage to tell him it wasn't herself she'd been worried about. Stupid man.

"Didn't realize it was like that," Ian said, and Chase's body tensed marginally.

"Like what?" he challenged, and Sophie told herself to get it together.

She gulped in a breath, pushed herself back. Chase let her go, but she sensed it wasn't easy the way his hand tightened for a moment in her hair and then slipped free.

Ian was looking at them both with interest. "Never mind." He sat down on a chair and kicked his feet up onto the small table, his hands going behind his head.

"You can go now, Black," Chase said. "I got this."

Ian just smiled. "Nope, can't do that. Brett and I have an obligation to see you onto that plane."

Chase went over and dropped the bag he'd been carrying. She knew it contained weapons, and she knew he would store them in the car tomorrow morning when they left it in the parking lot.

Then he turned and sank down on the couch in the small living area, throwing his arms along the back of it and sighing. He looked tired. "If that's what you want."

"That's what I want, HOTtie."

Sophie blinked. Did Ian Black just call Chase a hottie? He was a hottie, but… weird.

The guy named Brett sat down on a chair nearby. "HOT? Really? Fucking cool, man."

Chase glanced at her, his mouth hardening. "Yeah, really."

"Heard about that when I was a SEAL. Thought it was a myth."

Sophie decided she'd had enough of the cryptic weirdness. She wasn't tired, but she wanted to be alone for a while. "Well, if you guys are going to sit around out here and trade war stories, I'm taking the bed for a few hours. Good night."

She went into the bedroom and shut the door. The voices kept droning on as she sat back on the bed. There was a television in the room and she turned it on, keeping the sound low.

A few minutes later, the door opened and shut and then Chase was there, coming over and propping a hip on the edge of the bed.

"You okay, Soph?"

She told herself to stay right where she was. To play this cool. But Chase was here, and she wasn't ready to give him up. She put her arms around him, pressed herself tightly to him.

His arms enfolded her, one hand at her back and the other going into her hair and cupping her head.

"I thought I would never see you again," she whispered. "I thought Grigori's men would kill you."

He bent and put his lips to her hair. "Takes more than a couple of Russians to kill me, I promise."

"I was going to come back for you, Chase. Ian stopped me."

His fingers tightened in her shirt, her hair. "I told you not to do that, baby. I told you to keep going."

She pushed back and searched his gaze. "I know—but you wouldn't abandon me, so how could I abandon you?"

He brought his hand around to her face, his thumb gliding over her lip, pressing lightly before dropping away again.

"You're sweet, Sophie. So fucking sweet. I want another taste, and another and another. But this has to stop now. We have to stop."

She sucked in a pained breath as she took his hand and brought it back to her mouth, kissing his skin. "I know," she whispered past the razor blades in her throat. "There's no future. We both know it... But Chase, if you ever wanted to try—" She swallowed, the words sticking there.

"I killed a man tonight," he said, and her heart throbbed.

She knew what he did, knew it came at a cost. But she also knew it was a necessary part of his job. He kept people like her safe, and he had to do terrible things in order to keep that promise.

"I'm sorry you had to do that for me," she said, and he made a shocked sound in his throat.

Then he was clasping her shoulders, sliding his hands up to cup her cheeks. "Sophie, it's not your fault. It's what I do, and I'd do it again if I had to. I... Fuck, I just thought you should know what kind of man I am, what kind of things I do. You don't want to be with someone like me, Soph, even if it were possible."

She gripped his wrists. "Are you crazy? The kind of man you are is amazing and honorable. Protective. Loyal. You've done more for me in the past few days than anyone ever has. If you think I don't know that or appreciate it—well, you don't know me then."

He lowered his mouth to hers, took her lips in a hot, searing kiss. "I know you, babe," he said when she was breathless and aching for more. "I *know* you."

He said stuff like that and her heart melted. And, God, she was afraid it was true. He really did know her in a way no one else did—or ever would. He pulled her head down and kissed her forehead softly, tenderly.

"I like you, Sophie. I'll always like you."

He got to his feet and strode out the door, shutting it quietly behind him while her heart cried out at his words. They were everything in one way—and nothing at all in comparison to the words she wanted.

Chapter Thirty-Two

"Man, the shit that's in these files."

Billy Blake's eyes shone with excitement as he scrolled through the newly decrypted files. It had taken almost twenty-four hours to bust through, but he'd done it.

Pages and pages, all in Russian. Chase scraped a hand through his hair and tried to keep his cool.

"Does anyone read Russian?" he asked. Calmly, he thought. But Hawk and Kid turned to him. Matt "Richie Rich" Girard and Garrett "Iceman" Spencer were there too, having returned from their R & Rs yesterday. They were all looking at him like he'd kicked a puppy or something.

"Got that handled," Hawk said. "Send them over, Kid."

Billy tapped a couple of keys and the files shot through the ether, going somewhere.

Chase's eyes were gritty and his whole fucking body ached. Too much excitement and not enough sleep.

Their plane had landed a couple of hours ago, and Matt had met them rather than letting them take the car they'd left in the lot, driving them to Hawk's offices in a nondescript building in Annapolis. They weren't too far from HOT HQ or from DC. It was a great location, and it still kept Hawk closer to home on the Eastern Shore.

The offices were modern and filled with state of-the-art equipment. But it wasn't HOT. At least there was a private area with couches and a small kitchen. Evie Baker, soon to be Girard, had taken Sophie there for some coffee.

Sophie. Fucking hell, he tried not to think too hard about Sophie, but that was damned near impossible since he'd just spent seven hours in a flying tube with her head on his shoulder. She smelled good. Looked good. For a while he'd wished they really were Nathan and Beth Chandler, two innocent people on their honeymoon, starting their life together.

But they'd landed and reality crashed down. She was his fucking stepsister and his fucking father was a part of her life. And his mother would be hurt if Tyler suddenly became involved in Chase's life—where the fuck would they spend Thanksgivings? Christmases? Sophie might not have had a great life with Tyler and Justine, but she still loved her mother and she'd want to see her.

And that meant Tyler would be there.

Chase's mother had always said she didn't hate him, but Chase didn't know how she couldn't. She'd given Tyler his address because she was kindhearted and she'd believed him when he'd said Sophie was in danger. That was the only reason.

He blew out a breath and flopped into a chair.

"Dude, you all right?" Hawk asked.

"No, not really. I want this over with, and I want Sophie to have her life back. Who the fuck is going to read all that Russian and translate it for us ASAP? Who can you trust to do that?"

Hawk lifted an eyebrow. Chase knew he was being a cranky bastard, but his teammates forgave him for it. They'd all been there at one time or another.

"Mendez."

Chase blinked. "You mean HOT's involved?"

"Yeah... and Mendez is reading, along with a couple of handpicked translators."

"Mendez is *reading* it? The colonel speaks Russian?"

Iceman snorted. "Yeah, who the fuck knew, right? I mean, it has to be in his record, but it's not like that's the sort of thing we have access to. Fucking badass dude reads and speaks Russian."

"Holy shit." Not for the first time, Chase felt pride in his organization and his commander swelling his chest. Jesus, that Mendez *was* a badass motherfucker. You didn't get to be in command of an organization like HOT by being anything less than stellar, but sometimes commanders got so entrenched in the desk jockey aspects of the organization that you forgot they'd once been operators.

And Mendez must have been a damned good one.

"Yeah, holy shit. But if there's anything in there, he'll figure it out. We'll know something in the next few hours. Until then, you and Sophie can crash."

Chase rubbed his fingers over his eyes. "I'd rather stay here until we know."

"We're all staying here," Matt said. "Brandy and Victoria are on the way, and so are Knight Rider and Georgie. Flash is still on his honeymoon. Big Mac and Lucky are flying back from the Caribbean, and Dex is still in Kentucky."

Chase's throat was tight. This is what family was to him. The ties you made voluntarily were just as strong, sometimes stronger, than the ones you were born with. In his case, that was certainly true. He'd do more for these fuckers than he'd ever do for Tyler Nash.

"I meant that you and Sophie can crash in one of the offices if you like," Hawk said. "Not letting you leave here until we have an answer."

"I'm good," he said, unwilling to move. Unwilling to go and talk to Sophie, to face being alone with her in a place where they weren't surrounded by other people or the droning of jet engines. What the fuck would he say? What *could* he say? Last night, when he'd held her close and told her he liked her, he'd said everything.

Everything he knew how to. He didn't know how to do more than that, though something within him wanted to. But what more was there?

He rubbed his temple. Jesus, he'd made mistakes. Huge mistakes. He should have never gotten involved with Sophie, never let his dick rule his brain where she was concerned. Because he had to admit, even if it were just to himself, that he was fucking addicted to her body. That even now he was jonesing for another taste, another hit.

Like a junkie, he was trying to figure out how to get that fix. How to hit it one more time without hurting anyone. Without hurting Sophie, because fuck, she didn't need any more disappointment in her life.

The door opened and Evie walked in with Sophie, ending his battle with himself not to go to her. Evie's long black hair was pulled back in a ponytail, and her belly had the slightest curve to it now.

Chase didn't miss the way Matt looked at his woman, at the way his eyes went soft and his face looked as if someone had handed him the keys to heaven. Chase's heart lurched at that look, then his gaze slewed to Sophie.

Her hair hung in waves down her back and over her shoulders. She was dressed in formfitting jeans, the motorcycle boots, and a black tee that hugged those magnificent breasts of hers. She was wearing that cherry-red lipstick again and looked like sex on legs.

Ice was deeply, totally in love with Grace Campbell, but even he couldn't help the way his eyes slipped over Sophie. Chase saw it and wanted to growl, but then Ice looked away and Chase decided he had to give the man that much since this was the first time he'd laid eyes on Sophie. Matt had seen her at the airport, and of course Hawk had met her a few days ago.

Ice had been in this room the whole time, so he hadn't seen Sophie when she'd arrived. Billy was too engrossed in his screen to look up—but then he did, and he did a double take too.

Chase was seriously ready to pounce on someone, but

Billy got his shit together before Chase could act. After the initial shock of Sophie, the guys looked at her no differently than they looked at any of the other women who came into their paths. Every man in this room, except for him, was married or committed—and they were all in too, because Chase knew what they had done for their women.

Risked it all.

Risked their lives.

Gone to hell and back for love.

No, they might look at a beautiful woman—they'd have to be dead not to—but they weren't interested.

"Got anything, baby?" Evie asked.

Matt took her hand and stood, guiding her into the chair he'd been occupying. She smiled up at him with such a look of love on her face that Chase envied the motherfucker more than he already did.

"Billy broke the code—now we wait for the translation."

Sophie looked tired as she pushed her hair back behind an ear. "Of course it wouldn't be as simple as English files with a big red arrow pointing and saying, *Look here for the incriminating shit.*"

"Never is," Billy said.

Sophie leaned against a desk and crossed her legs, her hands going behind her to brace herself. Chase couldn't help but think of the first night he'd fucked her when he'd put her on the counter and tasted her pussy for the first time.

As if she knew what he was thinking, her gaze sought his. Their eyes locked for a long minute. They said things without saying a word, and Chase's heart rate kicked up as he stared at her.

Her neck bore his mark just as his did hers. It had to be clear to anyone watching them that they'd gotten involved over the past few days.

Hawk's voice cut into the silence that had descended on the room. "If you want to sleep for a while, Sophie, you can use one of the offices. It could be hours before we know anything, but you don't have to stay up if you're tired."

Sophie shook her head. "No, I'm fine."

"All right then, who's hungry?" Hawk asked. A chorus of voices agreed they were. "I'll order pizza."

The pizza arrived within half an hour, and everyone grabbed a slice. Sophie picked at hers of course, and Chase felt unaccountably angry about it. She'd been free with him over the past few days, lost some of that self-consciousness and eaten without thinking too much about it.

Now she was right back to the way she'd been before he'd shown her how much he loved her body just the way it was. He hated seeing her like that, but what could he do? He had no right to say anything. No right to have an opinion.

He finished his slice of pizza, stood, and carried his plate over to the trash and threw it in. When he turned around, several sets of eyes were on him. Except Sophie's. She didn't look at him at all. She picked at her pizza and didn't look up.

"Going out for some fresh air," he said, and then he

turned and blasted out of the building before anyone could stop him.

There was a green space behind the building, adjacent to the parking lot, and he went into it, stood there with his hands shoved into his jacket pockets. It was dusk, the sky awash in orange at the horizon. His breath frosted in the air, curling around him as he stood and tried to clear his mind.

What the fuck was wrong with him anyway? What the fuck did he care if Sophie picked at her pizza? What the fuck did he care if he never tasted her again? There were other women. Plenty of other women.

The door behind him opened and closed. He didn't turn. He expected Hawk or Matt to come and stand beside him, tell him he was being a moody fucker and that it needed to stop.

He was wrong. Her scent hit him like a blow and he sucked it in, holding his ground. He thought she might touch him, but she didn't. She came to stand beside him, her hands shoved in her own pockets.

"You okay?" she said.

He glanced at her, his body tightening almost painfully. "You shouldn't be out here."

"Nobody else thought it was a bad idea."

It probably wasn't a bad idea for anyone but him. "You weren't hungry?"

She shrugged. "Not really."

"Bullshit. You're back to thinking about Justine and Tyler and your fucked-up childhood. Thought you were over that. Thought I proved to you it didn't fucking matter."

"Nobody gets over shit like that overnight, Chase. Besides, maybe I've got new reasons not to be hungry."

He turned to look at her. "What the fuck does that mean?"

She faced him, her eyes flashing. "This is a lot to process, Chase. You, us, everything. It's been a whirlwind few days, and I'm not quite sure how to feel about any of it." She sucked in a breath. "I don't like where we are now, how we're acting toward each other. There's a damn elephant in the room and everyone knows it. I've been asking myself just exactly *why* we have to pretend like nothing happened between us, why there's no possible way forward. You aren't my brother; I am not your sister. We aren't related—we're no more than two kids who knew each other once. But now we're grown, and there's no real reason we can't have more."

He stared at her. "Other than the fact you live in New York—or is it LA now?—and I live here? And then there's my mother, who's already put up with so much shit from Tyler that I can't begin to heap more shit on top of her." He shook his head vigorously. "No, no way. It's not that fucking easy—and besides, who said I wanted more? It's pussy, Sophie. I can get that anywhere."

She stared at him, her eyes glittering like diamonds as she straightened, her head going back and her chin going up. "Okay. Well, I can see I was mistaken then. My bad. You just go ahead and go back to fucking around, and I'll pretend like none of this ever happened."

Her voice broke on the last and it about fucking

killed him. He wanted to reach for her, but he didn't. Jesus, she was tearing him up—and there wasn't a goddamn thing he could do about it.

"I thought you were brave, Chase. I thought you were strong and unafraid of anything. I see I was wrong. I see that you're just a little boy who's still running scared. Your daddy ignored you—news flash, you aren't the first person who had an uninvolved father. I never even met my real dad—and Tyler, hell, he tried sometimes, but he wasn't much better with me than he was with you. I got over it. But you—you let it control you. All that talk of being your own man—and you let it control you!"

She goaded him into action then. He reached for her, but she stepped out of his way, stumbling backward, away from him.

"Go to hell, Chase," she hissed. "Fucking go to hell!"

She turned and strode away. He started after her, but his body was suddenly on fire, frozen in place as lightning bolts rolled through him. He couldn't move, couldn't breathe—

And then he couldn't see her anymore as the world blinked out of existence.

Chapter Thirty-Three

EVERYTHING FUCKING HURT. CHASE FORCED HIS EYES open and stared up at the darkening sky. His muscles felt like rubber, refusing to obey his commands to move. It took a few seconds, but he finally managed to push himself up and onto his elbows. The door to the building burst open and Hawk, Richie, Ice, and Kid busted through, weapons drawn and badass-mother-fucker looks on their faces.

Kid rushed over and helped him sit up. The others filtered back to them within moments, weapons lowered but badass looks still firmly in place.

"Sophie," Chase forced out, his voice cracking. He pretty much knew he'd been shot with a stun gun. Military grade, judging by the feel of it.

Richie swore. "Goddammit, how the fuck did they even know where to go?"

Hawk looked more pissed than Chase had ever seen him, which wasn't good considering how calm the guy usually was. Calm and deadly was his norm. Pissed and deadly? Fucking scary.

"I'd like to know that myself," Hawk said. "Fuck!"

"We saw them on the security cam, but we couldn't get downstairs in time," Kid told Chase. "They tased you and grabbed Sophie."

Chase struggled to his feet, his muscles still like rubber, his body aching and smarting. He was lucky they'd only tased him, but he couldn't dwell on that. He was still alive—and Sophie was in danger.

"We have to find her."

He stumbled away from the group and Iceman caught him, stopped him. Chase jerked out of Ice's grip, but he didn't keep going. Hawk materialized beside them.

"We've got nowhere to go just yet," Hawk said. "At least not until Kid accesses the security cams from the nearby businesses. We have to hope like fucking hell they're on it. We get a fix on their ride, we can go after them."

Chase gaped at the men, his brothers, standing around him—except for Kid, who'd dashed back inside. "You mean we don't even fucking know *where* to go? Those bastards took Sophie, and all we can do is stand around with our thumbs up our asses and pray for footage that'll show us what the fuck they're driving?"

Hawk had walked away during Chase's tirade and lifted his phone to his ear. No one else said anything. They just continued to look at Chase sympathetically. He sucked in a breath that hurt. He felt like he was coming unglued at the seams, his skin splitting wide because it couldn't contain the pain he felt.

Not physical pain, because that didn't amount to much when he was accustomed to dealing with that kind of pain from his job.

This pain was worse. Deeper. In his soul.

Sophie.

She was gone. Kidnapped by Androv's men, probably scared out of her mind, and headed for who knew what kind of trouble.

Androv would not be kind. He would not be understanding. He would hurt her. He wouldn't kill her right away because he was too arrogant for that, too diabolical. He would want her tortured, want her to suffer for daring to defy him. For stealing from him.

Hawk was talking, but his voice was low and Chase couldn't make out his words.

Jesus, why had he been an asshole to her? Why had he told her they needed to deny everything they were feeling and pretend it never happened? Everything between them had been a whirlwind—but it was a whirlwind he'd never experienced before. He'd never been so addicted to a woman and so miserable about it at the same time. What the fuck was wrong with him?

Hawk turned and came back over to the group, his eyes glittering with determination. "Androv is in fucking DC, speaking at an international technology convention. Mendez is putting the SEALS on him. Every move he makes, we'll know it."

Chase's gut twisted. "That's where we need to look

for Sophie then. He'll keep her close. He's too much of an egomaniac not to."

"I think you're right," Richie said. He took out his phone. "I'm calling Viking. He'll be happy to let us join in."

Viking was Dane "Viking" Erikson, the SEAL team commander and a pretty badass guy to have at your back in a fight.

"We need to go inside and arm," Hawk said, and everyone agreed. They didn't have time to go to HOT and get their equipment, but Hawk had his own arsenal.

After they methodically went through the weapons, loaded them, and strapped on microphones and transmitters so they could talk, they were ready. Kid joined them as well, his search of the surrounding security cams revealing nothing of use. But knowing where Androv was, and knowing he wanted Sophie, was better. They would find her—and if Androv got hurt in the process, Chase couldn't really be too upset about that.

Evie sat alone in the adjoining office. She looked up when they came in, her gaze missing nothing, from the battle ready equipment to their determined expressions. She walked over and kissed Matt.

"Give them hell, baby," she said. "And get our girl back."

Chase started at that description of Sophie. Evie considered her one of their own, one of their little family of warriors. And why not? She'd been on a mission, and she'd helped retrieve information that might just give them insight into the heart of Grigori Androv's operations.

"Not leaving until I put you in the car," Matt said.

Evie rolled her eyes as she snagged her purse from the desk. "Then let's go so you can get down to the real business of the evening."

As they were walking out, she stopped and put a hand on Chase's arm. Her eyes made him think of Sophie's eyes. She had that same beautiful shade of violet, and yet she was completely different from Sophie.

"Good luck, Chase. I know y'all will succeed because it's what you do—but when you get her back, tell her whatever it is that's on your mind. The two of you—" She hesitated. "God, it hurt just being in the same room with you. I don't know what that means, but I'm thinking it means something. Stop fighting it. Life is too short."

———

SHE WAS DRUNK. Sophie held her hand up in front of her face and tried to focus on it. She shook her head, tried again. Her fingers still didn't come into focus, so she dropped her hand and turned her head. The world rippled.

She was lying on a bed. A soft bed, really. She didn't know how she'd gotten here. She remembered fighting with Chase…

Oh, Chase. Her throat ached at the thought of him. She couldn't remember all the reasons why, though she tried to push past the fog and find the memories in the mistiness of her head.

She'd been arguing with Chase, she'd turned and

walked away and—nothing. She'd woken up here, drunk.

But where was here? She tried to roll over, but she couldn't coordinate herself enough to move.

She heard the clinking of glass in the background. A man's laughter. A soft hand pushed her hair from her face and she turned toward it, trying to see who it was.

"She's coming out of it," a woman's voice said.

"Excellent. She needs to be able to walk on her own by the time Mr. Rodriguez arrives."

"She will."

"But she needs to be quiet."

"I'm doing my best. This is the first time you've ever wanted to sell a girl outside the auction."

"Cannot be helped. I don't have time to wait, and Rodriguez is ready to buy."

"She'll be ready, Mr. Androv."

A pause. "One hour."

"Yes, sir."

Chapter Thirty-Four

CHASE AND HIS TEAM, WHICH NOW INCLUDED BRANDY and Victoria as well as Viking's SEALs, were spreading out on the floor of the Walter E. Washington Convention Center in downtown DC. The center was jammed with technology displays, one of which was Zoprava's booth where they touted not only their antivirus software but also their research into ways to guard against cyberwarfare attacks. They were setting themselves up as the company to turn to for solutions in protecting vulnerable networks against hostile incursions.

Ironic considering Open Sky was another of Androv's businesses, but then most people didn't know that. It made a perverse sense, however. One of the most notorious networks of hackers also worked for the man who wanted to sell you a defense against hackers.

Chase strode through the crowd, heading for the stage at one end where the speakers were scheduled to be. He spotted Androv in a gathering and hot anger roared through him. He increased his pace. A voice spoke through the mic in his ear.

"Easy, Fiddler. We have to let him lead us to her. No good making a greasy spot in the carpet out of him."

Chase slowed. He knew his team leader was right. Tipping his hand before it was time was stupid. And he had enough experience to be patient.

He'd just never had to be patient when his insides were churning with this kind of fear. Not fear for himself, but fear for Sophie. He'd sworn to protect her, sworn he wouldn't let Androv get her.

He hadn't kept that promise, and it left a hollow in his chest. A big fucking hole that was so huge he felt like he'd fall into it if he looked over the edge. And keep falling forever. There was no getting out of this pit. No redemption whatsoever without Sophie.

He had to get her back. And then he had to tell her…

What?

Tell her fucking what?

This, dumbass. Tell her this.

About the hole. About the guilt. About the despair and anger and the way he hadn't ever felt as good as he'd felt the few days he'd spent with her. Not at first, no. But when they'd talked, when he'd understood her, when he'd tasted her—hell, he didn't want to stop tasting her. He needed more of that. He didn't know what that meant, he just knew he did.

And he had to figure out how to make it work. But first he had to get her back. He refused to think about what he'd do if he didn't get her back. If it was too late.

His throat ached and his vision blurred as he stared at the stage. As he waited for Androv to walk to the podium and spew his garbage.

The man finally went over and stood, looking out at the crowd like they owed him something. He spread his arms, jerking them skyward to make the cheers go higher. People obliged, yelling louder the longer he did it.

And then he turned his hands palms down and they quieted. He launched into a speech about the future, about networks the world over being joined together, about vulnerabilities and the need to prepare for disaster. To avert disaster.

Zoprava could do that, of course. Zoprava was working on the technology to protect the world's networks. Zoprava and Grigori Androv were concerned about the world. They had just donated twenty million dollars to refugee relief in the Middle East. They were cutting-edge, caring.

"You believe this guy?" Kid said into their ears. "Holy fuck."

"He's like a supervillain in a comic book," someone else said. One of the SEALs. Cody McCormick, maybe. Or Remy Marchand.

Chase liked those guys. Liked them a lot. But right now all he could think of was Sophie. He studied Androv. The man had never touched her according to Sophie. Never tried to fuck her. Impotent or gay—or so fucking narcissistic he wasn't interested in anyone but himself.

Though Chase had never found that to be the case.

Most men—especially the unbearably egomaniacal ones —liked fucking something, whether it was male or female.

Still, if this guy hadn't wanted Sophie, then he was stupid. But thank God he hadn't, because that meant he'd never had his filthy hands on her. Never tasted her sweetness. Never known the bliss of coming hard with Sophie underneath him, taking him in and making him feel like he was on top of the world.

Androv wrapped up his speech, sucked up the applause, pointed everyone to the Zoprava booth, and then worked his way through the crowd, shaking hands and smiling.

One of the SEALs was in that lineup, waiting to shake hands and place a small radio transmitter on Androv's jacket as he did so. Chase watched, saw the moment the SEAL—Zach Anderson—took Androv's hand and said something while gripping his elbow with the other. Then he smiled and stepped back while Androv continued on down the line.

"Got him," Viking said. "Let's roll."

———

ANDROV'S LIMOUSINE took him to the Ritz on 22nd Street, but he didn't go inside. Chase and Strike Team 1 rolled up across the street, their Suburban idling as they watched. The SEALs had traveled separately, but they were also there, ready to rocket into action. Everyone watched as Androv's car pulled up. Two women emerged from the hotel. One was tall and thin, the other not so tall. The shorter woman was veiled, and she stumbled as if she'd had a little too much to drink.

She was wearing a long coat that covered her entire body and high heels. Her legs, what they could see, were bare. She stumbled, and the coat flopped open. She was almost naked and stacked like a brick shithouse—

"Sophie!" Chase yelled, reaching for the door and tugging on the handle. He was out of the Suburban in two seconds flat, running for the portico of the Ritz. It was a distance away, but he could make it. He *had* to make it.

"Jesus, Fiddler, you're gonna compromise the op!"

He didn't know whose voice it was, didn't care. He kept running—and then the tall woman shoved Sophie in the car and got in behind her. It accelerated away from the curb.

He kept running, but the limo was fast disappearing. The Suburban rocketed up beside him and the door flew open.

"Get the fuck in here," Matt Girard ordered. "Now!"

Chase leapt inside and yanked the door closed as Hawk floored the SUV.

"Jesus, what the fuck?" Viking yelled into the mic. "Are you assholes insane?"

"Yes," Hawk growled. "Now help us catch that motherfucker."

Viking swore. "We're on it. But no more cowboy heroics, all right? Thought you fuckers knew better."

"If that was Ivy in there," Iceman grated suddenly, "would you be calm?"

The airwaves were silent for a long moment. "No. Fuck no."

"Thought so. That's Chase's woman in there, and we've got to get her before Androv hurts her."

Chase started to protest the first part of that statement, started to automatically deny what Ice had just said about Sophie being his woman. But, fuck, what was the point? He looked at the guys. The ones who could take their eyes off the road were looking back at him.

Yeah, fuck him, they knew what he didn't want to fully admit. Sophie *was* his. He wanted her—and he was going to fucking go get her. And then he was going to make Androv wish he'd never touched a hair on Sophie's head.

———

SOMETHING WAS VERY WRONG. Sophie knew it was. She wasn't as drunk as before, but she still couldn't seem to control her legs. And the world spun whenever she turned her head.

She was chilly. Her clothes felt strange. There was a coat, but beneath that, she felt almost naked. The coat rubbed her skin in places she didn't think it should. And there was a film over her face. It was dark but diaphanous. She could see through it, but not well.

"We seem to have company," a voice said. "You had better lose them."

"Yes, sir."

She was in a car, and it was going fast. Then it spun

around a corner, and she flopped against the person beside her. Whoever it was pushed her roughly.

"Hold her." The same voice as before. A familiar voice. Right in front of her.

Grigori's voice. A chill washed over her. Grigori had found her. He was going to kill her. Had he killed Chase? Where was Chase?

"Broke your files," she said.

"She spoke," Grigori said. "Why the fuck can she talk?"

"You wanted her to be able to walk. Talking is also a possibility." The woman's voice. Angry.

"She sounds worse than drunk," he said. "I couldn't make out a damn thing she said."

"Then that's a good thing."

"Is it? Rodriguez will want her sentient at the least. He's flown a long way, and he's going to want to enjoy his prize."

"He can still enjoy her," the woman said. "She won't fight."

"Files," Sophie said. But it came out sounding like *fzzzzz*.

Dammit!

"Shut her up."

Something poked into her skin. A needle. Sophie tried to fight, but her efforts were ineffectual. The drug moved through her system, flooding her with a strange ennui. She opened her mouth but nothing came out.

"Is she going to be able to walk?"

"Yes. But if you want her to seem perfectly unimpaired, it's not happening."

Grigori blew out a breath. "This is going to cost me, Annika. I am not happy. I'm even less happy that you didn't kill the man she was with like I told you to do."

The woman sniffed. "If you hadn't wanted to rush this, it would have been different. And I do not kill. You knew that when you sent me."

"You and your squeamishness," he bit out.

A hand smoothed down her arm, making her skin crawl. "She'll still fetch a nice price. She's quite lovely. And those breasts—dear God, they are fabulous. Rodriguez will pay handsomely for her."

"She would have earned me more in Monte Carlo. And now I have to sell her to a fucking Mexican drug lord."

Grigori paused and then growled something in Russian. She didn't know what he said, but the car sped up again, whipping around corners and rocketing down straightaways. Sophie gave up trying to sit straight.

She flopped like a fish—and then the tires squealed hard and the car stopped so fast she flew forward and then back before collapsing in a heap on the floor.

Before she could even attempt to right herself—and she didn't think she'd be able to do it anyway—rough hands grabbed her and hauled her up. Against a body. A male body judging by the size.

Something clicked and a hard metal cylinder pressed into her temple. Right about then the doors whipped open and men shouted.

Get the fuck out of there!

Hands above your head!

On your knees, motherfucker!

But the gun against her head didn't move, which meant the man didn't move. Outside the car, a woman cried. Annika.

The man holding Sophie shoved her toward the opening and out into the road, his arm around her neck.

"I will kill her," he said, and a little sob formed in her throat. It was Grigori's voice, and she knew he meant it.

"You do that and you're dead, Androv. I promise you that."

Chase!

"It looks like I may be dead anyway."

"Not if you let her go." A different man this time.

Grigori snorted. "What assurance do I have that you won't kill me when I do?"

"You don't have a goddamn one. Except this. You're the CEO of Zoprava and the world thinks you're a nice guy. If anyone dies here tonight, it won't look good for any of us. Too much fucking paperwork for me, and I hate paperwork. So do yourself a favor and let her go."

Grigori's arm tightened around her neck. "This bitch is worth a lot of money."

"Fuck it, Viking," Chase growled. "I'll do the paperwork for you—*after* I kill this motherfucker."

"I suggest you let her go, Androv," the man named Viking said. "Or my boy here is going to put a hole in your head that no amount of money will cure."

Grigori cut off her airway—and then he shoved her away and she stumbled and fell to the pavement, her knees and hands hitting hard, the pebbled surface scraping her skin.

And then hands were on her shoulders, beneath her arms, pulling her up, turning her into a solid body, her face mashing to his chest. He whipped the veil from her face, and cool night air rushed into her lungs as she sucked in a breath.

"Sophie, thank God."

"Chase," she said, but it came out sounding like *shhhhhhze*.

"Baby, you're okay. You're going to be okay."

"Chase…"

"I got you, baby. I got you. I'm not letting you go."

She clung to him just to be sure.

Chapter Thirty-Five

"HUMAN TRAFFICKING," MENDEZ SAID, THROWING A sheaf of papers down on the table in front of Grigori Androv. The man didn't even flinch, just looked up with hot, crazy eyes.

They'd brought him back to HOT HQ hooded and cuffed, and now they had him in a room with Mendez, Viking, Chase, Hawk, Richie Rich, Iceman, Kid, and Brandy. Victoria was with Sophie, taking care of her and getting her tended to by the on-call physician assigned to HOT.

Chase had wanted to be there with her, but he'd needed to be here even more. Because he needed to hear what Mendez had found out, and he needed to know how they were going to stop Androv. It wasn't as easy as locking the asshole up and throwing away the key. The man was, unfortunately, respected by those who had no idea just how evil he was.

And HOT was a military organization, not a civil one. They weren't the police or the justice system. They couldn't prosecute him, couldn't put him in jail. That was up to a DA.

"You sell women and children, Androv," Mendez said, his jaw tight. "You promise them a better life and then you sell them into sexual slavery. Your people shake down the pimps regularly, taking a cut."

"It is called free enterprise," Androv said, his Russian accent thicker than normal. "And you have no proof. This is not proof."

Mendez sat on the corner of the desk and swung his leg casually. Like this was just a friendly get-together. Anyone who knew Mendez knew that the calmer he was, the worse it was. In fact, he hadn't made eye contact with Chase since he'd arrived, and far from making Chase feel like everything was cool about the fact he'd gone off on his own mission, he was pretty sure there was going to be some hell to pay. Mendez had helped him and Sophie, but no way was the colonel going to let this pass without comment.

"You kidnapped and drugged Sophie Nash. By your own admission, you were planning to sell her to a Mexican drug lord. I have the recordings. I also have your files. Everything in them. The women, the underage girls, the records of where you sent them. And then there are the private sales, like you were attempting tonight. You kept very meticulous records."

Androv lifted his chin. "My name is nowhere on those files. Forgeries, all of it. Faked by your people so you could frame me. As for the recordings..." He shrugged. "I speak at a lot of events. A skilled engineer could easily make a mix of my words to implicate me."

"So that's how you want to play it, huh? It's a setup, you did nothing wrong, we want to take you down." Mendez looked thoughtful. "Sounds reasonable to me."

Then he leaned forward, his expression deadly. "You've sold your last human being, Androv. It ends here. I *will* destroy your ability to do business in every single location named in those files. I've shared the information with the intelligence community. Teams are moving to shut down every single operation you have around the world. By morning, you won't have a network anymore."

Beads of sweat broke out on Androv's brow. He looked angry—and worried. A cornered animal was a bad thing, but there was nothing the man could do right now.

Mendez stood and Androv shrank against his seat in fear. It was a reasonable response considering the look on Mendez's face.

"I'm turning the information in your files over to the district attorney. I'm turning you over to the police. Will they let you go? Probably. But know this—you fucking touch Sophie Nash again, you fucking breathe the same air she breathes, you're dead. *Dead.* I'm doing things the legal way tonight—you'd better take advantage of it."

Androv looked suddenly defiant. "You threatened to kill me. These men heard it."

Mendez's eyebrows went up. "Really? Did I?" He turned to look at them. "Did I threaten this man's life?"

"I didn't hear anything," Richie Rich said.

"Me neither," Ice said.

"Didn't hear a damn thing."

"See?" Mendez smiled. It was anything but friendly. "No threats here. Only a promise, Androv. Fuck with Sophie Nash and you die. Painfully."

And then he said something in Russian, and Androv's expression changed. He wasn't defiant now. He was terrified. And, fuck, Chase didn't know what the hell the colonel had said, but the angry harshness of his voice and the shock of hearing him speak another language was disorienting enough for Chase. He hated to think what his reaction would be if he could actually understand the message.

Androv cowered in his seat. Chase wanted to punch the motherfucker for good measure, but there was no way he was getting through his teammates to do so. Probably a good thing since he likely wouldn't stop if he did.

"Fiddler," Mendez barked, and Chase's head snapped up. "With me. Now."

Fuck.

————

GRIGORI ANDROV WAS FURIOUS. It was after three in the morning, and his lawyer had finally gotten him released from the jail where he'd spent the past several hours since those military assholes had handed him over to the police. He'd had a lot of time to think and to plan.

Open Sky would get to work immediately. They would discover the identities of every man who had been in that room with the asshole who'd threatened him—and then they would pay. He would not be the one destroyed, because he would destroy them first.

Yes, this was a huge mess now. His files were in the hands of the police, and no doubt now in the hands of the prosecutor in New York who'd pushed that bitch of a maid to file charges against him.

But he had money and power, and he was willing to use them. He would not lose everything he'd worked for because someone thought they could threaten him. Oh no, he would show them a thing or two—and they would be the ones who died painful deaths, not him. Even if it took him ten years, he would get them all. The last thing they would hear would be his name.

After his lawyer dropped him off, he called Sergei from the hotel phone. He'd had his cell phone returned to him when he'd been released, but the battery was dead. He tossed it on a table and dialed from memory.

The phone rang and rang, but Sergei did not answer. Grigori curled his free hand into a fist as anger whipped through him like a tornado. Sergei had failed at everything he'd been asked to do. He'd returned from Paris with nothing to show for it. He'd failed to get the flash drive back. He'd sent men to capture Sophie and her protector, but they'd failed to do the job and gotten themselves killed in the process.

Failed, failed, failed. Everyone had failed, and Grigori was ready to rip someone apart for this disaster.

But Sergei did not answer. He stabbed the disconnect button with a finger when it went to voice mail. Then he dialed another number.

This was not one he should dial tonight, but he was

too angry to care. The voice that answered was cold, deadly. "You are not calling from an authorized number. Who the hell is this?"

"Androv."

The voice on the other end chilled even further. "What the fuck is this, Androv? Are you insane?"

"You are going to find out some things for me. If you do not, the money I'm pumping into your campaign will dry up, do you understand me?"

"I'm listening."

When he finally hung up the phone, Grigori was quite certain that Mark DeWitt understood precisely where he was coming from. He started to remove his suit and prepare for bed, but there was a knock on his door. He went over and looked through the peephole. Then he yanked the door open when he saw who was on the other side.

"Where the fuck have you been? And what went wrong in Paris?" Grigori demanded. "What has happened to you, Sergei? You have never been this incompetent, this stupid—"

His mouth snapped shut at the sight of Sergei— his right-hand man, his coconspirator, the architect of so much of what they'd built—leveling a pistol at him.

"You've said quite enough, Grigori. It's time to shut the fuck up."

Sergei jerked the pistol and Grigori took a step back. Another man stepped through the door then, a big, hulking man who also held a pistol. This one had a silencer on it.

"What is this, Sergei? You would betray me? I built you into what you are today!"

Sergei laughed. "No, I built you. And now I've been ordered to tear you down. We're done, Grigori."

Grigori's heart hammered. "You would kill me after everything we've been through? We are brothers, Sergei."

Sergei looked almost sad as he shook his head. "No, I won't kill you. I can't. But Oleg can."

"You're insane," Grigori hissed. "Insane!"

"You've taken too many risks, Grigori. You've let your ego outweigh your caution, and that is not good. You cannot be trusted any longer."

"Don't do this, Sergei," Grigori pleaded. "We can fix everything. They have no proof, no way of making it stick to me—"

"You're a loose cannon. It is time." Sergei looked at Oleg, who nodded his big head without ever taking his gaze off Grigori.

"Got it from here, boss," he said.

Sergei walked out the door and Grigori turned to run. If he could make it to the bathroom, he could lock the door and—

He dropped before he'd taken the first step.

———

ONCE HE REACHED THE CAR, Sergei picked up his private cell phone and dialed a number.

"Is it done?" the man on the other end clipped out.

"Yes. You may rest assured that Zoprava's support of

your campaign will continue. We trust that your support of us will continue as well."

"It's a mutually beneficial arrangement. So long as it stays that way, I see no reason for either of us to pull out of the deal."

"*Do svidaniya*, Congressman."

Sergei punched the button to end the call. Then he started to whistle.

———

SOPHIE SLEPT. When she woke up, she felt woozy, kind of hungover, but mostly she felt okay. She turned her head and saw she was in a room with some seriously nice furniture. Silk drapes, antiques, tall ceilings that looked like they belonged in a historic home. She pushed herself up on an elbow and took in her surroundings.

A hotel perhaps. A nice one.

But the door opened and a familiar figure walked in. He was carrying a tray, and her heart leapt with joy. When he looked up, his eyes tangled with hers—and the truth hit her hard.

She was a goner. A total goner for this man.

He did not feel the same way; she knew that. And it hurt so much, like someone had taken a hot poker and jammed it right into her heart. It was excruciating, and yet she was just desperate enough to keep on feeling it so long as he didn't go away.

"You're awake." His smile was like sunshine after weeks of stormy skies.

"Where are we?"

He came over and set the tray on the table beside the bed. "At Hawk and Gina's place."

She blinked at him. "I…"

"Waterman's Cove on the Eastern Shore of Maryland. Cute town, historic. Gina bought this place when they got married, and they live here most of the year. Hawk's not in, uh, the military anymore, but this is still one of our homes away from home."

Sophie processed this. "I don't remember coming here."

"You were pretty out of it. The doc says Androv injected you with fentanyl in order to control you. Once she determined you were going to be okay, we brought you to Hawk's since I don't have a place anymore."

A twinge of guilt spiked inside her. "I'm sorry. I know it's my fault."

He sat on the bed and put his hand against her cheek, into her hair. Her skin flamed where he touched. Oh, she wanted more of that. So much more.

"It's stuff, Sophie. Stuff is replaceable."

She swallowed. "What happened to Grigori?"

Chase's mouth tightened, his eyes hardening for a second. But then he smiled and ran his thumb along her cheekbone. "He's not going to hurt you, Sophie. Not ever again."

She sucked in a breath. "You didn't—?"

She couldn't say it. She didn't want another man on Chase's conscience for her sake, but she was very much afraid that he did.

"No, it wasn't me," he said, and relief washed

through her. "We turned him over to the police. He bonded out eventually—and someone shot him in his hotel. It was on the news a couple of hours ago. No idea what happened, but he's dead."

"Oh my God."

"Are you sorry he's dead?"

She shook her head. "No… and maybe that makes me a terrible person, but no, I'm really not. It's still a shock though."

"Yeah, I guess it is. But I'm glad someone iced him. Saved me the trouble if he ever got near you again."

"I was afraid he'd killed you. When I woke up and realized I'd been kidnapped, I thought the worst."

And her heart had nearly broken in two.

"They only tased me, thank God."

"Did it hurt?"

He grinned. "Not as much as the ass-chewing I got from my colonel last night."

She blinked. "I thought he was helping us. Hawk said he'd been informed when he came and that he'd given us the passports. I assumed that meant he was on our side."

"Oh, he was helping and he's definitely on our side —but that doesn't mean he wasn't going to ream me when he got a chance. Going to Paris technically made me AWOL. Colonels don't like that shit, even when the ends justify the means."

Her fault. She'd pretty much given him no choice when she'd shown up and gotten his apartment blasted to bits. "I'm sorry I got you in trouble."

Chase hadn't stopped touching her. His fingers

stroked along her skin, leaving little tingles of sensation in their path. "And I'm sorry we fought, Sophie."

Her heart clenched with pain. The hurt from their fight hadn't gone away yet. "You said we didn't have anything special, that you could get pu—"

She didn't finish that sentence because his lips crashed down on hers. She opened to his invasion, moaning softly as he kissed her. Her nipples beaded tight and her pussy grew wet.

He pulled away from her all too soon, even while she clung to him, and smiled softly as he stood and reached for the tray.

"Look, you need to have this breakfast before it gets cold. You haven't eaten since you picked at that pizza, and you need to be strong for this conversation."

She scooted her way up in the bed, dragging the sheet with her. Then she lifted it and looked under. "I'm not wearing anything!"

"When we found you, all you had on was some underwear and a trench coat. I wasn't letting you wear that shit to sleep in."

She felt herself blushing, which was ridiculous, but it was the way he said he wasn't letting her wear the things they'd found her in, as if they were poisonous somehow.

And maybe they were, considering Grigori had likely had his hands all over them. She shuddered, and though she tried not to let it show, Chase saw it.

"What's wrong, baby?"

Her throat was tight. "I don't know what happened last night, Chase. How do I know he didn't…?"

She couldn't finish the sentence. Chase set the tray

down and then took her face in his hands, making her look at him.

"Honey, the doc verified it when she examined you—no one raped you. No one." He kissed her forehead. "Grigori was trying to sell you to a Mexican named Benito Rodriguez, according to the woman who was in the car. She says she was with you from the moment they grabbed you at Hawk's."

"How did they know where to find us?"

The corners of his mouth tightened. "We don't know that yet. We may never know." He nodded to the tray. "Now eat those eggs before they get cold."

He let her go and she picked up the fork. She dug into the eggs without much enthusiasm—but after the first bite, she was sold. She really was hungry, and she ate several bites before she looked up at Chase.

He was watching her eat. He didn't look angry or conflicted at all. He looked... content. She put down her fork and tilted her head as she gazed at him.

"What?"

"You're eating like you don't give a fuck. I like that."

Her cheeks felt rosy. Damn him. "Well, maybe I don't. This time."

"You never should, babe. You're gorgeous. The only ugly people are the ones who tell you that you need to change to suit their definition of beauty."

"You say stuff like that and it makes my chest hurt."

His brows drew together. "Why?"

"Because nobody ever said anything like that to me. I like that you do... but I don't know what it means, Chase. Because I don't know where you're coming from.

And I don't know whether to just be happy and believe you or to worry that in the next few hours everything will change."

She could kick herself for going there right now when all she wanted was to sit here, eat the eggs, and enjoy the fact he was with her. The simple things. Just for a few hours, until it all went to shit again and he got pissed off at their situation and told her there was nothing here worth fighting for.

"I said I was going to be here for you. I meant that. I said some stupid things last night—and I don't want to say anything stupid now, so please just eat the eggs."

Sophie ate her eggs and toast while he watched. When she was done, he took the tray and set it on the table. Then he got a robe from the closet and brought it over to her.

"Can you stand?"

"I think so."

He held the robe open and she got out of bed, slipping her arms into the robe and then turning and belting it tight. When she met his gaze again, his eyes glittered with heat.

"Damn," he said. "Didn't think helping you into a robe would give me a hard-on, but it definitely does."

She reached out and put her hand on his chest. He was warm and solid. "I like this, Chase, this playfulness between us. But I have to know what you're thinking about us. About this."

"I'm thinking I've never felt as alone as I did last night when I watched you walk away from me. And then I'm thinking I've never been as scared as when they took you. I would have taken a bullet for you, Sophie. I would have done anything to stop them from hurting you, to prevent you from going through even a moment of terror."

She cried out and clutched his shirt with both hands then. "Don't you ever think I'd want you to take a bullet to stop me from being scared. I'd rather be scared, I'd rather know you were still out there, still breathing, still coming for me even while I was afraid for my life than think for even a second that you'd sacrificed yourself to prevent that from happening."

He tugged her into his arms and held her hard against him then. "Sophie," he whispered, his lips against her hair. "Goddamn, baby, you kill me. I don't fucking deserve you."

She wrapped her arms around him, held him tight. "I… I care so much, Chase. So much it hurts. I can't stand the idea of your leaving me. Last night, when you said that you could get pussy anywhere—"

"Honey."

"I nearly died," she finished. "After everything we've been through…"

He rubbed a hand up and down her spine. The other cupped the back of her head and held her against him. "When I didn't know where you were, I thought I'd fallen into a hole that I would never get out of again." He took a breath. "A deep, dark hole where nothing good could ever happen. That's when I knew I couldn't give you up. That I needed to be with you. Fuck Tyler— and my mom will understand. She'll have to. And she'll love you, Sophie… because I do."

Chapter Thirty-Six

JESUS, HE COULDN'T BELIEVE HE'D SAID THAT—BUT IT was true. He couldn't imagine what else this could be, this need to be near her, this overwhelming emotion boiling inside him. This thought that he could never be close enough to her, that possessing her wasn't nearly the limit of what he wanted from her.

She pushed herself back so she could see his face. "You're serious."

"Yeah, I'm serious."

Her smile trembled at the corners. "I think I love you too."

"Think?"

She sniffed. "No, I know I do—but I keep expecting I'm going to wake up and find out this was all a crazy dream." Her fingers curled in his shirt. "Please tell me I'm not dreaming."

He let his fingers skim over her cheek, her jaw, her neckline. He wanted to go further—so much further—but she'd been through a lot recently. Too much to assume she felt well enough for all the things he wanted to do to her.

"You aren't dreaming, baby. This is as real as it gets."

She laughed and hauled him close. "Do you have any idea the kinds of things I want to do to you right now?"

"Honey, you have to take it easy. Androv drugged you, and you're bound to be feeling the effects—"

"Shower with me. Please. I want to touch you, Chase."

He let her lead him into the bathroom where she untied the robe and slipped it from her shoulders. It fell in a puddle at her feet and his mouth went dry. So fucking beautiful.

His cock swelled, aching with the need to be inside her. Sophie reached into the shower enclosure and turned on the water. And then she attacked his belt, whipping it open and unbuttoning his jeans. He gave in and ripped his T-shirt over his head with one hand, then dropped the garment as she shoved his jeans and under-wear down his hips.

His cock sprang free, and she dropped to her knees, grasping it with both hands. Then she looked up at him, her pretty eyes filled with love and desire, and he knew he wouldn't last very long if she got her mouth on him.

He tried to reach for her, pull her up, but she shook her head. "No, Chase. I want to taste you. I need to taste you."

Her pink tongue swirled around the head of his cock, and then she took him into her mouth.

Chase groaned. "Baby, no, can't do it this way. I want to be in you when I come."

"Give me a minute," she said, licking the length of him. "Just a minute."

He put a hand on her head and somehow resisted the urge to hold her hard while he fucked her mouth. His balls tingled and his spine arched. "Baby, you have to stop. Now."

But she didn't stop and he reached down, grabbed her, and yanked her up until he could smash his mouth to hers. She wrapped her arms around his neck with a sigh.

"Oh Chase," she murmured between kisses. "Love you. It's crazy, but I do."

"Fuck yeah, baby," he said, lifting her up with his hands under her ass and then carrying her into the shower. "Love everything about you, Sophie. Every fucking thing."

Water flowed over their heads, their bodies. Chase set her down and filled his hands with her breasts. Then he licked and sucked her nipples while she clung to him, making desperate little sounds in her throat.

But he wasn't done with her. He dropped down her body, dropped to his knees—and then he picked up one of her legs and put it over his shoulder. She supported herself against the wall with one hand, the other twisting into his hair.

"Chase, oh my God…" She gasped as he put his mouth on her pussy.

He loved the sounds she made as he swirled his tongue around her clit, the way she rocked against his face when she wanted to direct him right where she needed him, the way her hand tightened in his hair when he teased her too much.

Chase buried his tongue inside her while he worked her with his fingers, and then he sucked on her clit, flicking it with his tongue while he did so.

Sophie came hard. He knew because she swore— and her hand in his hair was almost painful as she kept him right where she wanted him. Her body shuddered and shuddered with her orgasm.

He surged to his feet and took her with him. She squeaked, but then she wrapped her legs around him and he sank her down onto his cock.

He realized right away that something was different. "Oh shit, the condom."

She kissed him. "It's okay. I have an implant... I guess I hoped when I moved to New York, I might have a bit more sex in my life. Didn't happen until you."

"I'm glad you didn't get freaky with anyone else," he said softly. And then his heart melted as he thought about how much she trusted him. "I never go ungloved, Sophie. You need to know that. I'm good."

"I know you are, baby," she said. "Now please, for the love of everything, make me come again."

He pushed her back against the wall and started moving inside her, slow at first. "You're going to come all right," he said. "But with me this time."

"I'll try. Don't make me wait though."

He snorted. "Not sure *I* can wait, honey."

He moved faster, pistoning his hips, driving up into her. He was so deep into her, so hard against her, that he thought nothing could ever be more perfect than this. Yeah, they were fucking—but they were also making love. He'd never done that before. And yeah, it was different somehow. Better. The best ever.

"Sophie, baby, come for me."

She threw her head back, her neck arching—and then she let go, moaning loud and long. Chase followed, coming harder than he ever had in his life as he shot himself into her. It felt fucking fantastic. Amazing. He pressed his face to her throat, breathed her in.

When he straightened, Sophie opened her eyes and smiled. And his world lit up.

"I love you," she said simply, and the gravity of that statement nearly took him to his knees.

"I love you too, Soph."

He set her on her feet and she clung to him. "If you want to wait to tell your mother and Tyler, I'm fine with that."

He gently pulled her head back by the rope of her wet hair. "We're not waiting to tell anyone. I'm not hiding from anyone." He frowned as he thought of something. "But Sophie, baby, I can't move to wherever you are. I'm a soldier, and I have a commitment. It's not like quitting a job and finding another one. Uncle Sam owns my ass for a few years yet."

"Then I guess I'm moving here. Like you said, there are acting opportunities in DC. And even if there aren't, I don't care. We'll figure it out."

He lowered his mouth to hers, kissed her gently. "Yeah, we will."

TWO WEEKS LATER...

"WELL, THAT CERTAINLY EXPLAINS A LOT," Gina Domenico was saying to Chase as he strummed a guitar while she stood beside him and crossed her arms. "Damn, I thought you looked familiar from time to time... but I would have never guessed you were Tyler Nash's son."

Sophie smiled at the way Chase shrugged and kept on strumming. He was good on a guitar and he had a good voice too. He'd apparently never treated his team-mates to his singing ability because, it turned out, he sounded a little too much like a certain blues musician. When he'd opened his mouth tonight at Buddy's Bar, more than one of them had stopped and gaped at him.

Sophie was standing at a bar table with Evie, who'd been so kind to her the night she'd returned from Paris, and Victoria, Olivia, Georgie, Lucky, Grace, and Emily —who, it turned out, was Victoria's sister. She was still trying to understand how all these women fit with the men, meaning who was whose, but she knew she'd get it eventually.

Plus she liked them. They were all so sweet. Including Gina, who was about a hundred times more famous than Tyler. Tyler was a well-known guitarist and vocalist in the blues world. That was nothing compared to mainstream pop.

When Sophie had emerged from Hawk and Gina's

guest room two weeks ago, freshly in love and stunned at that turn of events, Gina had hugged her and promptly tried to mother her. It was rather amusing considering they were close in age, but with two young children underfoot, mothering people was just sort of natural to the superstar.

Buddy's was raucous and fun, a real let-down-your-hair kind of place. Everyone drank beer or wine or soda, and they ordered all kinds of fried things like chicken wings, burgers, fries, mushrooms, and cheese sticks. The worst kind of food but also some of the best tasting.

Sophie took it easy, but she ate. Chase grinned over at her from where he sat strumming the guitar. He'd even fed her a cheese stick with sauce. Considering all the sex they'd been having, she figured she could afford a few cheese sticks here and there.

"So there's still no word on who killed Grigori Androv?" Olivia asked, pushing a platinum-blond lock of hair behind her ear.

"No, but his closest friend who grew up with him in an orphanage inherits everything, including Zoprava." Victoria shook her head. "Plenty of motive there."

Sophie sipped her beer and quietly agreed. Sergei Turov had put on a good show, but she figured it had to be a show. He'd cried on the news, vowed to find whoever had harmed his friend. He blamed shadowy military organizations, foreign governments, and rival software firms.

He had an airtight alibi for Grigori's murder, but that didn't mean he hadn't ordered it done.

"Well, he wasn't a nice man," Evie said, her hand

resting over her belly. She barely had a bump but apparently she was pregnant. Emily had a bump as well, but even smaller. "He snatched Sophie and would have sold her to the highest bidder if y'all hadn't stopped him."

She said the *y'all* for Victoria who, it turned out, was one of the team. So was Lucky, except she and her husband had been flying home when everything went down and they'd missed the excitement.

Georgie looked at Sophie as she nibbled on a fried mushroom. "How did your parents take the news of you and Chase?"

These women had embraced her as one of their own. Whether she wanted besties or not, she seemed to have them. Oddly enough, she liked it even if she was still getting used to it. These people were genuine—unlike the people she'd grown up with in LA, the people who ran in her parents' circles.

"They were surprised," she said. "But what can they say? We're adults."

That was the easy way of putting it. Tyler had been a bit pissed, but that's because he'd made it about him. Specifically, that Chase didn't care about her and was just nailing her to get back at him.

That had nearly earned him a punch in the throat, judging by the look on Chase's face at the time, but he'd refrained. For her sake, she knew. They'd left California that night—and then he'd told her on the plane that if she wanted to spend any holidays with Tyler and her mother, she just needed to tell him which ones and they'd work it out. He'd be there by her side if he wasn't on a mission and to hell with Tyler's bullshit.

"No," she'd said, "I'm not particularly interested in any holidays right now."

Chase's mother had welcomed them with open arms. Carrie Daniels was every bit as sweet as she'd ever sounded on the phone, and she'd embraced Sophie right away.

Chase told Sophie later that his mother had actually raised her voice at him when he'd suggested he'd been worried she might be upset about him and Sophie.

"Honey," she'd told him, "Tyler Nash gave me the greatest gift I ever got in this life—you. Nothing he can do, nothing he has ever done, will take that away from me."

And just like that, their families knew about them. Now they could get on with the business of building a life together. Since Chase had lost everything in the fire that claimed his apartment, they had to find a place to live, which they had. A cute town house near the military base where he worked.

She'd moved her stuff down from New York last weekend. She and Chase had driven a U-Haul into Manhattan, then packed it up and headed back to DC. She'd said good-bye to her job at the restaurant, gone to see her acting teacher, said good-bye to a few friends—and that was it. Good-bye New York, hello DC.

Chase worried she'd be sad, but she was excited. Life was full of new possibilities, and she was embracing them.

Evie cut her gaze to the men. "Double D's the only one left."

Sophie looked over to where Dex Davidson stood

with Chase and Emily's husband, Flash. He was a handsome guy—they all were, really—and apparently he was the only one with no girlfriend.

"Maybe he's gay," Emily said, and Georgie snorted.

"Girl, warn a body before you say something like that!"

Olivia handed her a napkin to clean up the spray from her soda. "If he's gay, it's a waste for our team."

"He's not gay," Sophie said, and they all looked at her. She could feel her face reddening. "I mean, I don't think he's gay. He seemed interested in me when we first met, though Chase put a stop to that pretty quickly."

"Yeah, I've seen him flirting with waitresses," Grace said. "I don't think he's gay either."

"We need to find him a girl," Lucky said. "He's the only one who shows up to our gatherings alone now."

"All right, ladies, who do we know that's single?" Evie asked. They started to talk but then grew quiet as the men broke up their conversation and moved toward them.

"Hey, baby, how you doing?" Chase sidled up to her and put an arm around her.

Sophie leaned into him. "Great, honey. How about you?"

"Never better."

The door opened then and Matt Girard walked in. He'd been outside, running an errand for her. When she saw him, he tipped his chin at her. She smiled and took Chase's hand. The others exchanged looks between them.

"You got a minute, babe?" she asked.

Chase's brows drew together. "Sure. What's up?"

"Come on."

She led him toward the door and then outside while the rest of the team gathered around them. In the parking lot, the guys she'd been told were SEALs stood in a row, blocking what she wanted Chase to see. She turned to him.

"I told you I'd fix everything I broke, Chase," she said, and his eyes gleamed as he caught her close.

"You already fixed everything, baby. You fixed me."

Her heart thumped when he said stuff like that. "No, that's not what I meant."

She turned to the guys, and they parted like she was Moses and they were the Red Sea. Behind them, a shiny midnight-blue Corvette with a white stripe sat on the pavement, looking badass and, well, shiny.

Her heart hammered as she waited for Chase's reaction.

"It's a C3 model, like yours," she said.

He'd had his pulled out of the brush, but it was trashed pretty badly. And since it was made of fiberglass, it took more time and money to repair than the worth of the car.

"Holy shit," Chase breathed. "Sophie, what did you do?"

She shrugged, happy and embarrassed. Around them, his teammates and their women grinned huge grins.

"I said I'd buy you a new one. Well, it's technically not new, but it's a good one. I had Matt check it out for me, and I did a deal with the guy."

She had enough money in the bank to buy a new one, but since she wasn't going to take money from her mother and Tyler anymore, she felt like saving it for her and Chase was the right thing to do while they built a life together. Chase had agreed, which was why he looked so surprised now.

Matt walked over with the keys and held them up. Chase took them, and she breathed a little easier. But he still hadn't said much.

Then he turned to her, his eyes shining with so much love it hurt. He picked her up, even as she squeaked, and spun her in a circle.

"You are amazing, Sophie Nash. Marry me, because I'm never letting you go."

Sophie's eyes filled with tears. "Marry you? We don't even know if we can live together without killing each other yet."

"Yeah, I know—but say yes now and then one day, when it's right, we'll do it."

Sophie sucked in a breath. And then she threw her head back and laughed. He was crazy, but she loved his brand of crazy. Because it was all for her.

"Yes, Chase. Absolutely, yes."

He put her down and kissed her hard. Then he led her to the car and opened the door for her. When she was settled, he kissed her again, then went around and got in the driver's seat.

The car roared to life and Chase shook his head at the throaty growl. "Damn, that's enough to make a man get a hard-on." He smiled at her, his eyes crinkling. "You ready to go for a ride?"

"With you, always."

"Yeah, that's pretty much the way I feel too." He leaned over and kissed her. "This is the second-best present you ever gave me."

She blinked. "What's the first?"

He gave her a mock frown. "Baby, you don't know?"

Her heart skipped. "Me?"

"That's right, Sophie. You." He pulled her hand to his mouth. "You changed my life when you crashed back into it. I was pissed at the time... but I thank God that you did. Woke me up to what was missing."

"I love you, Chase."

"And that right there is why you are the best present I ever got. You love me in spite of myself."

She wrapped a hand around his neck and pulled his mouth to hers. "No, I love you because of you—the man who helped me love myself for who I am instead of who I thought I wanted to be."

"Damn, Sophie, you know how to get a guy in the feels."

She giggled. "Take me home and I'll get you some-where else."

He put the car in gear. "You got it, baby. But be aware that I'm going to get you too."

She sure hoped so. Chase floored it. The cheers of his teammates followed them out of the parking lot. Sophie couldn't contain her smile. It came from the inside, the best kind of smile possible.

Life with Chase would be filled with surprises, she was certain. And she looked forward to them all.

THANKS FOR READING HOT PROTECTOR! Next up is Dex Davidson. When Dex was abandoned at the altar by the woman he loved, he threw himself into his military career. Five years later, Annabelle Quinn desperately needs his black ops skills. You really don't want to miss the fireworks and emotion! Keep reading for an exciting sneak peek at HOT ADDICTION!

HOT ADDICTION Sneak Peek

Five years ago...

Dexter Davidson checked his watch for the thousandth time that morning. It was nearing noon and his bride-to-be was over an hour late. His father stood in the chancel, his rented tuxedo making him appear distinguished and genteel rather than rough and worn like the farmer he was. But the look on his face was what killed Dex the most. It was one of pity and a growing resignation.

"Fuck this," Dex growled as he clenched his jaw tight and walked down the aisle, between the rows of pews where the guests waited for the ceremony to start. The chapel doors were open to the outside because it was springtime and warm. But it was also raining. A soft, gentle rain, but rain nonetheless.

Perhaps the rain had caused a delay. Dex stood in the open door and took his phone from his pocket. Annabelle still hadn't answered his texts. He sent another one, just in case, and felt his heart shrivel just a little bit more when no answer came.

He tried calling, but it went to voice mail without even ringing. "Belle," he said, his throat tight and his eyes burning, "where are you, baby? I'm worried. Please let me know you're safe. If you've changed your mind, it's okay. Just let me know."

It wasn't okay if she'd changed her mind, but what else could he say? Annabelle Quinn had been his girl for the past four years. He'd fallen madly in love with her in an instant. He'd known her most of his life, had ignored her for much of it because she was his little sister's best friend, but one day, *pow!* She'd smiled at him the way she had a million times before—and he was done for. He'd been hers from that moment forward.

And now they were supposed to be getting married. He'd come home on leave from the Army at Christmas and asked her to marry him. She'd said yes. She and his sister had planned everything while he went back to Afghanistan and did his best to stay alive. He didn't know how long he stood there before he felt a presence beside him.

"I'm sorry, Dex." Katie put a hand on his arm. "She's not coming."

He wanted to deny it, but the look on Katie's face told him all he needed to know. He felt hollow inside. Empty. Because he knew she was right. He'd known it deep in his gut for the past twenty minutes.

His sister's eyes were shiny. He took the phone from her hand and stared at the text message on the screen until the words blurred together and his heart burned away, turning to ash.

Belle: *I can't, Katie. Please don't hate me, but I can't. Tell Dex I'm sorry. I shouldn't have let it go this far. I've thought for a while that marrying him wasn't right, that I'm not the woman for him—I should have been brave enough to say so. He deserves more than this. Tell him.*

Dex stood there for a long moment, his gut roiling with emotions he didn't know how to process. He dropped the phone and strode out into the rain while Katie called after him. He put his uniform hat on, shoved his hands into his pockets, and kept walking down the muddy road, away from the country church that Annabelle had insisted was the place she wanted to be married.

He didn't know where he was going or what he was going to do when he got there. All he knew was that his life would never be the same again.

CHAPTER ONE

Annabelle Quinn-Archer couldn't get over the feeling she was being followed. She swiveled her head to look up and down the street but saw nothing out of the ordinary. She'd had that feeling a lot in the past month, ever since Eric had died in Africa, but there was never anyone waiting in the bushes to jump out at her. She'd varied her routine, never doing the same thing long enough to get predictable, and she'd hired a private detective to check for anomalies.

He'd found nothing. She'd paid him and sent him on his way, feeling like an idiot for being paranoid. But still, there was something that didn't feel quite right to her. Maybe she was overworked as her friend Molly had suggested, or maybe she was still reeling from the fact her husband was dead and there'd been almost nothing left of him once the animals were finished with his body.

A mixture of emotions rained down on her, like always, when she thought of Eric. She hadn't wished him dead, but she also couldn't be sorry he was out of her life. Guilt sat like a stone in her belly at her inability to care that he was gone. All she could feel was relief that she was finally out from under his thumb. For the first time in five years, she could breathe.

Guilty, guilty, guilty.

Maybe that's why she thought she was being followed. Maybe it was just the truckload of guilt perched on her shoulder like a malevolent gargoyle that was wearing her down and making her paranoid.

Annabelle ducked into the Archer Industries building and headed for her office, greeting people with a smile that shook at the corners. They were worried about what would happen to their jobs now that Eric was dead, but she intended to fight for their future. They still had a team of talented engineers, and they had a revolutionary—though flawed—product. Development would continue.

When she got inside her office, she shut the door and sagged against it, closing her eyes and taking a deep breath. Life over the past month had been chaotic. Stress lived with her these days.

As if she didn't feel guilty enough, there was also the fact that *he* was back in town. Dex. She'd seen him from a distance just two days ago, walking into the Briar City Diner with his sister and her family. Annabelle's stomach had twisted hard at the sight of him. Of them, actually, since she and Katie were no longer on speaking terms.

She missed her best friend—but she'd had no idea how much she'd missed the man she'd once planned to marry until she saw him again. Dexter Davidson, six foot three inches of pure muscle with dark hair, a five-day scruff, and deep brown eyes. Her first love.

Her first *lover*.

What would life have been like if she'd married him that day?

"Dammit," she muttered before opening her eyes and going over to her desk. She had work to do and no time to get lost in maudlin thoughts about Dex. He hated her. And why wouldn't he? She'd skipped out on their wedding and then married another man three weeks later. And not just any man, but his fiercest rival.

It didn't matter that she'd had to do it. It only mattered that she *had* done it. He would never forgive her for it. Katie had tried, bless her, but when Annabelle married Eric so soon after she'd left Dex at the altar—well, that was the end of that.

Her gaze strayed to the photo of the little girl on her desk. Charlotte was her world, her reason for existing. So long as she had her daughter, life would be okay. That's why she had to fight for Archer Industries and why she had to succeed. Eric's estate wasn't as big as people thought. He'd mortgaged everything to the hilt in order to live the lifestyle of a successful CEO.

He'd been counting on this latest technology to make a fortune for the company and for himself. Unfortunately, the Helios project had national-security implications, which meant he couldn't sell it to foreign governments or entities. But the US government wanted to buy it and they'd offered a very handsome price on delivery. In the meantime, they would fund development.

Eric should have been happy, but he hadn't been. He'd raged and complained for days, swearing the technology was worth five times what the US was buying it for. She'd stopped listening to his diatribes. Eventually he'd calmed down, and work returned to normal.

But now he was dead, and the project had veered off schedule. Annabelle took a determined breath and started to pick up her desk phone to call the lead engineer, Marshall Porter.

The phone buzzed before she could make the call. "Yes?"

Her secretary was on the other end. "Mrs. Archer, there's a call for you from a Mr. Lyon. He says it's in regard to the contract with Washington."

Her belly sank. "Thank you, Lucy. Oh, and can you call Charlotte's preschool and see what it is they need for the party next week?"

"Of course, Mrs. Archer."

Annabelle clicked the button to connect the call while also pulling up a spreadsheet on the Helios timeline and numbers. She didn't remember a Mr. Lyon from Washington, but she had to be ready for anything. "This is Annabelle Quinn-Archer," she said as she tapped a couple of keys. "What can I do for you, Mr. Lyon?"

There was a long moment of silence on the other end of the line. Annabelle was already getting lost in the numbers on her screen, formulating her answers to any potential questions, when the voice came through, hard and cold and so menacing it made the hair on her neck stand up.

"You can tell me where the money is, Mrs. Archer. Or you can die like your husband."

———

Dex shoved a hand through his hair and gazed out at the farmland. It was time to cut hay for the livestock, but Dad wasn't going to be harvesting anything this year. Not after his open-heart surgery last month and the fall he'd taken just a few days ago. He'd hit his head and been knocked out cold. It was hours before the neighboring farmer had found him in the barn, disoriented and in pain from the broken leg he'd suffered in the fall.

The cows were being taken care of by that same farmer for now, and there was a For Sale sign at the end of the drive. The sign was especially jarring, but there was nothing to be done for it. Dad wasn't getting any younger, and the farm took too much work. It was time for him to retire.

Katie ambled into the room, her eyes red-rimmed as

she clutched a framed photo. "I can't believe it's come down to this."

Dex shrugged. "It's life, Katie. Time moves on and so do we."

"You could take over the farm—"

"No. I can't." His voice snapped into the air between them, and she sucked in a breath. "It's not me," he said, softer this time. "It's never been me. Even if I wanted to, I still have another couple of years on my enlistment. Besides, there's no future here and you know it. If there was, you'd have had Jessie give up his job at the bank and learn to farm so *you* could take over when it was time."

She dropped her chin. They both remembered the lean times growing up, the beans and cornbread every night because there was nothing else. The early mornings feeding livestock, the days in the saddle when it was time to cull the herd, the millions of backbreaking tasks that went with raising cattle. "You're right."

He went over and put his hands on her shoulders. "He'll be all right. Once the stress of this place is gone, he'll be able to enjoy life again."

"Farming *is* Daddy's life."

"Not anymore. The doctors say it's time he stopped or he won't live another year."

"I just wish he could stay here in the home he knows."

"He needs to be closer to town and his doctors."

"I know." Katie sighed. "When Jessie and I bought a house with a mother-in-law apartment, we thought it would be for his parents when they came to visit. I never dreamed of Daddy living there."

"It'll be an adjustment for everyone, I'm sure."

Katie's eyes were shining. "Don't misunderstand me, Dex. I *want* Daddy there. I just don't know if he wants to be there." She swiped her fingers beneath her eyes. "I need to get back to the rehab facility and see how he's doing."

"I'll be along in a bit."

"Okay." She grabbed her purse and headed for the door. "The kids are looking forward to seeing more of their Uncle Dex, by the way."

Dex laughed. "They're three and one. I doubt that very much."

Katie smiled. "Fine, it's me who wants to see you. So don't forget I'm cooking dinner tonight, okay?"

"I'll be there."

Katie went outside and climbed into her Lexus SUV. She waved brightly before backing out and heading up the driveway. Dex watched her go and then took out his phone and scrolled through e-mail. This was the second time in a month he'd gone on emergency leave from the job, but his team was still in DC and waiting for their next assignment. He hoped it didn't come before he got back. He wanted to be in the action, risking his life protecting his country and its ideals, rather than here watching the death of the life he used to know.

He might not want to be a cattle farmer, but seeing the old house sold wasn't as easy as he'd thought it would be. He'd grown up here. Fallen in love here. He hardened his heart at that thought. No good ever came of thinking about Annabelle Quinn—Annabelle *Archer* now. The thought that she was a widow echoed through his mind, but he shoved it away. He didn't care. Didn't care what she did or how she was doing.

Fuck her and all the false promises that had ever issued from her cherry lips.

He put his phone away and let his gaze slide over the worn living room—the ratty couch and rattier recliner, the huge flat-screen television he'd bought his dad for Christmas, the dated wallpaper and creaky floors of the old house. He didn't know why he was standing here, reluctant to leave. He'd seen this place often enough to have every crack in the wall memorized. He despised and loved this house in equal measure. Once his mother had died, it had gotten even sadder and more worn than it had been when they were still a family.

He gritted his teeth and headed for the door. Time to lock up and get back to his hotel in town. He'd just turned the key in the lock and started across the porch when a blue Mercedes turned into the driveway and rolled toward him.

It was a nice car, an AMG sports car, low-slung and sleek, which meant it had cost the driver a pretty penny. There was no reason for a car like that to be here— unless it was the real estate agent.

Dex leaned against the porch railing and waited for the agent to pull up. Whatever she wanted—and he knew it was a she because he'd paid attention to the name on the sign—it wouldn't take long because he wasn't going to let it.

The car stopped but the driver didn't get out. Dex

started to get annoyed, but then he saw the woman's hands on the wheel, clenching and unclenching like she was thinking about what she wanted to do. He couldn't see her face because of the reflection off the glass and the angle he stood at. Before he could start down the stairs, she must have made up her mind because the car shut off and the door swung open.

A second later she emerged, blond hair shining in the sunlight, cherry lips glistening with gloss. Dex's heart was a dead thing, and yet it still managed a hard throb at the sight of her.

Fortunately, that throb went away and anger filled him instead. Hot, hard, swelling anger. "What the fuck do you want, Annabelle?"

———

Get HOT ADDICTION at your favorite retailer's website or ask them to order a copy for you to pick up at the store!

Books by Lynn Raye Harris

The Hostile Operations Team ® Books
Strike Team 1

Book 0: RECKLESS HEAT

Book 1: HOT PURSUIT - Matt & Evie

Book 2: HOT MESS- Sam & Georgie

Book 3: DANGEROUSLY HOT - Kev & Lucky

Book 4: HOT PACKAGE - Billy & Olivia

Book 5: HOT SHOT - Jack & Gina

Book 6: HOT REBEL - Nick & Victoria

Book 7: HOT ICE - Garrett & Grace

Book 8: HOT & BOTHERED - Ryan & Emily

Book 9: HOT PROTECTOR - Chase & Sophie

Book 10: HOT ADDICTION - Dex & Annabelle

Book 11: HOT VALOR - Mendez & Kat

Book 12: A HOT CHRISTMAS MIRACLE - Mendez &
Kat

————

The Hostile Operations Team ® Books
Strike Team 2

Book 1: HOT ANGEL - Cade & Brooke

Book 2: HOT SECRETS - Sky & Bliss

Book 3: HOT JUSTICE - Wolf & Haylee

Book 4: HOT STORM - Mal & Scarlett

Book 5: HOT COURAGE ~ Coming Soon!

————

The HOT SEAL Team Books

Book 1: HOT SEAL - Dane & Ivy

Book 2: HOT SEAL Lover - Remy & Christina

Book 3: HOT SEAL Rescue - Cody & Miranda

Book 4: HOT SEAL BRIDE - Cash & Ella

Book 5: HOT SEAL REDEMPTION - Alex & Bailey

Book 6: HOT SEAL TARGET - Blade & Quinn

Book 7: HOT SEAL HERO - Ryan & Chloe

Book 8: HOT SEAL DEVOTION - Zach & Kayla

Book 9: Shade's book! It's coming. Whether he believes it or not....

———

HOT Heroes for Hire: Mercenaries
Black's Bandits

Book 1: BLACK LIST - Jace & Maddy

Book 2: BLACK TIE - Brett & Tallie

Book 3: BLACK OUT - Colt & Angie

Book 4: BLACK KNIGHT - Jared & Libby

Book 5: BLACK HEART - Ian Black!

———

The HOT Novella in Liliana Hart's MacKenzie Family Series

HOT WITNESS - Jake & Eva

———

7 Brides for 7 Brothers

MAX (Book 5) - Max & Ellie

7 Brides for 7 Soldiers

WYATT (Book 4) - Max & Ellie

7 Brides for 7 Blackthornes

ROSS (Book 3) - Ross & Holly

Filthy Rich Billionaires

Book 1: FILTHY RICH REVENGE

Book 2: FILTHY RICH PRINCE

———

Who's HOT?

Strike Team 1

Matt "Richie Rich" Girard (Book 0 & 1)
Sam "Knight Rider" McKnight (Book 2)
Kev "Big Mac" MacDonald (Book 3)
Billy "the Kid" Blake (Book 4)
Jack "Hawk" Hunter (Book 5)
Nick "Brandy" Brandon (Book 6)
Garrett "Iceman" Spencer (Book 7)
Ryan "Flash" Gordon (Book 8)
Chase "Fiddler" Daniels (Book 9)
Dex "Double Dee" Davidson (Book 10)

Commander
John "Viper" Mendez (Book 11 & 12)

Deputy Commander
Alex "Ghost" Bishop

Strike Team 2

Cade "Saint" Rodgers (Book 1)
Sky "Hacker" Kelley (Book 2)
Dean "Wolf" Garner (Book 3)
Malcom "Mal" McCoy (Book 4)
Noah "Easy" Cross
Ryder "Muffin" Hanson
Jax "Gem" Stone
Zane "Zany" Scott
Jake "Harley" Ryan (HOT WITNESS)

SEAL Team 1

Dane "Viking" Erikson (Book 1)
Remy "Cage" Marchand (Book 2)
Cody "Cowboy" McCormick (Book 3)
Cash "Money" McQuaid (Book 4)
Alexei "Camel" Kamarov (Book 5)
Adam "Blade" Garrison (Book 6)
Ryan "Dirty Harry" Callahan (Book 7)
Zach "Neo" Anderson (Book 8)
Corey "Shade" Vance

Black's Bandits

Jace Kaiser (Book 1)
Brett Wheeler (Book 2)
Colton Duchaine (Book 3)
Jared Fraser (Book 4)
Ian Black (Book 5)

Tyler Scott
Thomas "Rascal" Bradley
Dax Freed
Jamie Hayes
Mandy Parker (Airborne Ops)
Melanie (Reception)
? Unnamed Team Members

Freelance Contractors

Lucinda "Lucky" San Ramos, now MacDonald (Book 3)
Victoria "Vee" Royal, now Brandon (Book 6)
Emily Royal, now Gordon (Book 8)
Miranda Lockwood, now McCormick (SEAL Team
Book 3)
Bliss Bennett, (Strike Team 2, Book 2)
Angelica "Angie" Turner (Black's Bandits, Book 3)

About the Author

Lynn Raye Harris is a Southern girl, military wife, wannabe cat lady, and horse lover. She's also the New York Times and USA Today bestselling author of the HOSTILE OPERATIONS TEAM ® SERIES of military romances, and 20 books about sexy billionaires for Harlequin.

A former finalist for the Romance Writers of America's Golden Heart Award and the National Readers Choice Award, Lynn lives in Alabama with her handsome former-military husband, one fluffy princess of a cat, and a very spoiled American Saddlebred horse who enjoys bucking at random in order to keep Lynn on her toes.

Lynn's books have been called "exceptional and emotional," "intense," and "sizzling" -- and have sold in excess of 4.5 million copies worldwide.

To connect with Lynn online:
www.LynnRayeHarris.com
Lynn@LynnRayeHarris.com

Acknowledgments

Many thanks to my wonderful team who help me get the books done by taking care of all the other stuff so I can write. Mike, Gretchen, Anne, Linda, Crystalle, Frauke, Kelley, Julie -- without you, I'd be sunk!

Huge thanks go to Justin Richardson, who answered my call on Twitter for information about how carrier services like UPS work. I needed to know how to get Chase on and off that truck and how he'd find the package. Justin was very thorough -- and now I have a new appreciation for UPS drivers and how hard they work. Any mistakes in that scene are solely my fault.

Finally, thanks to all my wonderful readers who keep asking for more HOT! There will be more. Colonel Mendez will get his story, don't you worry. And there's still Dex, Strike Team 2, the SEALs, and Ian Black to think about too. So, yeah, lots of HOT.

All the best to you, friends! Stay HOT.

CPSIA information can be obtained
at www.ICGtesting.com
Printed in the USA
LVHW032249200223
740018LV00018B/152